This book is a work of fiction. Names, characters, businesses, organizations, places, events and incidents either are the product of the author's imagination or are used fictitiously. Any resemblance to actual persons, living or dead, events, or locales is entirely coincidental.

For information contact; address www.mattkhouriebeastly.com
Book and Cover design by Adriana Hanganu at Adipixdesign.com

King-Z Production

First Edition: June 2015

For Talia, without whom Beastly would never have found the stars…
Thank you

Chapter 1

Donovan's chest pounded. His footsteps echoed on the cold stone floor as he raced for the throne room. The two sounds merged into a deafening roar inside his head. His torch cast the only light in the maze of darkness the castle had become. Outside, dozens of battles raged as his soldiers fought valiantly into the night in defense of their queen. They were horribly outnumbered and, worse still, aided by terrors long forgotten by the mortal world. Donovan's only concern was reaching the throne room. It was the last place Lady Adella had to fall back to.

She would have to be there...

Torchlight danced along Donovan's bloodied sword and illuminated vast rows of hanging murals and portraits. Each masterful painting told a story: moments from the viewer's life captured by canvas. The paintings flowed like quicksilver as Donovan sprinted by, conjuring an endless parade of scenes from his earliest memory.

A toddler with hazel eyes and a floppish mop of chocolate hair being raised in the castle. An awkward teenager trying to best his fencing instructor. A young man surviving the hardships of the barracks. Donovan sped by his life in oils, paying only a moment's notice to his favorite: the day he first met Princess Pandora.

The sound of thick doors being splintered into kindling snapped from beyond the torch's flickering sphere.

They've breached the inner defenses...

He skidded into a pair of tall doors featuring brass rings chewed on by matching dragons. Carved above the lintel was a bas relief of a gleaming star.

Over his right shoulder a painting depicted the day Queen Adella named a flustered Donovan "Captain of the Guard". He remembered the occasion fondly, though it seemed long ago. In the painting his armor was awash with sunlight and the white dragon crest emblazoned on the chest plate reared high at an unseen foe.

That very armor was now battered beyond recognition and covered in oily blood. Donovan sheathed his sword and raised a fist to the door. The doors glided open before he could strike. Relief steadied his thundering heart. *She was here.*

A beacon of light emanating drove back the hallway's pool of shadow. Tender warmth caressed his face. It was the soothing sensation of the queen inviting him in for one of their talks. Only this time there could be no friendly banter. Donovan wasted not a single breath and walked through to a most welcome sight.

A luminous throne sat atop a marble dais trimmed by ivy speckled with white roses. It was modest by royal standards, little more than a simple chair of shimmering silver whose back climbed to just above the queen's waist. A plush maroon cushion with an embroidered pin stripe of silver provided the sole embellishment. A guardian trinity of rearing ivory stallions stood watch. Sparkling water cascaded from their mouths, circling the dais like a stream.

Three thin windows stretched from floor to cavernous ceiling, providing a constant flow of salty sea breezes. The chamber's vaulted crown had been long ago enchanted to reflect the nightly stars. Thousands of miniscule white candles flickered in the night breezes, gusting in circles around the room.

Queen Adella leaned into her favorite window, gazing upon the stars. Gleaming moonlight caught her shoulder-length platinum hair, amplifying the light. Her bare feet pitter-pattered over stone tiles that warmed solely for her. She proudly regarded her war-weary captain and with Fae-like grace lowered her slender form onto the throne. Her pearlescent sapphire dress pooled at her feet, rippling like a breeze over a pond.

Donovan tossed the torch back into the hallway and shouldered the doors closed. He made to hoist a heavy steel-braced beam but was interrupted by an angel's whisper.

"Donovan, come."

"Highness, they have breached the inner defenses. Many have fallen... and Pandora... she..." He dropped an end of the beam, shoulders suddenly aware of the day-long battle yet raging.

"That doesn't matter now, Captain."

The Queen suppressed the laugh she always had to when using his official title. Despite his oft proven valor, Adella would always see him as the same little boy she had come to love as her own. Donovan's voice returned, fierce and determined. "This castle, your safety, will always matter to me, highness." He slammed the brace home and then hurried to the throne.

Adella brushed the mud-covered hair from Donovan's eyes, revealing a blood-caked gash. A startled breath escaped her lungs. "You're hurt." Adella flourished her hand, charging it with the same cerulean shine of her eyes. She gestured to Donovan's wound.

Donovan dabbed a dented gauntlet to his brow, gently resisting the queen's aid. "Your Highness, that isn't necessary. We need to get you and the Princess out of here. We need..."

A thud boomed from the door. Donovan's head snapped around, hand immediately upon his blade.

Seizing upon the distraction, Adella acted. Before Donovan could flinch away, the magic coursed from her hand, briefly enveloping Donovan's head, then disappeared with a flash. The wound collapsed instantly upon itself, healing without scar. He felt the warming relief of the healing enchantment and smiled gratefully.

The door boomed again, this time coupled by the crunch of splintering wood.

"We must find Pandora and convince her to come with us. We can still make for the hidden pass." He gestured to a great mosaic depicting the royal emblem. The dragon was brought to life by thousands of tiles of whites, greys, and reds. "Your forces will know where to rendezvous."

Adella's face dimmed. "Pandora has chosen her fate. I know you fear for my daughter's safety, but she is lost to us."

"Highness, if only I could speak to her. I could explain. I could make her understand that it wasn't your fault."

A third, mightier crash carved a deep gash in the brace. The stone archway expelled the door's hinges halfway. Donovan leapt from the dais. His sword was drawn in a heartbeat, yet before he managed a single step a gentle hand weighed upon on his shoulder. "Donovan, there is something I must tell you. Something you should have known for some time now. About Lia... her birthright." Adella's words were soft and measured. She reached for the sparkling medallion at her neck.

Fighting the impulse to charge, Donovan managed a slight turn of his head. "I know you believe Pandora's loss was unforeseeable, but that's not true. You know as well as anyone her penchants for cruelty. Hers was a path selected long ago and is no fault of yours," Adella whispered, "her blood, as is your daughter's, is special..."

Donovan's thoughts shifted to baby Lia. So small, so precious. She was every bit his daughter right down to the amber eyes that brightened every shadow in every room. It felt like a lifetime had passed since the nightmarish dracoliche crested the twin hills with its dark army beyond Lady Adella's grand palace. Donovan had granted his consent for his retired Commander to escort Lia to safety through the passage concealed behind the grand dragon mosaic. He had meant to join Cedrik and his daughter and see the queen to safety alongside them should the castle fall. The sweet words to Lia's favorite lullaby had stuck in his throat while the handmaidens bundled her...

The door finally succumbed to its injuries. An explosion of splinters and rivets spewed debris into the candlelit chamber. A foursome of soldiers clad in black armor breached the threshold, rushing for the room's occupants.

Donovan slipped free of Adella's restraint, charging with a beastly roar. The sea of candlelight scattered showers of radiant beams as Donovan crashed shoulder first into the closest assailant. The man crumpled to the ground, dropping a serrated blade.

He twisted under a slicing sword intended for his neck, scooping up the dropped weapon. He staunched his dash with a flurry of slashes and parries, cutting down a second assailant.

Blood trickled down Donovan's dual blades. The falling droplets upon the floor were for a moment lonely sounds. His chest heaved adding to the battle's symphony. He sized up the remaining threat and sighed. "It will take more than two."

Donovan closed the gap like a jungle cat, expertly parrying wild blows into empty space. Swords clanged and pinged. The invaders struggled in vain, blades cutting into shadow. They were no match for Donovan;

testimony to Cedrik's rigorous training. He taunted his foes with feints and footwork, maneuvering them like pawns on a chessboard.

The pair attempted to attack as one, slashing high and low. Donovan deflected the haymaker strikes aside and then drove cold steel home. The soldiers slumped from his blades, collapsing in a heap. He flourished the twin blades, making them sing in the silence.

Donovan glanced at the borrowed sword, disgusted by its hateful black edge. *How many good men met their end to such a wretched thing?* He flung the blade away and spat.

Though his shoulders screamed and his back burned with spasms, the fight had invigorated him as it always did. A familiar tremor in his fingertips twitched as adrenaline washed through his veins. He reached for the queen's hand.

"Lady Adella--"

A blade pierced Donovan's back plate. At first he only gasped, struck by absurd amusement. Not until he found the black blade erupting from his chest did he panic. Gurgling, Donovan staggered to a knee. A thin stream of scarlet trickled from his mouth. He met the queen's gaze, eyes wide with unfamiliar fright.

Adella quickly whispered a chant. A tempest choked the candles, engulfing the room in blackness. The assassin's sword shook violently in his hands. The wind howled and swept the soldier into the vaulted ceiling, pinning him to the starry illusion. The queen's glare burned through the hapless assassin. With a sharp flick of her wrist, he sailed toward a beckoning window. The doomed man clawed frantically for purchase but found none. He vanished into the night, leaving behind only a fading scream.

Donovan collapsed into a sprawl, exhaling a wet gasp. Adella fell to her knees and with strength concealed by her slight build lifted Donovan into her lap. She traced trembling fingers along the jagged breach in his chest plate. "I need something from my chamber to heal this wound."

The color in Donovan's face ebbed. An unnerving chill crept up from his feet before swallowing him whole. He shiver-nodded his understanding, but chattering teeth ate his words.

Adella's heart sank deep into her stomach. Her private chambers were at the palace's far side. And there was a war in progress. She needed time, and that was a luxury that even the queen could not afford.

She made for the window, taking on a pale bluish glint that gleamed through her dress. Her feet lifted from the floor as she began to glide.

"If you value his life..." A woman's voice called, dripping with menace.

Adella's glow vanished. For a moment, she refused to turn. The queen remembered the voice's sad echo, absent from the palace for nearly a year. It was hollow now, an empty replica of a voice she once loved.

Pandora sauntered into the throne room flanked by a dozen guards. The Blight's indigo aura pulsed through her skin, illuminating the throne room's dark. A thin black cape fell over her bare shoulders. She surveyed the room, shaking her head like a disappointed mistress. "How unbecoming." A twitch of her forefinger set the candles ablaze and the night scrambling back outside.

"Welcome home, my *dutre*." Adella's words tore at an old scar. She loved her daughter beyond limit but not beyond reason. She could not forgive what Pandora had allowed herself to become.

"Never my home," Pandora said coldly. "Not since you drove me from it. Not since you left me heartbroken and desperate."

Pandora's crystal blue eyes remained fixed on Adella's as she casually stepped over the dead men like so much refuse. She lingered over a shivering Donovan, finally shifting her gaze from Adella. She regarded her former protector with nothing more than a vacant stare.

Adella noted the circlet pinning back Pandora's hair. The fanged skull at its center stared back with glimmering eyes of onyx. "The whole of the Once Kingdom stood ready to support you. Our people would've given anything to spare you the agony of such a loss. You left our home to pursue a destiny I could not allow."

"I left because she died!" Pandora yelled, pointing an accusatory finger. "Because *you* let her die!" Her voice cracked but fast regained its fury. "I left because I couldn't stand to look at you. Either of you."

"Star-shine, please..."

"Don't call me that. Don't ever call me that. I've no more love for stars than I have for you or him."

Adella reached for her daughter, hoping against the hatred in her eyes. "Please, end this siege. Let us heal our kingdom and our family."

The creeping cold bored into Donovan's chest, siphoning his strength. Pandora's venomous anger threatened extinguish what little remained. He had to try reasoning with her, for their daughter's sake. Donovan summoned his remaining strength and twisted onto his chest, feebly reaching for Pandora's hand.

"Princess Pandora, I'm... sorry." Donovan's consciousness threatened to fade but he willed his focus true. "I'm sorry I failed you..."

The words drained him. Seeing the princess aligned against his queen, hearing her callous words, thinking of all that had been lost was too great a burden. He shuddered, then slipped into unconsciousness.

"If Donovan dies all hope for you dies with him," Adella warned.

Pandora silenced her mother with a sharp gesture, then motioned for her lieutenant. Malachai broke from the pack of soldiers, removing a black helmet shaped like a dragon's skull. He stood a head taller than his men and possessed the wiry build of something predatory. Each step was a calculated action: cold and efficient. His doll-like eyes were alive with a furious crimson energy that cast streaking trails as he moved.

"Traitor. How dare you show your face here?" Anger surged through Adella's naturally calm tone. "I should have known it was you who corrupted her. Always ready to increase your station, so eager to advance. I shall see that justice hunts you down, no matter the hole you hide in.

Malachai sneered before drawing a dagger. The blade pulsed in his hand, craving more carnage than the siege had wrought. "Get him up."

Pandora's guards heaved the unconscious Donovan to his feet. His head lolled forward as the soldiers propped him up. Malachai seized a handful of Donovan's hair, jerking his former commander's head back. He slowly raised the dagger, taunting Adella with the tip to his victim's throat.

"That's quite enough." Adella was once more calmer than a spring breeze. She glanced at Pandora and with a spry smile tapped a foot. The footfall echoed, then blasted a dazzling sapphire shock wave. Armored bodies flew away, smashing against the walls. Malachai barreled through Pandora, breaking against a stone pillar. A cacophony of screams and twisting metal evicted the silence of the attempted execution.

Adella caught Donovan's falling body with an uttered incantation, leaving him hanging like a marionette. She unfastened her necklace and cinched the golden chain around Donovan's neck. "May the light of the Aether guide you." The firestone blazed as it accepted its new bearer. After a few surges of fiery glow, the jewel became still.

Crystalline tears flowed from Adella's eyes while a lump swelled in her throat. *There was so much more you needed to know.* She crossed her hands over her chest, centering her focus. The sounds of battle raging elsewhere fell silent. Surviving candles found their flames unable to flicker.

The whole world was still.

Adella's hands moved in broad strokes, painting an ancient symbol on the air as though the frozen candlelight provided canvas. Magical energy flowed from both floor and ceiling, converging on the glyph. Her hands moved faster, the symbol becoming more vivid as the energies multiplied.

The symbol exploded in a shower of golden sparks and swirling vortex was born.

Adella touched a slender finger to her lips, then pressed it to Donovan's temple, gifting him the remnants of her power. She hoped the sacrifice would be enough to balm his wound. She hoped it would give him time.

With a wave she sent Donovan's body into the unknown of the portal. "Good bye, Captain."

"No! He must pay!" Pandora had shaken off the shock wave's effects. Her eyes were no longer the crystal blue of her mother's. They burned with an ugly indigo firestorm that ached with hatred. Pandora jabbed a palm forward, flinging a sizzling green flame at Donovan.

Adella stepped into the bolt, absorbing the brunt of it with her chest. A streak arced from her body, colliding with the portal. The combined magicks of Breath and Blight twisted and pulled at the helpless captain of the guard. His torso collapsed upon itself, then ballooned. Limbs cracked and twisted. The portal collapsed upon itself leaving no traces, as the opposing energies continued to ply Donovan's broken form.

Adella shuddered in disbelief. She had expected pain, but there was only warmth washing over her. Warmth and peace. She suddenly felt a nagging fatigue and longed only for her favorite blanket.

"I shall love you always, star-shine." Adella's body dissipated into a translucent cloud of sapphire fireflies and then faded away.

The Once Kingdom, home of Adella's proud palace stood eerily silent, absent any traces of its former family.

Save for a furious Pandora, whose glowering eyes continued to burn.

Chapter 2

The Beast of Briarburn awoke hungry as usual. He rolled from a spongy bed of moss, patting the pangs away. He yawned until something popped, then massaged his smarting jaw with a plate sized paw that ended in coal black claws.

He brushed a blanket of fluffy snow from his shoulders and shook his mane clean. He stood on thickly muscled legs like those of a lion king. A stout pair of ram-like horns added a further foot, ensuring the Beast was taller than any man of the realm. He fastened a dingy pair of breeches over an even dingier loin cloth and arched his back like a rustled feline. More popping. *The price of sleeping on the ground.*

The setting sun bequeathed swathes of mingling oranges and creeping purples. A canopy of snow-laden branches struggled under their added burdens. Despite obstructions of snow and ice, the Beast quickly located a princely tapestry of constellations glistening like diamonds. It was an appreciated comfort. But for the stars and the solitude, there wasn't much that was comfortable in the Beast's world. He could not even recall the last time he gazed upon a rising sun.

The Beast waited patiently for families of foxes and rabbits to drift off to slumber before lumbering about. After all, they afforded him the same courteousy during the day. A badger quipped a goodnight and then disappeared into the hollow of a nearby fir. A moment later, its tiny yellow orbs were swallowed by the darkness. He wished them all a peaceful night, then heeded the second rumble of his hungry belly.

He cinched a hunter green cloak whose faded tattered edges had seen better days. Still, it was all he needed to face winter's bite. His own coat of chestnut brown fur was ample enough. A walnut sized ruby hung from a preposterously thin necklace of golden spider silk. He pawed at the jewel, vying for a better look. After a curse best reserved for a tavern brawl, he managed to grasp his most treasured and frustrating possession.

In a bath of starlight, he pored over the jewel. By his count it was the millionth such inspection. The Beast grunted his frustration and let the medallion slip through his claws. *Such a delicate bauble for such a crass being. It must have been crafted by a powerful sorcerer,* the Beast reckoned. He often sensed power emanating from within, whispering in the stillest of nights.

The Beast ran a claw over the medallion's reverse, feeling the familiar grooves of the impeccable inscription etched by a forgotten author. The words were as foreign to him as his own origin. His heart sank a hair as it often did when he tried to force the memory free.

Sometimes he thought the inscription was mocking him. Other times he imagined it was the forgotten incantation of an ancient spell. Perhaps a spell to remove a curse or to turn water into ale? He cared little for magic or for curses. In truth, the Beast of Briarburn would have given anything for the medallion to merely reveal his name.

Frustrated, he pulled the cloak closed, burying the firestone in his mane. He flipped up the cloak's cavernous hood. At night, but for his massive build, he would travel unnoticed. That suited him just fine. At the onset of his lonely march, the Beast had tried consorting with the world of Men, but found it more frigid than the bitterest winter. Even within the kindest of company, a cast of worthwhile comrades was rare in the finding.

The Great Road was teacher of a great many lessons. Painful lessons the Beast had little intention of repeating. Lesson number one: Trust No One. It was far better to rely on oneself than to trust in another. *For bread or for blood, there was only a man for himself.*

The Beast was no fool, however. Occasional cooperation was not without merit. But it was meant to be just that, occasional. And preferably short-lived. Things may have worked out for the better had that always been so.

Shouldering a worn pack, he contemplated lesson number two. The penalty for forgetting lesson number one was usually a stiff one; such as being chasing by an angry mob wielding rusty farm tools. Or being shackled and caged. The Beast shuddered at that last thought.

There was nothing worse than chains.

He put the memory aside and started for the road, careful to avoid the slumbering critters. Vapor escaped from his snout in large plumes and snow crunched underfoot, while the winter wind whistled through the trees. The Beast preferred the season. He found it had a unique pace that suited him. In the wild, winter was able to freeze time itself, making things serene.

The Great Road remained where he had left it the night before. Wagon tracks in the knee high snow had been freshly filled by the morning's storm. He stared down the lonely stretch of cobbled stone. The snow covered road rolled through a serpentine series of gentle curves before disappearing behind a drift horizon of ivory. In the still of the spreading night the strange words returned, dancing amongst his skulking ruminations. *In my heart, I know you're there...* He knew not from whence the words came. The mysterious voice chanting them in was ever changing, distorted like an echo in a cavern.

With a huff he buried the strange voice and trudged off, leaving behind a trail of prints the size of foxholes. East had been his heading since autumn's end. Tales from a score of inn keepers and pilgrims had provided countless leads, each one naming a wizard or shaman who may possess the skill to translate the mysterious inscription. The Beast snickered. The intellectual types never could resist the urge to prove how much smarter they were than everyone else.

The moon finally appeared and began its nightly journey. Drifts of snow at the road's shoulders glistened, mirroring the starry sky. Fox tracks dotted the land in the strange crisscrossing pattern they were notorious for. He would have appreciated the company of foxes tonight. He could have used one of their famous riddles to help pass the time. *What was that last riddle? They have not flesh, nor feathers, nor scales, nor bone. Yet they have fingers and thumbs of their own.* The Beast considered it for another moment and then moved on. "Stupid foxes," he grumbled.

All remained quiet long into the night until the thunder of hooves disturbed the golden silence. The vibration perked his ears up. Riders in the night were almost never a good thing. Madmen and marauders and things much more vile readily preyed on road weary travelers who found themselves caught out in the dark.

No panic crept upon the Beast's heart, however. The local gangs of rabble knew better than attack the Beast of Briarburn. His own reputation as something not to be trifled with was a common place story, carried on the wings of ravens, and sung by bards in taverns far and wide.

The Beast had little desire to fight, but had no intention of fleeing. The road was free to travel. And since he had traveled its windy worn out stretches for so long, he had come to consider it home. No, there would be no cowering this night. If the road were to be all the home he had, than he would not abandon it.

The hooves thundered closer. As a minor concession, the Beast moved a step closer to the shoulder, before resuming his journey. Confrontation would not be necessary unless the horsemen desired it. The Beast did not even bother to turn his cloaked head to the noisy intrusion.

A family of rabbits bolted from a roadside den, heading for the deeper woods. Angry birds squawked objections from tree tops before departing like black storm clouds. It was then that the Beast stopped. He cared little for the din and less for his friends being shaken from their homes.

Muffled sounds of plodding boots rounded a drift, followed by their creator. The man staggered and fell, clawing frantically through the snow, trying to rise. He turned over his shoulder to the thundering hooves and cried out. He righted himself and ran at the Beast.

A band of horsemen burst from the trees, trampling the drift, closing on the terrified man in seconds. The doomed man reached desperately for the Beast. The lead dragoon seized a handful of the man's cloak, jerking him from the ground.

The man's fingers madly worked the cloak's clasp, trying to free himself. "No, please. It wasn't mine. It was--"

A dagger tore through his back, piercing his heart. He gurgled a mouthful of blood into the snow. The dragoon wiped his serrated blade on the bloodied cloak. He released the corpse and stared at the only witness.

The Beast regarded the mounted party who in turn slowed to a tentative trot. *Mercenaries by the look of them.* Their horses were chained in heavy plate mail; riders in suits of black armor covered head to toe by twisted barbs and hooks. A singular pauldron forged into a fanged skull skewered by three blades sat on each man's left shoulder.

The Beast knew of these men. The fanged skulls gave them away.

Tales from the Great Road whispered of these riders in black, said to never eat or sleep. Rumor said they rode under the banner of a powerful sorceress. A banner usually seeking the capture and trial of a fugitive. The Beast knew that words like 'capture' and 'trial' were usually euphemisms for kidnapping and murder. And based on what he had just witnessed...

Not my concern. The Beast resumed his march, ignoring the carnage at his back.

The riders closed to twenty paces. Their captain broke formation and rode ahead until his mount was within arm's reach. Despite the war horse, the Beast stood at nearly eye level with the man in black. The stallion reared, rattling the armored chains. Thick plumes of steam erupted from its flared nostrils as it shifted its bulk.

The rider removed his helmet and set it on the saddle's horn. Malachai's skin was the sickly translucent color of spoiled milk. The Beast's reflection flickered in the seething crimson of Malachai's eyes.

What manner of demon spawn was this... thing?

Doubt cared not for lingering in the Beast's thoughts. These men were most certainly the Wakeful. The muscles of his body tightened, taut as a drawn catapult. Meeting the Wakeful elicited that effect in all living beings. It was as though the waking world knew it was being poisoned by those more at home in nightmare.

"We seek..." Malachai's voice droned as he struggled with the rigidity of his lips. "We seek the girl."

"Haven't seen her," the Beast muttered, his tone an overdue volcano. As far as he was concerned the conversation was over.

The hissing sound of swords escaping scabbards countered his defiance.

"We seek the girl. We seek the Gift." Malachai motioned to the Beast's chest. Malachai's armored gauntlet creaked as plates of steel folded into an accusatory finger. The Beast stole a glance at the spot beneath his cloak where the medallion rested. *How had Malachai known?*

"I know no girl and have no gifts to offer. Leave me be. Continue your ride." His blood rolled to a boil and the Beast, very subtly for his size, shifted to a slight crouch.

He liked his odds despite the six on one disadvantage. The Wakeful began a hasty dismount, but were abruptly halted by Malachai's swift gesture.

Malachai stared long and hard into the Beast's own savage amber eyes, finding his reflection as the Beast had in his. The battle hardened captain was no fool. Though Malachai was neither sorcerer nor Seer, he recognized the unbridled fury only a beast of the wild could know. It was a primal fury without limit or mercy. Malachai saw the certainty of the battle's outcome.

There would be no battle here.

"We ride for the village," Malachai shouted to his men. He waved the Wakeful onward and they surged past at a gallop, leaving the Beast standing as steadfast as a mountainside beside the road. None looked back as they disappeared around the road's bend.

Malachai nudged his horse to a trot. He hadn't gone far when he pulled on the reigns, bringing the mount to a halt. "I should hope we don't meet again on the road," Malachai called back over his shoulder.

The Beast dashed two lengthy strides in less time than most folks needed to rise from a comfortable chair and was once more eye to eye with the Wakeful captain. His eyes burned a hole straight through whatever black heart Malachai had left.

The Beast whispered, forcing Malachai to truly hear him. "You should hope we don't meet again anywhere."

Malachai twisted the remains of his partially frozen mouth into a painful slit of a smile. "Indeed." With a savage kick, Malachai's horse broke into gallop.

A gust of wind sliced his cloak, cooling some of the rage gifted by the Wakeful. He knew he would see them again. He knew it as certain as he knew the stars would shine.

Chapter 3

While the world slumbered, the ratty doors of the Troll's Breath tavern remained open for business. It was an ugly squat building known for its terrible food and the cursed odor of its namesake. The tavern's pitiful thatched roof was notorious for leaking onto many an unsuspecting traveler just as they settled in to their lumpy bed.

The bronze light struggling to escape from the dirty windows was an easy spot for the Beast of Briarburn. A faint trace of cooked meat filled the Beast's nostrils. Stomach rumbling, the Beast made straight for the inn. He cut an arrow's path through the woods, bypassing the final mile of the Great Road's curves.

Loud music split the night with each drunken fool staggering through the door. The noise may as well have been a moat filled with burning pitch; merriment did not suit him. He much preferred the song of wilderness silence. He shrugged off a wave of broken chords and gripped the door's handle.

There was the small matter of the medallion... And the larger matter of hunger.

The Beast shouldered the moldy door, nearly bludgeoning a plank free. He bent to avoid catching his horns on the lintel. A modest crowd eyed him suspiciously as he twisted through the narrow doorway.

Hamish slouched over the bar, swabbing at a stubborn clean spot with the corner of his apron. His bald head shined with a tinge of red like a festival ornament. He chuckled at the arrival of his newest, largest customer and returned to his swabbing. His patrons turned back to their drinks, following the old bar keep's lead.

The air reeked of dried urine and rotten meat. The stench worsened at each step. The Beast navigated the room, carefully avoiding the lanterns dangling from rusty chains. The floor was a carpet of dead insects and nut shells. Puddles of spilled drink tugged at his paws. He located a lone table in a shady corner and seated himself back to wall. The spindly chair protested, unaccustomed to such bulk.

A roaring fire crackled under a mural of the tavern's framing. Heads of fanged and horned beasts were mounted in a macabre ring around the walls. *Such a shame to be made a trophy of. To what end? For whose benefit?*

A troupe of bards strummed off-key, stumbling about in search of alms and ale. Out-stretched legs earned fits of laughter as the drunken performers periodically fell face first to the floor. Hamish masterfully ferried endless trays, too dexterous to suffer the bards' fate. The Beast struggled with the commotion. Tension knotted his shoulders. There were too many people doing too many things.

The Beast quickly noted the band of huntsmen dominating the room. He was familiar with their type: rough cut and cock sure. Men with look of haggard wolves. They circled a long table, numbering just shy of a dozen. The table was a mess of chipped plates and trails of flung food. Fresh blood pooled around a dagger driven home; remnants of a round of Bishop. A single moll with ginger hair worked the rowdy troop, slapping away roving hands.

The Beast resolved to maintain his guard, keen that trouble often joined pairings of liquor and lust. A nearby rack of swords offered little reassurance. No matter. He would not seek trouble out. But should it come calling...

A woman with ample crow's feet and jet black hair streaked with silver nursed a drink at a small table by the hearth's side. She tapped her foot mindlessly against a brown trunk. Through the haze the Beast read "Madame Urda" scrawled on its lid. Around her head, three apple-sized crystal balls danced playfully, flying at impossible angles and sliding through one another. The Beast snorted. He had seen this type of trickery before.

Mere carnival deception.

Behind Urda's table, a rickety staircase climbed to the inn's shabby bed chambers. Nailed to the side was a collection of "Wanted" posters offering pittances for a gallery of common rogues. One in particular, caught the Beast's eye, causing him to squint. The poster read:

"Wanted: Dead or Alive"

Marrock of the Woodland realm

For crimes against the township of the most

heinous type and degree including murder

most savage.

REWARD: 1000 Gold Pieces

A long face with a pointed nose and narrow jaw was crudely etched below the reward. He studied the image from across the room. Three scars slashed the face's left side, marring cheek and eye. The scars were telling. Only a lord of the wild could have survived such grievous wounds. But what manner of monster had carved them? Intrigued by the bounty, the Beast dodged a parade of swinging lutes and plucked free Marrock's poster.

"You'd best put that back and forget it," Hamish called over the din. His greasy rag streaked the bars lone clean patch.

The Beast fought to maintain a hushed tone; despite the bar keep's advice. "And why is that?" he tersely replied.

Hamish waved the Beast to an empty stool. It was closer to the huntsmen than he preferred, but he accepted. He flattened the notice on the sticky bar, struggling to balance himself on the stool. He muttered a curse and subtly kicked the infernal seat aside.

"I meant no offense, stranger. I was merely offerin' up some advice. Plenty of huntsmen and even some mercenary types have gone lookin' for Marrock." Hamish's mouth went dry and his beady eyes flickered to the boisterous table. "We usually find pieces of them come spring, sometimes not at all."

The Beast followed the bar keep's gaze. The wolf pack was still hard at work, clinking steins and groping at unfortunate women as they happened by. *They appeared capable enough,* the Beast thought. He looked down at the sketch. The scarred eye and gouged face refused to give up its secret. *What sort of query could challenge such a party?*

Hamish swallowed the lump in his throat.

"Lord Marrock once owned himself a fine manor not too far from here. He was a good man, fair to his people."

"What happened to his face?" The Beast tapped the picture.

Hamish frowned. "Hey now, I'm running a reputable business here, not a university."

"Reputable?" The Beast nodded to a hunter being lead upstairs by a buxom consort. In his haste the young man forgot to unsling his crossbow. He tripped over an errant boots lace, nearly stumbling back down the stairs.

The Beast produced a single gold piece and, with a toothy grin, placed it on Marrock's charcoaled nose. Hamish snatched it up with a wry smile and disappeared under the bar. He re-appeared with a bucket-sized stein, filled with frothy ale. He nodded appreciatively and slid the monstrous drink in front of the Beast. The Beast returned the gratitude and drained half of the ale in a single pull.

"I had that made as a joke," Hamish chuckled. "Never thought I'd actually pour in it."

The Beast took a second swig, finishing the ale off. *Not the worst, certainly not the best, but good enough.* He pointed at the empty cup.

"Fill it again, and tell me Marrock's tale."

Hamish happily obliged and returned with a fresh ale. He wiped his hands dry, then tossed the apron aside in a ball.

"I'll tell you what I know, lad. But like anything, there's more than one side to a tale," the bar keep cautioned. "Marrock was a good man, I told you as much already. He took a wife. Pretty thing. Big brown eyes. Anyways, they say one night she noticed his Lordship sleep walking. Walked right out of the house and into the forest, he did. Opening doors, not falling down or nothing funny. She followed him a ways into the woods, she did. A mile in, Marrock entered a clearing."

Hamish glanced at the handbill, then quickly away, trying to avoid Marrock's etched gaze. "And then things became... peculiar."

The Beast leaned in, taking another monstrous pull of his ale. "I've seen my share of peculiar, bar keep."

Hamish regarded the Beast's monstrous features. "Not like this you haven't, lad. There in the moonlight, she watched as Lord Marrock stripped down to his starkness. Starts howling at the moon, he does. And then in a burst of silver fire he disappears! Burns up!" Hamish threw his arms up.

A huntsman slammed his stein down on the bar, bringing the story to a halt. Vildar's head was covered in a mat of rough stubble. A harness of throwing knives buckled over his chest gleamed in the fire light. His leathery face tightened into a scornful mask. "Go on, tell him the rest."

Sweat beaded on Hamish's brow and he stammered. He found his tongue after choking on a second gulp.

"Right. The silver fire, you see, it disappeared after a moment and all's was left behind was a wolf. A grey wolf. Massive." Hamish gestured wildly, stretching his arm span. "So the lady near passes out, but manages to escape to the manor. Next morning, she awakes and finds his Lordship in the bed beside her, bare as the day he was born, he was. They don't speak--"

Vildar's jaw clenched, his scowl reducing his eyes to slits.

"Tell him how that filthy dog killed my brother. Tell him how Marrock stalked our camp and tore out Ugmar's throat as he slept."

Vildar snatched the "wanted" notice from the bar and tore it to shreds. He tossed the confetti up than spat at the pieces. He threw a final glance at the Beast.

"Don't even consider it. Marrock's hide is mine. I am going to flay his carcass bare, then mount his head right on this wall." Vildar's bold claim earned a round of cheers. He liberated a foaming ale from hunter's hand and hoisted it high.

"Ugmar was *my* brother. And he was ten times the hunter than the likes of you." Vildar measured the Beast. "Whatever you are."

"To Ugmar!" Vildar drained the stein and flung it into the hearth.

Jagged shards tumbled free, glowing like hot coals. He wiped his mouth with a dirty sleeve.

Vildar's company jumped to their feet, knocking over chairs and dousing the floor with ale. Up and down the table, the huntsmen clapped swords and punched at the air. They chanted Ugmar's name and stomped the floor, rattling a chorus from dancing cutlery. Startled patrons looked up from drinks. Some made for the door.

The Beast remained anchored to the bar, shoulders rigid, squeezing the bucket-stein. He snorted like a bull contemplating a charge. *This man must be a fool of the highest order,* the Beast thought. *I could be done with you without even setting this cup down, little man.* The idea simmered just long enough for him to abandon. It would take more than a slight from a drunken fool. *But every man has his line.*

Hamish burst through the kitchen door, arms laden with trays of blackened meat, anxious to disrupt the escalating tension.

"Any of you blokes fancy another round of mutton? On the house, it is."

He offered the tray to Vildar, who snatched a blackened piece of meat. He bit a large hunk from the bone, then spit it immediately back at the bar keep. Hamish's eyes widened and he stepped back, ready to use the tray as a shield.

"That was the vilest mouthful I've ever tasted." Vildar snatched the rag from Hamish's shoulder and wiped his tongue.

"I doubt that." The Beast's tree trunk arms hung from his sides, paws clenched into mace-heads.   If these men insisted on acting like savages they would be treated as such.

The huntsmen scrambled to readiness. Vildar stood front and center, chest puffed out. The Beast was not so easily intimidated. He spotted the false bravado in the shaking swords and flop sweat.

Quick thinking patrons elbowed their way into the snowy night. Silence reigned inside the Troll's Breath. The Beast took a single step forward, repelling the wall of blades. A metallic twang shattered the standoff. The Beast's paw shot up from his side, plucking the mysterious sound from the air.

A crossbow bolt.

He squeezed the bolt, grinding it to pulp. The iron head clunked onto the grimy floor. The Beast flexed his knees, drawing energy like a cobra. Vildar would be first.

The hearth exploded, covering the tavern in dancing oranges and yellows. The company of huntsmen gasped and flung themselves to the floor. Their screams combined in terrible symphony. The Beast shielded his face with a forearm. He peered between his claws.

Only Madame Urda remained seated, hunched over her table. In the middle of the flames. Unshaken. There was at first confusion, but then cause and effect were clear. The Beast's cloak was unsinged. The clothing of the huntsmen was unsinged as well. The Troll's Breath, consumed by flame, did not burn.

An amused snicker rolled over the bar.

"Gets me every time, it does." Hamish beamed. He waved to Urda who returned an animated wave of her own.

Remaining skeptical, the Beast passed his paws through the 'fire' while stepping over the writhing huntsmen. *No heat. An illusion for interrupting fools.*

Madame Urda blew a kiss at the Beast. A cool breeze accompanied the gesture, extinguishing the false flame. Vildar's company scrambled to their feet, patting themselves down and searching for burns. Vildar started to speak, but Urda cut him off with her best headmaster's voice.

"Don't bother with idle threats. Take your brutes and leave us, lest you look even more foolish."

Vildar considered Urda's words, still inspecting for scorched skin. Satisfied, he sheathed his sword and ordered his men out. The huntsmen hurried to retrieve scattered weapons, then filed out of the Troll's Breath. None dared to glance back.

Vildar paused at the door. "We'll see you soon, savage. On the road, in the wood, it matters not. Sleep with one eye open--"

The Beast snorted. "As Ugmar should have?"

Vildar ground yellow teeth. He fingered the hilt of a throwing knife and just as quickly thought better of it. He stepped out into the blustery night, slamming the door behind him.

Madame Urda gestured for the Beast to join her. "Come, sit. Enjoy the fire." She sipped from her mug. "And the peace."

The Beast obliged her, glad to be rid of Vildar and his din. He closed his eyes, letting the fire warm the fur on his snout.

Urda smiled, understanding too well the familiar look of a weary traveler.

"I know you have traveled a long road, Beast of Briarburn. But we have much to talk about."

Chapter 4

Hamish pushed the tavern's doors wide open, retiring for the evening the coupled reek of pipe smoke and ripe bodies. With a grunt and a fat foot, he jammed home a moldy wooden doorstop. Frosty air, charged with the welcome scent of pine, cut the room like a biting blade. He stood the mop against the bar, yawned and feigned a low bow.

"It's late Madam, will there be anything else?"

Urda dismissed the bald barkeep with a wave. She eyed her guest and the messy handiwork on his plate. And beside the plate. And on the floor.

"No, no I think we've had enough, have we not?"

The Beast chewed through a thick cut of meat, nodding contently. The flavor of charred beef goaded him into comically oversized bites. Juices exploded from the corners of his mouth spattering down his snout and onto his chest. A large plate piled high with bones, picked clean, caught the pink runoff.

He could hardly remember such a banquet. The forest never failed to provide, but there was always the low rumble of hunger. He washed down the final bite with a gulp of ale, patting his sated belly. He unleashed a long belch. He regarded Urda, prompted by a sudden rush of embarrassment.

"Sorry. Good meat."

Urda chuckled like a doting grandmother. She rested her elbows on the table, drumming her fingers together. The trio of crystals circled her head like a floating crown, slowly bobbing. Firelight caught their dancing facets and scattered a prismatic spray.

The Beast squinted at the shimmering stones. He found no rhyme or reason to their motion, but suspected otherwise. After a moment of study he found his own head bobbing along with them. He shuddered, breaking the spell, and drew a second chuckle from his host.

"They intrigue you? Frighten you, perhaps?"

The Beast's words were a reflex. "I fear nothing." In the wild, fear could kill in any number of ways. "Magic and I don't see eye to eye."

The shimmering rhythm of the crystals accelerated.

Urda grinned. "No, I suppose you do not. It has been since long before you were born that Man and Magic existed in harmony. Since before the days of Adella's reign. And even then the balance between Blight and Breath were already strained."

The Beast furrowed a brow. *Adella? Blight and Breath?* In the forest everything drew breath and everything blighted. Animals, birds, even the very trees constantly took in deep breaths. Hearing them was merely a question of how closely one listened. And in the end, everything passed over to the World After, leaving behind sustenance to renew the cycle.

"Those names are unknown to me." The Beast's broad shoulders sunk. "As is my own."

"Well I would have hardly that your name was as absurd as 'Beast of Briarburn', Beast of Briarburn."

The Beast stared at the plate of bones, fidgeting with its edge. No one could know what it felt like to be bereft of name. To exist but to be less than real.

Madam Urda reached over the table and placed a wrinkled hand on the Beast's paw, stilling the nervous tic. She leaned further still until they were nearly nose to nose. The cloudy whites of her eyes flashed in the firelight.

"A name is only a name, my friend. Nothing more. It is our action, or indeed our inaction, that defines who we are... Defines our legacy. Instead of chasing a name you seem to have misplaced, why not pursue a name you have earned?"

"I do not believe--"

"Of course you do not believe! And why should you? You've believed in nothing since the day you awakened in the wood alone and unable to find your way back to a home you cannot remember."

"How did you..." The Beast shrugged a defeated shoulder. It was true. One learned quickly in the wild to rely on no one and believe in less.

Urda extended an empty palm. A crystal's tint turned pinkish and glided to her hand. The orb hovered, awaiting the unspoken. Urda's voice fell to less than a whisper.

"There are many magicks in the world, my boy. Seeing in the crystals is amongst the eldest of disciplines, as old as Star Seeing."

So delicate was Urda's whisper that the Beast did not realize he was perched nearly halfway over the table. His hackles jumped at an unsettling combination of nagging intrigue and apprehension. A little voice in the back of his mind chanted a familiar mantra: *Cursed was magic no matter its name.*

"The crystals share with those so privileged the stories of the past and promises of the future. They are both written record and guiding cartograph. They... can pull back the veil."

The Beast hesitated, but only for a moment. His curiosity was unrelenting.

"Veil?"

"The veil of memory," Urda replied with a coy smile. "You need only have the courage to let them look within."

The Beast's head tilted slightly and a furry eyebrow was snagged up by an invisible hook.

"Yes, yes, I know. You fear nothing. My boy, it's been this old hag's experience that those who claim to fear nothing tend to fear deeply something very real. I wonder if you are that sort."

The Beast's eyebrow fell back into place and his jaw squared. "Only one way to find out."

"Ah, splendid then!" Urda tapped the floating crystal up and clapped her hands like an excited child receiving a gift. "Let's have a look."

The crystal sauntered to the Beast's nose and began to spin. Its shining facets churned through the spectrum before finally selecting a shade matching the Beast's amber eyes. Satisfied, the crystal moved into orbit around the Beast's head. It moved slowly, taking a full minute to complete each turn.

"This is ridiculous," the Beast grumbled under his breath.

"Patience, my boy, patience. Any magic quick to impress is almost certainly an illusion."

"Fine, but my patience is already worn thinner than my cloak."

Urda chuckled and waved her hand towards the Beast. The remaining crystals shot across the table, joining their yellowish sibling, adopting shades of identical amber. The crystals crisscrossed paths as they accelerated, forging three golden halos that crowned a feral prince.

The Beast's stomach churned and threatened revolt.

"Worry not. That feeling will pass. Always happens the first time." Urda snickered, remembering her own first trial with the crystalline halo.

"There won't be a second," the Beast groaned.

The room joined the crystals in a wobbling spin of its own. The Beast's vision grayed at the edges. Across the table, Urda's smile held fast. *Had the old woman tricked me?* His stomach lurched and his eyes rolled into the back of his head. He fell through the floor and into the blackness of his mind.

As suddenly as it started, the spinning stopped. The dingy Troll's

Breath reformed before his eyes and his stomach no longer begged for mercy. The Beast gingerly panned around. Urda was gone. Hamish too. All appeared as it had before the crystals' dance.

Notices were still pinned to the stairs. The plate of bones still dominated the table. The Beast knew the tavern was somehow changed, but could not say how. He continued to inspect the empty space. And then he finally realized.

The door.

The front door was closed tight. He clearly remembered Hamish propping it open to freshen the rancid tavern air. He pushed his chair back and made for the entrance. His paws and ears tingled. The Beast's nostrils flared as he tried to pick up the scent of hidden danger.

Nothing.

Even his keen ears failed him. Ears that he relied upon in the wild, ears that could pick up the cracking of twigs miles away. Now, they heard nothing. Nothing at all.

The Beast reached for the door's latch. Urda's fiery illusion popped into his head. He shuddered at the thought of a real magical flame exploding through the door. He snapped his paw back, considering his options. There was standing there like a fool, waiting to see if Urda returned. Or he could try the door. That was all. In the wild, those who kept moving were those who survived. Those who remained stagnant, fell behind...

Urda's previous illusion had done no harm. She had played the role of generous host thus far, and the Beast could find no reason to distrust the old woman despite his pessimistic nature. He tapped the iron ring anyway, checking for traces of magic hotter than Urda's fire.

Cold as death.

Relieved, the Beast chuckled. How ironic that he of all people was grateful for the cold kiss of iron?

The chains were the coldest...

"Enough already." The Beast's words echoed in the vacant tavern. He yanked the door open and stepped through.

Chapter 5

A deafening crash of unseen waterfalls, boomed through the doorway, pounding a throb into the Beast's skull. A blinding flash of white light followed. He threw up a thick forearm, pressing fur and muscle into his grimacing face. Blinding slivers penetrated, burning purple spots through his eyelids. *How much longer would it burn?* He turned against the light, fumbling for the door's latch.

The burning vanished with the click of a door. The torturous explosion had lasted only as long as a door closing and yet felt like an eternity. A darkened expanse of grayish brick walls splotched by mold replaced the tavern's mounted trophies. Streaks of pale moonlight filtered through an unseen canopy, painting watery shapes at his feet. The emptiness tugged at an ever present scar. It had been two long years since the chains.

He would never go back.

A tiny voice called to him. The Beast lowered his head, ears straining. His heart thumped steadily in his temples. He dropped to all fours, squishing cool wet sand between his toes. The voice beckoned again.

He stalked his way through columns of dusty light, stifling dry coughs into his cloak. Twenty paces ahead, glimmering droplets of moonlight fell in reverse, climbing from floor to ceiling. The Beast halted his advance, unnerved by the bizarre scene. *More of Urda's magic?*

Urda's whisper danced in the shadows. "You know this place, Beast of Briarburn, no?"

The Beast's head swiveled to the gypsy's voice but found nothing.

"You are indeed alone, my boy, but fear not! Urda is watching. Now think. Force those rusty works of yours."

The Beast wracked his mind, willing memory to come crashing back and fill in the blanks. *A forest... Stars... cobblestone...* Nothing before his awakening on the Great Road. He shook his head, unable to conceal the disappointment in his voice. "Never in my life have I seen this pit."

"Ah, as truthful a reply as there ever was," Urda chuckled. "But have you considered that perhaps you've had more than one?"

The Beast relaxed to his haunches. "One what?"

"One life, Beast of Briarburn."

More than one life? Had the old woman gone mad? The Beast knew full well that a being lived and died only once. *You were only dealt one hand.* The Beast exploded to full height and rumbled through clenched teeth. "I grow tired of riddle speak and parlor tricks."

"Ah, patience, my boy, patience. We have come to a forgotten place. How deep is for you alone to decide. I have merely forced a stubborn door." Urda's jovial tone became grim. "From here, you journey alone. Beware, you may not like all you discover. Some memories are best left behind." The gypsy's words trailed off. The Beast fancied not the prospect of searching for answers in a dungeon. Let alone an illusion forged by his fragmented mind.

A weak sob echoed. The Beast leaned toward the muffled sound, reluctant to charge ahead. In the wild, many a wily predator used calls and cries to bait their prey. The cry echoed again. *Familiar*, he thought. His eyes narrowed against the near pitch, studying the walls. And there it was: The faint outline of an egress. The cry had to have come from within.

The Beast took a step and the moonlight poured into the sand, collecting in a buckler sized puddle. The liquid filled the passage's mouth, swirling like a whirlpool. He clenched his massive fists, hoping the gesture would prove unnecessary. He stalked the puddle, drawing long even breaths of the stale air. The swirling light rose like a storm funnel, undulating like a cobra. It darted forward, probing the intruder.

Just as I thought.

Despite the ominous dance he remained unafraid. He was hesitant to trust in Urda's illusion, but she had delivered much with little effort. He would dare to believe. The serpentine light lashed out like a whip. But the Beast was quicker and dropped his heavy fist like a mace, shattering the light into crystalline shards. He stepped over the puddle and cast a wary eye at the dissolving fragments.

The low stone ceiling forced him to hunch and the tunnel narrowed with each step. Halfway through, the suffocating passage smeared slimy mold onto his cloaked shoulders and scraped at his curved horns. The coffin-like tunnel spilled into a round chamber of shining obsidian walls.

Several crackling braziers dotted the room's periphery. The Beast traced a smooth wall with a clawed digit. Overhead, an oculus of ruby and onyx blocked an unseen sky.

A boy of no more than five winters sat by a brazier. His knees were tucked under his chin and waves of stringy hair caked with grime clung to tear stains. A filthy tunic did little to hide welted limbs. His eyes darted to the menace of dancing shadows and widened when the Beast's giant form filled the entrance. The Beast awkwardly gestured for calm, thinking himself the cause of the child's fright. "Be not afraid."

The boy shivered into his knees and leveled a finger. His raw lower lip quivered. The Beast extended an outstretched palm. "I will not harm you." He struggled for a re-assuring tone and crept closer, fully expecting a shriek sure to shatter the oculus. The boy remained still, as though carved from stone. The Beast realized then the power of Urda's enchantment. He was indeed merely a visitor.

The Beast was waving a paw before the boy's eyes when a faint clicking sound ebbed into the chamber. His skin crawled at the awful noise. He snapped to the narrow tunnel, finding nothing in the deep dark. He rushed to the boy and scooped him onto his back. He tore the closest brazier free and hurled the burning sculpture overhead... A rainfall of shattered glass tossed glints of fire over the walls of obsidian mirror. The Beast spun around, shielding the boy. "Hold tightly, boy."

The Beast mustered his strength and leapt into the newly ventilated ceiling. He found his mark and clamped down hard. His brawny legs dangled, building momentum. His grip slipped and he slid back. He gouged the stone and pulled. A moment later, he pulled himself through. The Beast rolled to his back and gasped for breath. *The boy.*

His stomach somersaulted and he crawled to the ring of broken glass.

The boy was back beside the brazier, knees to chest, finger leveled. The Beast blinked, checking against his disbelief. He shouted for the boy to hide. Still, the boy remained motionless.

The sea of clicks drowned out his calls. And then it arrived. A rust tinged wave swept through the tunnel, rolling against the chamber's walls. The Beast told himself that he had done all he could, but a foul pit in his stomach dissented.

The reddish brown flow filled the room, climbing the walls, dousing the braziers. A writhing swarm of spiders and scorpions clicked and crawled, snapping at him as it continued to climb. The Beast backed away from the oculus and scanned for an escape route. A cover of grainy darkness stretched into forever. There was only one option.

Run.

He sprinted down the dome, looking back only once. He instantly regretted the decision. The swarm of stingers and fangs had crested the breach and spilled over, surging like a poisonous tide. The dome's edge raced closer. The Beast leapt and sailed through the grayish murk of his forgotten memory. Crashing sounds of waterfalls and a piercing white light suddenly surrounded him. His head throbbed between his paws. He squeezed them into his ears, trying to silence the deafening roar. His vision cleared.

And his heart sank.

He sat surrounded by burning braziers in a round room with shimmering black walls. Overhead, an intricate stained glass oculus reflected the fire light. The Beast was quick to his feet. He lifted an arm to brush himself off, but was thwarted by the sight of a child-sized, human hand. *His child-sized, human hand.* He gasped at his reflection and traced the round features of a fleshy face. He ran his hands through grimy hair, stopping where his horns were supposed to be.

It couldn't be...

He fell back to the safety of a brazier's warmth. A faint clicking squelched his astonishment. The swarm was coming and there was no chance of repeating the escape. His human legs lacked the strength. Thankfully, his wit remained intact. He tore off a greasy piece of tunic and wrapped it around a scrap of loose wood plucked from a brazier. The clicking built to a sinister roar. He ignited the torch and barreled into the passage.

Dancing torch light cast an amber glow over the sea of carapaces as the Beast-child's spindly arms swept the torch in wild circles. Arachnids sizzled and scorched into black dust. He skidded into the memory-scape's first chamber, driving the swarm into full retreat. The clicking mass piled against the Troll's Breath's door. A shaft of silvery moon painted the latch. He need only put the swarm to the torch and be done with it.

A ghostly light rose from the floor and drew the swarm's burnt remnants to its luminous center. When the last scorched carcass was consumed, a flash ignited the room. The shock wave blasted the Beast-child into a jagged crack in the wall. His vision cleared in time for the memory to morph into a nightmare.

For something horrible crawled out from the glob of pulsating light.

The Beast-child's chilled blood slogged through his quaking body. He bit down hard on his lip, desperate to silence his chattering teeth. He tried desperately to push deeper into the crack. The creature's name eluded him in his fright, but he remembered well the terrifying visage. Its eyes numbered eight and glowered with pale fire. A mottled humanoid torso sprouted grotesquely from a giant spider's body carried by skittish, bluish-black legs. A muscular left arm ended in a wicked serrated pincer.

The Beast-child clamped his mouth. He was sure his heart would freeze any moment. And then the monster spoke with the chilling midnight wind of a cemetery.

"Say it. Say my name."

Icy rails pierced the Beast-child's heart. He choked down a parade of gasps, clinging to fleeing breath. The demon beckoned with its human hand and smiled a hideous mouthful of hooked fangs. "You'll never be free of Arak-jai."

A shrill scream shattered his consciousness and the Beast-child lapsed into darkness.

Chapter 6

Without warning, he was back. He clutched the table's sides, tension
building in his forearms. The Beast slumped in his chair, vaguely aware of
the fire's warmth upon his face. Never in his life had he felt such
exhaustion. Urda summoned the crystals back to her side. They flashed
home, hovering beside the carved headrest of the high back chair. She
probed the hearth with a poker.

The old gypsy smiled in the dancing light. She had indeed delivered a
rare gift. The Beast now possessed a kernel of truth. His origin had long
been an elusive dream. Now it was as certain as the dawn. The image of
his childish hands was imprinted upon his mind. *Human...*

"I remember..." The words fought through his throat. "I remember
the dark. I remember when he first came." A shiver climbed the Beast's
spine. He remembered the stinging, the biting. He remembered hiding
from the horrible eyes.

"Ah yes. The Prince of Stingers, the Arachnomancer himself," Urda
said, slipping back into her chair.

The Beast uttered the once forgotten name scorched forever on his
tongue. "Arak-jai." He wondered why the brutal memory was the first to
reveal itself.

"Because it was he who ignited the burning desire within you. The
desire to fight. The desire to live free of fear."

The Beast sprung upright, unnerved by the intrusion into his private thoughts. He started to issue a complaint but Urda found words first.

"Peace, Beast of Briarburn. Yours was an obvious question. In fact, it was the most obvious question. Everyone who travels inside questions why they see what they see."

The Beast sensed truth in her words. Inside of that frightened boy a glowing ember had been born. That boy would mature and face his crawling fears in the darkness. The works of his mind turned, creaking slowly as rust fell away. The Beast remembered that boy. He survived, found his way to a new home... A castle. He would grow up to be...

The memory faded. It was only a fragment of a fragment. But it was something. It was a start. The Beast studied the lines around Urda's eyes. The fire in her milky orbs hinted that old age had done little to dampen a strong spirit. There was no trace of dishonesty. He fumbled for the medallion and then lifted it over his head. The firestone gleamed, soaking up the fire's warmth. With a gentle push it slid across the table, splitting the narrow spaces between bone-filled plates and empty mugs. Urda cupped her hand beneath the table's edge just as the medallion slipped off.

The medallion spun, dangling from Urda's bony fingers. She let it dance at the end of its chain, then traced a thumb over the inscription. "I've never seen anything quite like it, my son," Urda lied. "It is dazzling piece. Certainly there is magic within the stone, that much is obvious to even the thickest dullard. Very old. Originated beyond our realm."

The exhausted Beast missed the subtle shift in Urda's tone. Layers of flowery talk about magic and distant realms provided ample concealment. *It was the stuff of children's fantasies and old maid's tales*, the Beast thought. *Fantastic tales for hopeless fools.* Then again, he had experienced Urda's magic firsthand. *Maybe there was something to her claim?* He leaned onto an elbow and extended an open palm. The medallion drifted from Urda's fingers and settled around his tree trunk neck. The Beast stifled a chuckle. Urda's mischievous nature was growing on him.

The Beast allowed a minor breach of his guard, dressing his words with a hint of sarcasm. "Parlor tricks are one thing, gypsy, but what real help are you?"

"Yes, yes, faerie fire is one thing. Showing you the nature of true magic is another entirely. Your quest, your very existence is grounded in more magic than you care to admit, Beast of Briarburn. It surrounds you though you deny it, fueled by the brightest stars in our nighttime sky." Urda's eyes sparkled with the rising passion in her voice. "Magic is the very life-blood and soul of *all* creation. It stretches beyond the land of the living, binding all of the realms in a delicate master piece."

The Beast was speechless. He had no rebuttal for Urda's passionate words. Had he arbitrarily dismissed magic's importance as the world of Men had so callously dismissed him? He thought of the cold iron shackles that had bound him after the last time he had trusted in men. Summoning all courage, he stood and bowed his head. He crossed his heart with a wide paw.

"Please, help me."

"Of course Urda will help you. There is much to learn from your past, yes. But a glimpse into your future will provide guiding star."

The Beast fell back into his chair, expecting the crystal balls to resume their dance. Urda slapped the table with a freckled hand and laughed. "Silly boy. One cannot divine the future by scouring the fabric of memory. Come, we must go outside."

Much preferring the hearth to the freezing wind, the Beast hesitated. "Why is that?"

"The stars, Beast of Briarburn. If there are answers for us to find, surely they will be amongst the stars."

Urda snapped her fingers and the door leading outside swung open. A second snap dismissed the flickering crystals. Urda offered her arm to the Beast. Again, he hesitated. Urda scoffed and picked up her old bones. "Heaven forbid a gentleman help an old woman from her chair. Especially when she means to wander into the cold on his behalf."

The Beast flushed and looked sheepishly at his feet. Urda patted him on the arm and strolled to the door, leaving him to embrace his role as shadow. The sky was a jumble of gray cotton. The moon peeked in and out of sight, but the stars were all but absent. The Beast grumbled, slicing a paw through a thick fog. "I can barely see my hand let alone the stars."

Urda ignored the complaint. She pressed her palms together, fingers pointed to the moon. He heard a whisper, thinking at first it was the rustling wind. The whispering lasted a sparrow's song and then Urda blew a kiss to the heavens. The stars shook their cloudy blanket free, for a moment illuminating the world with light brilliant enough to make the sun envious. The stars' diamond encrusted mural promised that he was an important thread in a grand masterpiece. Humbled, he bowed his head.

Urda summoned the crystals with a snap, then threw an imaginary stick at the sky. The crystals shot off in pursuit of their quarry, climbing over snow-covered pines, then scattering in three directions. Positioned to her liking, Urda shouted. "Well then, go on. Show our friend what is to be."

Beams of scarlet light shot from the crystals, forming a triangle against the starry backdrop. They carved the night, slowly draining away the color within the boundary. First went the cottony clouds. Then went the charcoal sky. The stars themselves faded last, leaving a pale triangle. The Beast's jaw dropped. He eyed the gypsy, but only for a moment. There was a nagging sensation that her magic was dangerous. But, he had decided to place his trust in it and he would see the decision through.

"No harm shall come to you from the stars. Not ever," Urda said softly.

The tension eased in his shoulders and the Beast released the breath he had been holding since the fiery shape appeared. A speck flashed in the triangle's center. It danced erratically, leaving tracers of light in its wake. The speck raced about, bouncing among the scarlet boundaries, filling in the empty space with a familiar image.

His portrait...

"You've out done yourself," the Beast said, impressed once more by the gypsy's magic.

The sketch suddenly vibrated. A writhing tail of wicked barbs burst through the triangular frame, knocking the Beast-effigy from his feet. A second whip like appendage wrapped around its throat.

The Beast jabbed a talon at the morbid image. "Jahana's blaze! What was that?"

Urda did not answer, only solemnly nodded upwards, trying to focus the Beast's attention.

The Beast snarled and looked as commanded. Fanged jaws appeared, snapping and salivating. He watched helplessly as the effigy was flayed by the writing serpents. The jaws stalked forward. With a crunching pop they unhinged to a grotesque angle. He heard a child's cry from above. Familiar somehow, like an echo. He didn't know how, but he was certain it was not the scream of the cringing boy.

The image vibrated again. The speck sped about, etching a small figure behind his effigy. Not until the Beast noticed the curly hair did he realize it was a child.

A girl.

The fanged jaws snapped like a bear trap, swallowing the scene. A cruel laugh leaked from the dying portrait. And then there was nothing. The sky breached the crimson triangle like ocean tide through a sand castle.

"No!" The Beast paced a circle around Urda, snow and ice crunching underfoot. "I must know more. Is that to be my end? You said no harm would come of stars. What then is that?" The furious tirade left his muscled chest heaving. He clutched at his medallion, pulling the chain taut.

Urda rested a gentle hand on the Beast's paw and guided the medallion back to his mane. "Take heart, Beast of Briarburn. Your fate is no more certain than the next man's. All you carry from this moment, your fears, your strength, and yes even your weakness can protect you from that fate. But only if you recognize which is which."

The Beast grumbled a minor complaint about Urda's cryptic words but the old woman hushed him with a wave. She extended her arm and this time the Beast was swift to take it.

"Come. This wind is fit to chill a witch's heart. Let us find the fire. In the morning, you will visit Sensheeri. An old friend there may be of further service. I yet have a trick that will aid your travels."

***

A bright sapphire star penetrated the newly settled cloud cover where the macabre theatre had been drawn. Polaris shined down with increasing intensity. The light filtered down in a spiral, enveloping the Troll's Breath in its center.

Chapter 7

Sensheeri was founded at the edge of Lake Tamahl, the largest lake in the Once Kingdom. The mammoth body took weeks to traverse under the most accommodating happenstance. At its deepest Tamahl was several times deeper than man's natural ability to dive. For generations, Sensheeri's people worked the bountiful waters as fisherman and salvager. The town was raised in circular fashion like the rings of a tree; proud evidence of growth and prosperity. Sensheeri's domiciles and small shops were also perfect circles, owing to a belief that evil spirits preferred shadowy corners to use as portals.

Daybreak found vendors of bolted wool and cured meats pushing carts through the modest marketplace. Cries of cheap wares and scandalous bargains melded into a continuous buzz. A bakery teased the air with scents of sweet bread, a welcome distraction from the scent of brine. A small armada of fishing boats cinched to a pair of barnacled piers rolled on gentle tides. Icy winter months provided no respite: the lake remained under daily siege by eager crews preparing their vessels for launch. Men bundled in thick coats scurried across the docks, carrying supplies for the long day ahead. Lines were cast off and wives wished for safe returns, their breath dotting the morning air like smoke signals.

Lia knelt in front of Sensheeri's bakery, watching a pack of children kick a patchwork ball around a muddied stretch of road. Her shoulder length hair was the color of baker's chocolate, carelessly cinched with a pale blue ribbon. She wanted nothing more than to join them at play, but knew better than to ask. She was different and they would never let her forget it.

She pressed a tiny twig of a finger into the snow, doodling nothing in particular. The nothing was soon a box. Another scribble and it became a house. Next to the box-house came a family of stick figures. She giggled at the accidental giants beside the tiny home. *How peculiar,* she thought. A wave and a whisper and the canvas of snow became blank once more.

Startled by a sudden chill, Lia looked up from the snow, cautiously looking around. *No one had noticed.* She breathed a sigh of relief. Magic in all forms was expressly forbidden by the queen. Even simple gestures like asking the snow to erase itself. Lia didn't understand why it were so. How silly that something as wonderful as painting the sky over Festival with tiny comets was forbidden?

A tall boy noticed Lia off by herself. Philip sneered, carefully lining up his next kick. With a dull thump, the ball sailed over the slush covered road. He took off in hot pursuit, knowing full well where it would land. A growing shadow darkened Lia's snowy canvas. The dirty ball bumped her knees and spread mud through her work space. Sighing, she looked up and found a most expected Philip grinning down from behind a mask of filth. Lia fought back a gag. Philip smelled of manure and the fishmonger, a wretched stench that could fell a charging bull.

"What are ya drawing today, *durp*?"

Lia shrugged. She hated the word '*durp*', essentially a slur meaning 'outcast'. The other children were fast at Philip's side, loyal minions all.

"Leave me alone, Philip." Lia's voice was soft but steady. Sadly, being bullied was a way of life. She took a deep breath. '*Don't give in starshine*', she heard Cedrik say in her head. Her back stiffened a bit.

"I asked you a question, *durp*!" Philip shrugged his shoulder with more than a little menace.

"Yeah durp, what's that supposed to be?" Another boy chimed in, emboldened by his boss.

The urge to lash out germinated deep in Lia's belly, rising steadily into her lungs. She knew she shouldn't give in. It never ended well and usually supplied them with additional fodder. Instead, her amber eyes darted back and forth, hoping for a nearby elder.

No such luck.

"Maybe it was supposed to be her *matar*," a fat, pig-faced girl oinked in a nasally voice, "the mother she doesn't have!"

The band of bullies laughed at Pig-face's cruel jab. Lia's eyes watered, but no tears fell. She swore to deny them the pleasure of seeing her cry. She climbed to her feet, deftly dabbing her eyes. Her brave act lit the powder keg inside Philip's mean streak. The bully's shove sent Lia reeling through the muddy snow and flopping into a freezing puddle.

"Stay in the gutter where you belong." Philip trampled the rest of the clean patch of snow. "No more stupid pictures today, *durp.*"

Lia shivered, looking on in sad disbelief. Not for her pictures, or for Philip's cruelty. She pitied Philip and the others. *How sad and hurt they must be on the inside.* Philip racked his brain for another insult. The wheels turned then stalled. Frustrated, Philip wound up a kick instead. If he couldn't hurt Lia with words...

"You little demons leave that girl alone," called a stern voice. It was instantly soothing to Lia as always and in the air like a woodwind. Cedrik made for the crowd of bullies, walking stick leading the way. A battered lute was strapped to his back, partially obscured by folds of his cloak. He stopped, pinning the stick beneath his arm, and adjusted his blindfold.

Philip picked up the ragged ball and flung it hard. "Mind your own business, old man!"

Without dropping his seeing-stick, Cedrik caught the ball with a flash of his hand. He held the captured projectile in place for a moment before offering a sly smile, much to Philip's chagrin. Satisfied that he had Philip's attention, Cedrik returned fire with perfect aim. The impact forced Philip to stumble. Cedrik stooped and helped Lia to her feet. He quietly asked if she were ok. Lia was equally awestruck by Cedrik's keen reflexes. She mumbled a meek 'yes'.

"You kids run along."

"Lucky throw," Philip muttered, hands yet stinging. "Come on then, let's have another kick up the road." Philip tossed the ball up and kicked it away.

"They're just little fools. We can only hope they outgrow it someday," Cedrik offered as he lowered himself to a bench. His intervention came as quickly as his rickety knees had allowed. The price was a paltry soreness and well worth it.

Lia sat beside her savior, feet dangling, eyes filling with tears. "I know. It's just..." With her tormentors gone her voice finally cracked. Sobs quickly followed.

Cedrik rested a thin arm around his ward. "It'll be ok, starshine."

Lia dried her eyes. What would she do without her *'pafaa*? Cedrik was more than a grandfather. He was a constant source of love and guidance that far exceeded any such title. She was grateful for his many lessons on the world's magical wonders. Of utmost importance, he lectured, was starlight. Cedrik taught her of the Breath and Blight and how they were the balancing halves that made magic a family. *Death and decay are natural parts of life. It is the darkness of mankind's heart that corrupts the starlight and spawns evil into our world.*

Cedrik swung the lute from underneath his cloak and strummed a few chords. The melody was hypnotic; legendary throughout the lakeside villages for its ability to soothe fussy newborns. His record on the subject was spotless. Lia proved no different from the day she was born. Seven chords later, Lia was all cried out and smiling.

"Feel better, starshine?"

Lia hugged the old man with the tight squeeze of a grateful grandchild.

"I think those little demons will get what's coming to them someday," Cedrik said, pointing the seeing-stick.

"I think you're right." Lia closed her eyes and whispered a secret meant only for the wind's ear. A strange glyph formed in her mind and her nimble fingers began to scribble in the air. Lia's enchantment settled upon the ball, encasing it with a golden shine. It took on a life of its own, bouncing wildly, running amok through Philip's band. Her tormentors shrieked in confused terror.

Pig-face tried escaping on her stubby legs, but the ball danced around her feet and sent her sprawling. Philip cried the loudest when the ball singled him out for a double share of punishment. The golden enchantment spread to his boot laces, tying them together while a newly golden sweater flew over his head. The scratchy garment snagged under Philip's bulbous nose, blocking his vision.

A giggle escaped Lia despite her best attempts at stifling. Cedrik was thankful for a mind capable of painting the chaotic and gratifying picture. Philip bucked against the enchanted sweater and knotted boot strings. "Oh, oh there he goes!" Cedrik snickered.

Philip spun around, tripped, and fell face first into a frozen dung pile. The others remained at the mercy of the still rampaging ball, flattening backsides and faces as it saw fit.

"That's quite enough, young lady," Sensheeri's mountain of a sheriff called. He brushed at the thick ginger moustache foresting his upper lip.

Cedrik attempted to mount a defense. "Oh Jack, she was just having a bit of fun. And bullies are not to be appeased."

"Ced, you know the law. Absolutely no magic. And besides, you shouldn't want her stooping to their level." Jack stared at Lia as he stressed the point.

"But Jack, you're the one who always says how magic is the most precious part of our world. It's what pushes us forward when we most want to run home!" Lia pouted. "Besides, I'm tired of being bullied all the time."

Cedrik's pride swelled. The child by his side, so small and fragile, had proven once again to be much sturdier than she was given credit.

Jack took a knee, still doubling Lia's height. "Magic *is* very important. But using it to reflect malice is wrong. Even if it means we have to turn the other cheek. Magic is a dangerous tool, more dangerous than all of our axes and gaffing hooks combined. When we use magic for vengeance a little flicker of our soul's shine is eaten away. And soon enough we find we have none left to light our way. Do you understand, *dutre?*"

Lia nodded, knowing Jack to be right. He was always right. She appreciated hearing the traditional word for daughter. It offered additional balm against Philip's terrible slur. Jack opened a sweeping wingspan. Lia barreled face first into his ample belly, arms not even close to reaching around Jack's waist. The sheriff's arms wrapped around her. With a surprise scoop, Lia was deposited on a burly shoulder.

Jack's tone darkened. "Word on the Road is that the queen is becoming woefully intolerant of even the smallest transgressions. The Wakeful are sweeping the countryside, just itching to find people daring to dabble in magic-craft."

A shiver ran up Lia's spine. Though too young to fully grasp the tyranny at large in her tiny world, the uneasiness in Jack's voice was crystal clear. She was no stranger to the odd soldiers whose voices all droned alike. Horror stories of the Wakeful's incursions whispered by hushed tongues were commonplace amongst travelers journeying through Sensheeri. Stories that included kidnapping 'undesirables' and making them disappear. Or worse.

The village's lone bell clanged everyone to attention. It was a startling sound, used for emergencies like fires on the wharf. Lia knew the other reason the bell was used. A reason nobody cared for. A reason most sensible people feared. Jack knew it too. He was responsible for the assembly the tolling demanded.

Lia climbed down from Jack's shoulder and stared at the twin cairns marking Sensheeri's main gate. She grabbed a hand from each of her guardian bookends. Bearing down on the peaceful fishing hamlet was a tight formation of riders...

...in black armor.

Chapter 8

Sensheeri's moss covered cairns stood twice as tall as a man and stood far enough apart to accommodate two wagons. The original settlers regarded the great stones as symbols of welcome and amity. The Wakeful burst through the gateway oblivious of their sentiment.

Hooves pounded the snowy road, grinding the peaceful morning to a halt. The cobbled stone of the Great Road ended, giving way to well trafficked mud. Smacking sounds replaced clopping ones as the formation trampled into the village. Malachai halted his men and ordered a dismount amidst the crowd summoned by the bell. Fishing crews filed down the piers and joined their apprehensive families. Though long accustomed to the Wakeful's regular incursions, the people of Sensheeri sensed this visit was cause for grave concern.

Lia followed closely behind Jack, leading Cedrik by an elbow. She peeked around Jack's waist, careful to avoid the icy stares of the unwelcome visitors. A timid glance found Jack's cheeks drained of color. She watched in dismay as the same pallor spread over the sea of Sensheeri's faces.

Malachai marched to the crowd's center flanked by his semi-circle of Wakeful. He moved with the supreme confidence possessed by all hardened warriors; a swagger born of a career's worth of crushing victories. The unseen hand of fear brushed aside even the largest citizen, causing more than one to stumble. At a position to his liking, Malachai removed his dragon inspired helm. His eyes were crimson infernos that hollowed Sensheeri's hearts and souls. The fear was all but palpable and he knew his mission had been completed long ago. *Sensheeri was properly subjugated.*

How he reveled in their delicious terror...

His nod saw a pair of Wakeful to purpose, stacking wood taken from a nearby pile into a pyre. The villagers groaned but found their protests muted to a murmur by Malachai's penetrating stare.

"You searched our village not two months ago, Captain," Jack shouted. "Why have you returned so soon? We've done no wrong."

"I beg to differ." Malachai's sinister drone climbed every spine present. A Wakeful produced a vial of emerald liquid from his belt's pouch and presented it to his captain. Malachai's armor screeched as he brandished the vial high overhead. Sensheeri fell silent, stiller than a graveyard past the witching hour. Malachai threw the vial with frigid indifference, shattering the glass over the pyre. A breath later, the pyre erupted into an eerie, smokeless green flame.

"Captain--" Jack said.

"People of Sensheeri. By decree of her Majesty, your Queen, we are charged with the destruction of your heresy." Malachai's powerful voice suffocated the crowd like an avalanche. "Bring to us all that inspires you that we may purge such... burdens."

Lia cupped her hands over her ears. She tried to block out Malachai's words, but the voice reverberated in her head. Her brow crinkled. "What do they mean 'heresy'?"

The veins in Cedrik's thin neck bulged. "They mean to say 'magic' or anything to do with it."

"But why? Why do they hate it so? Haven't they seen the magic at Festival?"

"Starshine, they *have* seen magic. Magic that stirs the heart and invigorates the spirit. This is precisely why she wants to destroy it," Cedrik spat, unwilling to name the Liche Queen. "I hope you live to see a day when magic exists as it did during the time of the once ways."

A handful of villagers slogged glumly to the pyre, carrying assorted blankets and trinkets. They stared at the frozen ground, fearful of Malachai's condemnatory glare. He nodded to each, signaling that their offerings should be cast in. *Purged.* The emerald flame had yet to go hungry. A short woman with stringy hair gently tossed an earthen decanter. A simple flower was scrawled on its side. She sobbed while it was consumed by the green fire, erased from all but her memory. She toddled from the pyre, whimpering.

Lia wanted to run to Nell, to wrap her arms around her and squeeze. She recognized the decanter. She remembered the day that Nell's daughter had painted the blue flower and the ceremony for her passing into the World After that winter. Several of the villagers remembered it from the summer fair where it had taken the blue ribbon that matched the proud flower.

Fists were balled and a few braver souls clenched farm tools tighter. The subtle uptick in tension did not go unnoticed. The Wakeful reached for weapons, but only Malachai drew his blade.

"Be at peace, for this is your queen's command."

Cedrik dropped his seeing stick and reached for Lia's hands. "Starshine, I need you to do your old *pafaa* a favor. I need you to remember this day. Remember that there comes a time when you must draw a line." A tear traced one of the many lines on Cedrik's face.

"Not my queen! Never *my* queen!" Cedrik released Lia's hands and unknotted his blindfold, letting it fall away. He felt the sun on his eyes for the first time since his punishment. The warmth seeped into his wrinkled skin. It was time.

"*Pafaa*, what's happening? Lia's eyes watered as confusion washed over. The crowd was fast parting at the front. The Wakeful cut a path to Cedrik, shoving people aside, old and young. Cedrik pinched Lia's chin with a loving squeeze and kissed the top of her head.

"Someday you will. And on that day, you will make me the proudest *pafaa* in the world." Cedrik pushed away his cloak, slinging free the old lute. Lia's eyes widened. Music was banned under the law. The penalty for possessing an instrument, let alone playing one was...

After the fullest breath he had ever known was discharged through pursed lips, Cedrik strummed tired fingers over tired strings.

"Peasant, you are ordered to stop. Immediately." Malachai's ominous command hung like a storm cloud.

Jack swam through the crowd, desperate to reach Cedrik first. "Ced, stop. Do as he says."

Cedrik plucked a few errant notes that quickly fell into place. And became chords. Cedrik played the oldest song he remembered, an old lullaby that he often sang to frighten away Lia's nightmares. The Wakeful pushed through the last row of people surrounding the defiant old man. Jack reached him a second later, once again imploring him to stop. Malachai's voice boomed. "I've warned you once, old man. There will not be a second."

The Wakeful drew serrated swords of the same black steel as their armor. They surrounded the old musician, now playing as painstakingly perfect as anyone had ever heard. Lia whimpered as the Wakeful closed on Cedrik like a starving pack of wolves. "*Pafaa..*"

Jack sprinted to Lia, brushing her protectively behind him. "Ced, please. Don't do this, we need you."

The melody slowed, then came to a halt. Cedrik looked to the sound of his family's voices. A smile, broad and reassuring stretched over his wrinkled face. The crowd of on lookers breathed a collective sigh of tentative relief.

Cedrik panned to a sky he could not see and only barely remembered.

With the last bit of Breath in his aching bones he willed darkened eyes to glance upon the light. A sapphire halo of star dust spiraled around his head.

Lia couldn't believe it. *How couldn't I have known? Why did he keep it a secret?*

The blindness fell from Cedrik's eyes like a masquerade mask. He searched for Lia. He had to see her face one last time. He found her standing by Jack's side, safely bound at the shoulders by the brawny hands of his closest friend. Cedrik beamed and mouthed the word 'remember'. In a final act of defiance, Cedrik turned his back on the Wakeful and the tyranny of their queen.

And resumed his song.

"Take him," Malachai commanded.

"No!" Lia screamed as loud as her lungs would allow. She tried to wrestle free from Jack's grasp.

The Wakeful blades flashed like black lightning, cutting through cloak and flesh. Cedrik gasped and fell to his knees. He looked around the village that he had called home for the last seven years. The hut that he had once used to deliver newborns. The wharf, where he had mastered the craft of Sensheeri's trade. A coldness not born of winter settled into his bones and Cedrik shivered. He saw Sensheeri's lone tavern. Memories of celebration dissolved like lighted shadows. The world grayed. He stared at the child he loved above all, grateful to take Lia's vibrance into the

World After. She was the divine symphony a world deafened by oppression cried out for.

Cedrik cradled his lute and crumpled over.

Malachai pointed his blade at Cedrik and then turned to the stunned crowd. Hateful mocking tinged his drone. "Such is the price for your blasph--"

A lone chord twanged beautifully, rippling through Lia's heart before sailing across the still lake waters. Cedrik's body quaked and his hand readied another bit of lullaby. Malachai's sword flashed with emerald flame. The Wakeful captain drove the inferno through Cedrik's chest, pinning the old man to the snow. He withdrew, making a proud display of his bloodied trophy.

The blackness returned to Cedrik's eyes. And then the music was gone.

Chapter 9

The portal sealed with a sucking sound of mud. The Beast rested his paws on his knees, willing his stomach to peace. "Never again."

A wailing scream split the morning. In an instant, the birdsong of nearby snow doves was hushed. Even the wind, long entitled to whistling over the lake's tides, found itself silenced. It was the wail of an innocent robbed by a cruel twist of fate. *A child tormented by a terrible evil.*

The Beast took cover behind the twin cairns marking Sensheeri's boundary. Crouching, he was half as tall as the monolith. Not the best of cover, barely wide enough to conceal his girth. But it would have to do. He poked half of his horned head around the stone.

The townsfolk were assembled beneath a bell tower. No one spoke. No one moved. *Did they yet breathe?* At the crowd's heart were six men in black armor. The Wakeful. The Beast's guttural mumble rolled though fangs on a plume of steam. "Wakeful filth. I should have known."

A somber air blanketed the town, sadness plainly written on the sullen faces of men and women alike. He pitied them. Despite his being a cast off he harbored Sensheeri no ill will. But this was not his battle. Facing the Wakeful on the road would have been in defense of *his* home. He had no such place here. The Beast shouldered his pack. He would leave behind the Wakeful and their grim business.

The cairn beneath his paw vibrated. He stepped away, crouching low.

A familiar voice distorted by the sound of ancient stone whispered to him. "Did I not tell you to go to Sensheeri, Beast of Briarburn? Hmm? Did Urda not say there was someone for you to meet?"

"The Wakeful are not my concern."

"They are your biggest concern, my boy. They stand between you and what you prize most." The vibration stopped and Urda's essence fled the cairn. The Beast's head drooped as he considered the task at hand. Urda had neglected to name the person he was to meet, saying only that his path would be brightly lit. He would have to trust her words.

Movement flickered in the paralyzed mass of villagers. A little girl broke free of a muscular man with a bushy moustache. She charged the Wakeful, piercing the crowd like a javelin. The brazen act shocked all. The crowd widened and the soldiers in black readied their weapons. The Beast found his curiosity piqued. *What could stir such raw emotion in a child?*

The riders cleared the Beast's line of sight, falling back to their mounts. The wailing girl knelt over the bloodied body of an old man cradling a broken lute. She wailed into his tattered cloak, muffling the cries and giving the Beast his answer.

Murder.

The muscular man who had been holding her called out. "Lia!"

For a moment all was still. And then Lia finally lifted her head. The Beast's eyes twitched wide. Hovering over the deceased was the child from Urda's sky sketch. There was no mistaking it. Every detail of her round face had been etched into his mind the night before. It was the amber reflection of her eyes that drew his stare above all else. Instead of the rage he expected, rage that would've claimed him like an angry storm, there was stillness. Where there should have been hot painful tears, there were none.

Something very foreign stared at Malachai and his men. Something beautiful and painfully absent from the world he knew. *Innocence.* The Beast was suddenly very ashamed for his near departure. Lia's eyes were free of fear, narrowed and focused. They were the calm gaze of a spirit perfectly centered. He was fascinated by the spectacle, thinking it impossible to be so steady in the face of such brutality.

Lia brushed the snowy hair from the man's eyes and kissed his forehead. The big man lumbered over and dropped to his knees. His beefy arms tried pulling her into a bear hug. Lia resisted with the push of a tiny hand and whispered into the breeze.

Eyes widened throughout the village. Lia's delicate hands glowed a delicate white shine. She chanted ancient words and the speechless wind answered with a mighty gust. The light spread, wrapping her like a luminous shroud. Linens blew from lines and hats from heads. Adults stumbled and children were blown into muddy snow. The light intensified and with a final chant, Lia lowered her hands to the dead man's chest.

The enchantment spread from Lia's hands to the deceased. Wind ripped through the village, rattling shutters and bumping rows of

Sensheeri's boats against docks with wooden clunks. The lake's tide surged, threatening to reclaim the wharfs. Malachai roared a challenge to the wind and ordered his men around the emerald flame. The Wakeful raised a cathedral of swords over the fire, edges clanging against the tempest.

The green flame raised the Beast's hackles. This magic was different than Urda's. The unholy blaze hinted at a greater, darker evil. It was unnatural. It did not belong in this world. The Beast abandoned the safety of the cairn and rushed to the village. A shock wave blasted from the pyre in a bubble of shimmering energy. The Beast was knocked down hard. His ears rang with a high pitched whine. The ground felt like it had melted into a rolling sea.

Sensheeri fared little better. A smoldering pit three acres wide steamed with the ashes of the blast. The village shops were no more than immolated skeletons of glowing ember. Screams and groans filled the acrid air. Panic stricken survivors scrambled in all directions, searching for sanctuary. Men scooped up wives, who scooped up children, and fled for the safety of the trees.

Only Lia's light remained unshaken. Her face was the same mask of tranquility.

Malachai's fist crushed his sword's hilt. The burn of his crimson eyes flickered in tune with the embers at his feet. "Seize the girl."

A Wakeful sheathed his jagged sword and sprinted like a wolf running down prey. Lia's hands crossed in waving patterns, working the enchantment to its pinnacle. The Wakeful closed, drawing a twisted dagger. The Beast hurdled the child in a blur of billowing cloak, barreling a bone-crushing blow into the Wakeful a pace from Lia's side. The collision smashed a tangle of fur and steel through Sensheeri's well.

The Beast climbed from the stony wreckage and towered over the fallen soldier. He seized the Wakeful's faceplate, hoisting him to eye level. Snarling, he squeezed. Malachai ordered the attack and the rest of his men charged. The grating screech of metal being crushed quickly halted the advance. The Beast held his trophy high and then casually tossed the drone aside.

He threw his massive shoulders back, bared every last fang and growled, daring them to come.

The Wakeful split apart, circling the Beast. One charged, slashing high. The Beast caught a gleam in the blade, paused a breath, then ducked. A Wakeful to his rear careened in and rolled over his shoulder. The Beast channeled the momentum and flung him into Wakeful at his front. He clamored over the pile of black armor, rushing for the green fire. Malachai and company plunged their swords into the pyre of emerald, siphoning power into their blades. The fire burst, spewing embers into the snow. The discarded embers sizzled and the ground began to shake.

The Beast danced awkwardly for a moment and then dropped to four paws. The Wakeful withdrew their swords and the quake died. Their obsidian blades pulsed with borrowed power.

They took aim with the charged weapons and loosed jets of green flame. The Beast rolled away. Ravenous tendrils singed his cloak and burned patches of black glass into the land. They lined up for a second volley, but he was ready. He snatched up two heavy pieces of broken well and heaved them like a catapult. The missiles connected with a boom, blasting two Wakeful into Lake Tamahl's freezing grip.

Malachai threw a whirling sword that wedged into the ground a pace before the Beast.

The Beast snorted. "Not even close, Wakeful filth."

Malachai droned a chortling sound. "Hardly."

The Beast's wild ears twitched at a faint whistling sound. He dove aside, narrowly escaping a screaming meteorite. A second, then third orb of malachite fell, birthing quakes of their own. The Beast evaded, dodging storms of debris, with a flurry of dashes and dives.

Lia cried out. "Jack!"

The Beast rolled to his feet, head snapping to the cry. Malachai was dragging Lia to his waiting mount. She dug her heels in and wrestled her captor's grip, but the ground was too muddy and Malachai much too strong. Lia clawed for the big body lying in the snow. The Beast gave chase, running hard for the Wakeful captain. A flurry of green meteorites blotted the morning sun, then pounded the earth, trapping him behind a wall of undying flame. He sprung back, watching helplessly as Malachai took his mount and slung Lia across his lap. The dark horse wheeled in place, then bolted for the cairn.

In two blinks they were gone, disappeared down the road. Faint groans interrupted his pursuit.

"Lia.."

The Beast knelt by Jack's side. The burly man was badly burned. Clothing and hair were singed to flakey ash. The Beast was no medicus. He knew Jack's moments were fleeting. His tongue fumbled, lacking the comforting words of a cleric's offering. He silently chided himself for not acting sooner. A voice from the forgotten part of the Beast's heart told him to take Jack's hand.

Sensheeri's dying sheriff's eyes glossed with tears. Burned fingers tugged at the Beast's cloak. Jack shook as the World After beckoned. His eyes widened and with the last of his strength he pulled the mammoth figure closer.

"You must find her."

Chapter 10

The Beast closed Jack's eyelids with a gentle paw. He was no stranger to the cruel bond of death and desperation. The grim scene had been played out for his benefit many times over. In the wild, Death hunted with any number of masterful techniques: exposure, starvation, combat. Survival was, at its core, merely a struggle to delay the inevitable.

Sensheeri burned all around; a doomed village beyond saving. Most of the villagers had fled the terror. Some lingered about, skulking through rubble, salvaging what they may. Their ash covered faces mirrored Jack's grim mask. The Beast knew as they did: winter was young and yet had long to reign.

A woman carrying an infant scurried to Cedrik's body. Trembling sobs and prayers parted her lips. The Beast gestured for her to pay her last respects. He stepped back, affording her a measure of privacy. The woman's eyes pulsed wide. She pulled the baby closer and fled for the safety of her neighbors.

The Beast of Briarburn was unsurprised by the woman's fear. His earliest memories conjured angry mobs and sleepless nights. The villages were seldom a place for a being such as he. On the Great Road, he had found sanctuary and lived amongst others chased from hearth and home. Such men were happy to have an intimidating companion. *It was then the chains found him.*

The woman ambled up a gangplank and disappeared onto a waiting barge. Several such boats remained, singed but spared by the Wakeful fire. Their crews shouted instructions at the growing crowd of refugees lining the wharf. By twos they ordered aboard, carrying the salvaged pieces of their world. Moments later, the last of the boats slipped between the lake's mists and vanished. The Beast pitied the refugees, knowing they left behind more than burnt buildings. They sailed away from festivals and autumn harvests. And from the camaraderie of drunken brawls and friendships renewed in their tavern. The bell tower snapped and collapsed, falling with a splat and a clang. *How many weddings and births had the bell chimed?* In the span of a single morning, the whole world had burned.

Scorched by one man's brutality.

Those unable to book passage, slogged away in a trundling caravan of charred ox carts. The Beast pitied them even more, understanding the dire straits of the perilous journey ahead: able bodied fighters numbered few, their armaments little better than rusty hand tools, and winter's own biting unpredictability. It was unlikely they would reach any destination save for ruin.

The Beast considered burying the dead men, but a scrape at the icy ground denied such sentiment. He recalled that it was sometimes the way of men to set their departed ablaze, allowing the wind to carry souls to the World After. He cobbled a makeshift pyre and placed the frost covered bodies shoulder to shoulder, hands clasped over hearts. He closed the old man's fingers around the song worn lute. The Beast was unsure if the ritual called for words. Truth be told, he was glad no one was around to hear his fumbling attempt.

"Be at peace amongst the stars."

He struck the pyre's base stone with a claw. A trail of fire spread swiftly around the wooden rings, then consumed waiting men. He hoped the two friends would meet the afterlife together. Taking solace in the sentiment, the Beast started for the cairns.

"That was a very courageous thing you did," a man's voice said softly.

The Beast spun and greeted a silvery silhouette stepping down from the pyre. The ghostly figure clapped Jack's shoulder and bowed. It raised the lute and forced a breath over the blackened instrument. Charred scales fell away, leaving behind only earthy brown wood. "Ah, much better. Though I shall miss playing it. Do you play, stranger?"

The Beast had witnessed much of the bizarre since re-awakening. Nothing had prepared him for such an encounter. He scanned for a weapon, settling on a length of splintered wood that burned of emerald. The fire's emanations settled in his stomach like a lead weight. The spectre gestured for the Beast's calm. "I assure you that won't be necessary. I am Cedrik, and I mean you no harm."

The Beast was not convinced. Common knowledge dictated fire would repel the undead. He hoped that rule included the evil magical type of flame in his possession.

"I mean to thank you for the kindness you've extended. You could have just as easily turned a blind eye."

Cedrik's words coaxed the Beast's guard down. He felt a familiarity in them. The old man reminded him of Urda. And someone else. Someone he could not quite recall. "Old man-"

"Cedrik."

"Apologies. It was the least I could do." The Beast dropped the torch. Wisps of steam twisted around his ankle. He shrugged and gathered his pack.

"Wait!" Cedrik shouted. The ethereal vapor of his legs melted away and the spectre rushed forward, clamping a hand onto the Beast's shoulder.

A cold chill swept over his chest. He gasped and fell to a knee. Cedrik gingerly lifted the Beast back to his feet.

"I am truly sorry. That was... unexpected."

The Beast pawed at his chest, thankful the chilling grip had fled.

"There was a little girl, Lia. By my side she was, when I... She brought me back, stopped me before I could reach the World After."

"Gone. Taken by the Wakeful. By Malachai." The words haunted him. There was no telling to what dark end the black rider with the burning eyes carried her off to. The Beast thought the apparition's heart would beat once more simply to burst. "I am truly sorry for what the Wakeful have done here." He reached for the firestone. *Her eyes, gleaming amber orbs...*

"That amulet, I've seen it before. How came you by it?" Cedrik asked, drifting closer.

The Beast closed his fist around the medallion. "I don't know. I've had it for as long as I can remember." The Beast's pulse quickened.

"You know what this is? Can you translate the words? Please, you must help me."

Cedrik's ghostly fire shimmered. "I know it well. I was there when the firestone was set to its golden cradle. It belonged to a loving, loyal friend who said the pieces came from the stars themselves."

The Beast's ears perked and he felt a prickle at his chest. His imagination reeled. *Maybe it was enchanted after all. Maybe it could send me home.* A dark thought crept into his head. What of the little boy in the dark dungeon? *Should I want to go back?*

"I raised Lia as my own," Cedrik hesitated, as if nervous to reveal more, "but her blood is of noble birth. The touch of the Breath is ever upon her lips. The very starlight swaddled her like a warm blanket."

The Beast cocked an eye brow. What did he care for noble blood and starlight?

Cedrik rambled on, hands fluttering into smears of bluish-grey. "Lia is the key to the end of the Wakeful and their accursed mistress. The last of a forgotten magic flows through her." Cedrik buried his face in his hands.

"It's my fault she's been taken. I knew the price of defiance and didn't think anyone else would have to pay my share."

The Beast's pitied the sobbing spirit. Tears ran down the ghost's cheeks in rivulets of smoke and dust. Powerful indeed the man's love must have been to have crossed the void between the realms. It seemed perverse to abandon Cedrik to his sorrow. The Beast squat onto a rubble pile and swept an inviting arm. Cedrik flashed an appreciative grin and melted into the ground. He spiraled up in a funnel of ethereal smoke by the Beast's side sitting cross legged, hovering a foot from the ground. The ghost cradled the lute in his lap, absentmindedly fingering the strings.

The Beast groaned. Was there no one left in the world who did not act magically out of sorts at every opportunity? "Could you just not sit like a normal person?"

"No more than you can, I'm afraid."

Cedrik's translucent fingers hovered above the strings. The Beast expected a few chords, but the ghost remained still, frozen by a cold he could not feel.

"You went through the trouble of reclaiming it from the fire's bite and now refuse to play?"

"Sadly no." Cedrik's chest shimmered and heaved. "Music is written in chords of love and light. Its essence may only be captured by a beating heart gripped of intense passion or pain." Cedrik stroked the lute's long neck. "Those exist now only in memory. And memory is no more real and passionate than I am."

"Tell me more of your friend and the child," the Beast said.

"She is more important than you know. To everything. And to you especially." Cedrik recounted the frightful history of Lia's abductor, damning the Liche Queen and her black fortress, the Nekropolis.

The Beast was eager to gauge his would-be foes. "And the Wakeful? What of them?"

Cedrik sneered. "Mercenaries twisted by the Liche Queen's curses. Cowards in life, seduced into an eternity of sleepless servitude." Cedrik's aura darkened.

"It was the Wakeful who razed my queen's palace, sending me into exile."

The Beast let the story settle. He sensed Cedrik was obscuring details about the warring queens and the abducted child. Once more it seemed he needed to resist the instinct to distrust. Could it be mere coincidence? Urda had all but delivered the child from her 'vision' and a spirit to corroborate her importance. If rescuing the child would aid his quest than he would pursue the Wakeful to the end.

"I will hunt Malachai no matter where he flees. I will see your Lia to safety. But I have no defense for the sorcery you speak of."

"Not to worry, my savage friend," Cedrik replied, "You will be safe as long as Lia is near."

The Beast's face twisted. Did the old man think he meant to cower behind a child? He let the perceived sleight pass. "How will I find them? Malachai has taken to mount and has a half-day's lead."

"Malachai's power stems from the Blight. It's an ancient strain of magic that leaves an indelible trace. And he rides east at speed to deliver his prize to the Nekropolis."

The Beast rose from his throne of rubble. "Will you join me?"

"My friend, you've done this old man more kindness than he thought remained in this wicked world. And I thank you for it. But I cannot come with you. Already I hear the siren of the World After beckoning. Perhaps another time I shall join you."

The Beast buried his disappointment with a huff. An ally that could pass through solid earth would have proven useful. "Your Lia called upon a white light after you passed. Could she always do such a thing?"

The old ghost smiled, his flicker quickened. "I have known her to be quite adept at handling the magical energies of our world but..."

"But what?"

Cedrik faded into the faint outline. "But I've never known her, or anyone else for that matter, to recall a soul to this world. Farewell and good luck."

The Beast spun around, looking for a trace of the ghost. "Wait! Can she reverse magicks lesser than Death's embrace? Please! I must know!"

Cedrik's voice echoed faintly against the tide's gentle lapping.

"My friend, if anyone in the world can help you..."

Chapter 11

The Great Road shook beneath the magnificent black stallion with the lifeless eyes. Sinewy muscle strained under heavy armor. The war horse had been crafted by the Liche Queen's own hand; a gift from mistress to champion. It maintained a feverish pace, its eyes shrouded by an unkempt mane of coal.

The horse landed a jump over a fallen log, jolting Lia back to consciousness. She shivered against the leather saddle, fighting the urge to be sick. Her magical efforts had taken their toll. She had never before asked so much of the Breath and feared the magic had vanished for good. She needed a bearing, but feared any movement would draw Malachai's wrath. Lia squeezed her eyes, willing courage to find her. She tilted her head, only an inch and still flutters grew in her stomach.

Lia found the sun directly overhead. *Half a day since they came.* Suddenly, she thought of Jack. A flicker of hope glinted at the thought. She quickly bottled the sentiment, burying it away, safely hiding it. She refused to allow Malachai to take any more than he already had.

The sun speared the forest's dense canopy with splinters of light that reminded Lia of another man she wished to see. Emboldened, she twisted in the saddle. She immediately regretted the decision. Malachai's horrid red eyes stole a shriek from the child. Fear trapped her in a net of icy tendrils. The creaking barbs and blades of Malachai's armor glared as well, taunting her to come closer. She cringed deeper into the saddle's nook, desperate to escape the nightmare. Cedrik would have insisted she be brave, but she felt smaller than the smallest firefly.

The war horse trampled a broad puddle of slush. Droplets of water took to a gusting wind, rustling alongside the galloping animal. The drops swirled by its flanks, growing into a pearlescent periwinkle gleam.

"I will find you soon, starshine."

Lia's head snapped around, convinced her mind was playing tricks. A woman's voice calling her 'starshine'? *Only Cedrik called her that.*

"Please, don't leave," Lia cried out.

But the mysterious whisperer had vanished. Malachai clapped a spiked gauntlet against the armored saddle, missing Lia by inches. "Silence, little abomination."

Lia obeyed, looking to the blur of cobblestone. *There must be a way to escape,* she thought. She searched the trees and snow drifts for hidden opportunity. *Maybe there was somewhere to hide.* She was rewarded solely by despair. Escape, unlikely as it was, was not even desirable. She was lost, far from a destroyed home and surrounded by an empty road rife with hidden dangers.

She had nowhere to go.

Malachai's furious flight lasted into the afternoon, ending by the bank of a narrow stream. He hoisted Lia singlehanded from the saddle, let her dangle for a moment, then dumped her into the snow. He commanded her to drink. "You are little use to me dead."

The Liche Queen's soulless champion was clear on the penalty for failure. And the penalty for failure on the magnitude of letting the little brat die would be...

Lia needed no further instruction. Her parched throat would not permit resistance. The stream's chilly water dripped from a cup of tingling fingers. Lia felt the cool fluid flush through her chest, draining into her stomach. Her belly rumbled and she realized her last meal had come yesterday.

"I'm hungry," she said quietly before another scoop of water.

Malachai dismounted and unhooked a crossbow from his saddlebag. The battle worn weapon was a mess of blades, strung with barbed wire. It was as foul a device as Lia had ever seen. He gestured for her to follow and started for the tree line. She obliged, afraid to be left alone with the ghastly mount and peered back, making certain the wicked creature was not at her heels. A step beyond the trees and Lia smacked face first into Malachai's outstretched palm.

Lia flailed at the pale hand, certain she was fighting for dear life. Malachai grabbed her by the wrist, lifting her straight into his cold gaze. He did not speak. He merely shushed the girl with his free hand and dropped her rump first to the ground. Malachai pointed through the brush into a tight clearing. A stag with trophy worthy antlers rooted a patch of moss no more than ten yards away. Malachai deliberately readied his weapon.

Lia banished the rumble in her belly, pleading instead for the animal's life. "Don't kill it. It's done you no harm and I'm not even hungry. Honest!"

Malachai raised his weapon and took aim, his target oblivious to the stalking peril. "Foolish girl, I've heard your pathetic grumblings for miles. I grow weary of them."

The barbed wire twanged and the quarrel slammed into the stag's throat. Malachai slung the crossbow over his shoulder and stalked his kill with a serrated dagger. The dying stag struggled through a death rattle with Malachai looming over, blade readied. Lia's stomach churned. *He was going to watch it die...*

Malachai had no right to claim the stag's life as prize. Though weakened from her attempt to save Cedrik, she would not disappoint her *pafaa*. And that meant acting brave when you really felt small. The Breath sighed through Lia's body and fresh strength took hold. She would give all she had. Lia bowed her head, whispering an ancient secret she didn't realize she knew to a lonely wind. Malachai raised the dagger, then slashed with savage fury.

Lia thrust her hands forward, pushing away at an invisible weight. A ripple of golden light erupted from her finger tips, shielding the wounded stag within a wrought dome of energy. Malachai tried to avert his strike but was too late. The dagger collided with the barrier, exploding into a flurry of golden snow. The blast sent Malachai reeling, smashing a pair of stout trees to kindling.

A veil of silence smothered the forest. Lia stood motionless. She dared not move, lest Malachai recover and cut her down. The wounded stag struggled to its feet, nodded in gratitude and bound off for the deep woods.

A droning growl rumbled behind her.

Malachai's crimson eyes narrowed to slits. Lia scrambled back, pressing into a tree. She turned her cheek, flinching, expecting the worst. The gauntlet's plated fingers clinked as he seized sword from scabbard. He admired the wicked blade's edge, scraping a thumb down its length, letting the vision settle into Lia's heart. Her instincts screamed 'run', but her feet were stone weights. She silently pleaded with them but the glaring orbs locked her in place. She wanted to cry.

She wanted her *pafaa*.

The whisperer returned. "Be not afraid. He cannot harm you. I shall soon be by your side." The soft words rang with the chiming notes of a lullaby. The voice was Lia's only remaining shield.

Lia closed her eyes, clinging to the promise. Malachai closed the gap to a step... With a wild roar he summoned the emerald flame back to his trusted blade. The sword fell with all of the captain's darkness driving it. Lia flinched.

The blade cleaved reality's fabric, leaving a gooey purplish gash in the air by her head. Malachai grabbed the frightened child and shoved her through the portal. Strange magic enveloped the frightened girl, twisting her into shadowy distortions. Her ears popped. The forest was not the forest anymore. The trees and the snow and the sun were all there. And so was Malachai. But everything was wrong. Flawed somehow. A nervousness crept over her skin.

"I think you'll find your petty Breath has abandoned you here. In this place, I am King." Malachai's eyes no longer burned with crimson fury. The spectrum of the world was gone, drained away to drab greys. The sky, the stream, her hands. Everything.

Lia stared at the stream, hoping the murk would wash away. She crashed in knee deep and began to scrub. She rubbed frantically at her hands to no avail. It took a moment, but she realized the water was as tepid as day old bath water despite winter's touch. Malachai sheathed his weapon and strolled towards his mount like a nobleman on a pleasure walk. He cradled the dragon helm under an arm, revealing a face untwisted by the Liche Queen's Wakeful Curse. He stretched his angled jaw and rubbed his eyes. He passed Lia by and to her surprise dropped to a knee in the stream.

Malachai tugged a spiked gauntlet free and splashed grey water onto his face. Smiling, he stripped away the second gauntlet and doused his newly restored black hair. He pushed it back and whistled through a mouth no longer twisted to a slit. Lia clenched her fists and wept into the stream. She hated this place. It was unnatural, false. Its emptiness left her longing for a home she could never return to. Mostly, she hated Malachai for being able to enjoy such horrible oblivion.

Malachai offered a vindictive smirk. "Does the little abomination have something to say?"

Lia's eyebrow twitched. Malachai's voice was changed as well. Gone was the hollow Wakeful drone. In its place was the knavish voice of a common thug.

"I thought not."

In the forgotten ether of the Gloom, a lost realm remembered by legend only, Malachai was safe. Sworn to secrecy by his Lord, Malachai could only pierce the Gloom's veil as a last resort. Lia's outburst had more than qualified.

Lia stomped out of the stream and flung herself to the ground. She picked at the rubbery stones by the brook's edge. "I hate this place." She whispered to the Breath, hoping for reply. None came. Malachai had been telling the truth...

The black rider continued his ritual cleanse, stripping away pieces of armor, massaging murky water onto his skin.

"Why? Why did you ruin everything? Why did you kill Cedrik?"

Malachai ignored the question. He extravagantly splashed another armful of water onto his face, enjoying Lia's torment.

Anger flushed Lia's face. "Tell me!" She flung the biggest stone she could find, striking between Malachai's shoulders. The petty stone bounced harmlessly from the plated armor, plunking into the muck. Malachai stood without turning and gave the only response worse than silence.

Laughter.

Terrible, evil laughter that rolled over the smudged tree tops.

"Was that the old fool's name?"

Lia screamed and charged, certain Malachai's smug face would find mud. Malachai spun away and Lia crashed face first into the water. Again came the laugh. This time louder. "Pitiful."

Lia quickly scrambled to her feet, covered in grey sludge. She saw only red and charged again. Malachai casually side stepped. His sword flashed and slapped Lia across the rump. Malachai sheathed his weapon.

"Finished?"

Lia puffed an exasperated sigh and wiped away the disgusting sludge. The muted tones of the forest snickered, cheering Malachai's victory. "This is a secret place, little abomination," Malachai chided, "Few living beings know of it." He pinched Lia under the chin.

"And no one of this world knows of its entrance."

His words punched savagely at Lia's resolve. Had it not been for the whisperer's assurances she would have collapsed, resigned to her fate. Instead, her posture softened as she took comfort in the promise.

Malachai released the child's face and grabbed the horse's reigns, quickly taking to saddle. "We ride for the Nekropolis. Home of my Queen, mistress of Blight." Malachai scooped Lia onto the saddle. He leaned down, brushing his helmet's jaw against Lia's ear.

"Your new home, little abomination."

Chapter 12

The Great Road stretched for thousands of miles across the sprawling continent. Its cobbled stonework, once renowned for masterfully crafted intricacies, was now little more than a broken trail of crumbling gravel. In Queen Adella's absence the realm's magnificent works had fallen to disrepair. The once proud highway fared worst of all, remembered only by the rogues who plundered it.

The stones blurred into streaking slates as the Beast ran. Malachai's lead was substantial, but the Beast was confident he would catch him by nightfall. The road reeked of the Wakeful's evil and left a trail fit for the most inexperienced ranger. The Beast felt it simmering in his breast like a shadowy twin pulse, beating alongside his own. He slowed to a trot. The trail's pulse intensified to a fervor. Silence reigned, forcing bird and beast into hiding, trapped by Malachai's echo. The Beast's ears perked and he readied for the inevitable ambush. A jumble of foot prints danced beside a stream ten paces ahead.

The Beast studied the tracks, mentally measuring spacing and depth. Tracking and stalking were traits acquired of necessity in his lonely world. One could not survive relying on the charity of a world fearful of appearances. Hunger was an unrelenting demon that had forced selection of a number of regrettable paths, the last of which provided fodder for nightmares of chain. The Beast dropped to all fours, sniffing at the prints.

A large impression marked the trail's origin. *Deeper than the others. Someone small, dumped from a mount.*

The smaller prints scampered to the pebbled stream that listlessly carved the forest floor. The tracks did not reappear at the other side. *She ran to the stream but did not cross. Thirst... not escape.*

The puzzle pieces were falling into place. The Beast regarded the large trampled mess of snow and mud. *The stallion.* The trail's pulse bounded and began to thump in his temples. Two sets of foot prints, one large, the other child-like, trekked side-by-side into the woods away from the stream. *Why would both enter the woods?* The Beast followed, brushing aside frozen branches. Sunlight broke through, shining a golden invitation into a clearing. The Beast's skin crawled the closer he neared it.

Something terrible happened here...

The meadow lived in a circular patch guarded by a copse of ancient trees. Angular branches saluted the sun in perpetual reverence, offering praise throughout the day. Drifts of snow, weary and wind beaten, rested peacefully at the feet of their rooted guardians. Their slumber glistened undisturbed, but offered no advice. The Beast shuddered that such perfect serenity had been tainted by Malachai's violence. He abandoned the tracks and searched through nearby thickets, hoping for another bread crumb.

The sullen hunter resumed the original trail and paced back to the road. His nerves flared. Only one set of tracks returned. *Malachai's.* Had Malachai done the unspeakable?

A sudden bolt of brown fur erupted from a nearby drift, nearly bowling the Beast over. A stag baring a brace of mighty antlers stared up at the other horned visitor to the meadow. A scar at its throat indicated a grievous wound. The Beast made several skittish attempts to pass the bold animal, but was each time countered its magnificent crown. Annoyed, he finally gave in to the stubborn request for audience.

He growled, certain his tone would drive the stag off. "I've no time for your foolish games."

The stag paid the Beast's command no mind and started sniffing around the larger footprints. Its eyes sparkled and, like a flash of lightning, it charged though the meadow, interrupting the peaceful snow drifts. Finally understanding, the Beast followed suit, tracking the snap of twigs. He found his guide frantically nipping the bark of a withered tree. The decrepit pine was unique among the ring of wooden guardians. It was darkened and hollow, dying in the presence of its brothers. The Beast gratefully pet the stag's head and then gently brushed him aside. A twisted crossbow quarrel was buried deep in the decaying tree's side. An oily liquid dripped from the fletching and sizzled through the snow.

Poison.

The Beast rested a paw on the tree trunk. Agony swept through his arm as the tree silently plead for him to remove the insidious thorn. He grabbed the quarrel and yanked it free. The Beast snarled at the despicable missile. What manner of coward poisoned his weapons? Malachai had shot the stag, that much was clear. But how had it survived the poison? A creeping suspicion came over him, followed by a wry smile. Lia was alive and had most likely intervened on the stag's behalf. The Beast felt an unlikely surge of pride in the young girl. If she had found the courage to resist, he would champion her freedom.

But the trail had gone cold, died by the clearing.

The Beast haphazardly kicked a tree stump. Wet snow plopped to the ground. He kicked the stump a second time, feeling the familiar flame of rage rising. He kicked again and again, mood festering into full blown hatred. Razor sharp claws dug into wood. The Beast roared and flung the stump high over the tree tops. A strong urge to slip into the shield of trees ebbed through his veins, replacing the rage. He focused intently on his breathing, slowing the rise and fall of his chest until he needed little breath at all. His focus tightened further until it cheated the earth's pull on his massive frame and he was moving between the trees as light on his feet as a wraith. It was an old technique, mentored by a stealthy former accomplice.

The Beast tread no particular path, leaving the clearing and cold trail behind him. The forest's even grade rolled beneath his paws, steepening a mile later into a robust climb. He left no trace, made no sound. Each stride coaxed tension free until the fury was no more.

A sharp metallic clang, followed by a pitiful yelp echoed through the forest. The Beast rushed up the next hill in great bounds, hoping to find

Malachai. Sounds of drunken men chased the clang, dimming his hopes of confronting the black rider. It seemed that would be a meeting for another day. The Beast stood still as a stone totem on the hill's peak, flanked by a canvas of snowy pines. Below, a wolf, no more than a pup, tried in vain to free itself from the iron jaws of a hunter's trap. The Beast was no shaman but was quick to judge the grave injury. A spatter of scarlet blood stained the snow, ruining the field of perfect ivory. A spatter, fast spreading into a puddle...

The boisterous laughter grew louder. Taunts and promises of torture replaced the drunken revelry. The wolf-pup quaked, straining against the trap, as if its wild ears had somehow translated the threats. The Beast singled out a familiar voice from the crowd.

Vildar.

The Beast crashed down the hillside, grunting and snarling, dodging trees and a crag of icy boulders. He sprung from a downed log, soared through the air, landed in a tight roll, then towered over the wolf-pup. The frightened pup stared down its snout at the giant whose shadow blocked out the sun. It bared its teeth with as much menace as it could conjure and uttered a low growl though its fangs.

The Beast admired the fight in the youngling. "You have some fight in you yet. Good, you shall need it." He regarded the pup with the look of shared pain, offered from a creature whose own life was once shackled. The young wolf read the pained expression. It lowered its head to the blood stained snow, tired and whimpering. It licked at the Beast's claws as he pried the trap open.

He tore a scrap from his cloak and carefully bound the wound. "There now. Find your family. Keep them close."

The wolf pup limped into a snowy copse of pines and disappeared. A bloody trickle marked a bright trail Vildar would have little trouble following. Adrenaline surged, infusing fury into his bulk. Iron screeched in rusted agony as he mangled the trap into a twisted sculpture of scrap metal.

The hunters required dealing with.

Vildar lead his band though the trees in an ale-inspired totter. The men reeked of the cheap drink and made no attempt to conceal their approach.

"Vildar!" The Beast hurled the twisted trap at Vildar's bulbous head. The hunter ducked at the last second, narrowly avoiding the heavy projectile. The man behind him was not as fortunate. The trap smashed into his chest, bludgeoning his breath free. The gasping man went down in heap, his battle over before he knew it had begun.

Vildar slurred instruction to his equally inebriated henchmen. Two men fumbled for crossbows and fired wild shots as they staggered. The Beast stood his ground, allowing the quarrels to sail harmlessly by. He closed the gap in a frightening eye-blink, swatting the bowmen away with powerful backhands.

A hunter in a filthy brown cloak slashed at the Beast's back, tearing through cloak and fur. The Beast stomped around and roared into the man's face, shaking free the sword in his grasp. The terrified hunter fell to his rump and clawed at the snow, scrambling madly for escape. The Beast's jaw clenched. "Coward."

He seized the man by a handful of tunic, raising him a child's height from the ground. The Beast's gaze locked with the hunter's, delivering an eternal warning. He tossed the shaking rogue onto his disabled friends. Vildar clutched a throwing dagger, staring at the Beast's unprotected flank.

"Don't even consider it," the Beast called over his shoulder.

Vildar dropped the dagger, turned and ran. He trudged through the snow, stumbled and fell. Warm fluid trickled down his leg. He swam through a drift and ran off into the woods. The Beast picked up Vildar's shameful scent. His laugh rolled over the tree tops like angry thunder. "Run, you gutless puke!" the Beast roared triumphantly, " Run, for the Beast of Briarburn will forever be at your back!"

A calm fell over the forest and the Beast kicked at Vildar's blade. *Right back where I started.* Out of habit, he reached for the medallion. A soft whisper called out to him. "She needs you now, more than ever."

The Beast spun to the sound, crouching defensively. He panned around, considering every angle of attack. "Show yourself!" A frosty wind sifted through the tree line, carrying the whisper to his perked ears.

"He has taken her to Meridian..."

Chapter 13

Battle standards flapped with mounting excitement atop the Nekropolis's shadowy spires. The tattered flags bore the Liche Queen's sigil: a silver skull impaled by a trio of serrated blades. Where the Pierced Skull went, despair soon followed.

A dense palisade of petrified trees weaved into a perimeter wall that cast perpetual shadow onto the accursed grounds. Five towers snatched at the sky like a twisted, black hand fingering an invisible orb. The bitter wood creaked always, contorted by the painful designs of the castle's mistress. It was a blight upon the once living land it occupied. It was the Liche Queen's most prized treasure.

The Liche Queen herself stood on the peak of the highest tower, surveying her domain. She waved her hand, dragging a patch of dark clouds in front of the sun, plunging the land into shadow. The milky swirl of her eyes relaxed. She disdained the light and all of its pitiful creation.

She had selected the location of the castle herself, inspired by the sprawling decay of the petrified forest covering the country-side. So moved by the deathly spectre, she had summoned forth from the rock a fortress built in their image. The Nekropolis's main gate faced west, in firm defiance of the sunrise. A deep chasm stretched for miles into the horizon, offering protection beyond the formidable walls.

Spanning the gorge was a bridge renowned for inspiring as much fear as the twisted walls of the castle itself. The dracoliche's skeletal tail provided the precarious passage and was wide enough for five men to take at once. The dreadful beast's carcass reared at an unseen foe, guarding the castle's gate. The mighty bones of its wings were tucked in close to its tail and stretched nearly to chasm's opposite side. The Liche Queen glided from her tower perch, descending to a seat upon the dracoliche's shoulder. She caressed the skeletal shoulder with a slender alabaster finger.

"Keep watch for me, my love."

The Liche Queen conjured an image of her throne room and disappeared into a flash of black light. She arrived in the cavernous hall smiling at the towering dais of polished skulls. At the dawn of her power, the dais was but a single layer of empty eyed bone. With each conquered kingdom the column enhanced itself, reaching upward to the vaulted ceiling. The morbid structure was of Her Majesty's own design, an atrocity fashioned from the skulls of slaughtered mounts. It was a most enjoyable, postmortem swipe at her mother's memory.

A pool of water, serene as a mirror's surface, dominated the room's heart. Braziers clinging to six petrified oaks painted Wakeful flame onto the still water, giving it an eerie emerald glow.

Her heels clicked hard on the stone floor as she circled the pool. Ten paces from the dais, a staircase of skulls mirroring the grisly column erupted from the floor. The Liche Queen took the steps two at time, skulls exploding into dust behind her. At the peak of the skull stairs, she whipped free the black cloak at her shoulders and claimed the newly materialized throne of skull and bone.

All round her, the halls of the Nekropolis brimmed feverish. Rumors passed freely among the slaves that Malachai had found *'her'*. Scouts returning on weary mounts provided fiery confirmation of Sensheeri's fall. But she would hear the news from her favorite. She would hear it from Malachai. That she was unable to reach Malachai's mind through the Wakeful curse was a manor of small concern. *Perhaps the little wretch was that powerful?* No matter. There were other ways...

"Bring me the Echo."

Two giant hooks descended from the darkened ceiling on chains thick as a giant's forearms and splashed into the water, shattering the calm surface. A moment later a muffled clunk and more ratcheting sounds. The hooks re-appeared carrying a ring of roiling magma, a wagon's length across. Steam hissed from the enchanted artifact as it became fully exposed to the cool air.

"Malachai, my most favored. Heed your Queen's call."

The ring of molten rock brightened, illuminating the hidden corners of throne room, revealing a number of hidden Wakeful guards. The Echo reached across the void of space and time voicing the Liche Queen's call. Malachai's visage appeared in the circle soon after, painted in the same rolling volcanic shades. His fiery silhouette stepped down from the Echo, walking onto the pool's boiling surface. Malachai's image genuflected and steam sizzled from his knee. "What is thy bidding, Highness?"

"You disappoint me, Captain," the Liche Queen said, "Was I not clear on my orders? Were you not to contact me the instant you had the girl?"

Despite the great distance separating them, a shiver climbed Malachai's spine. "Highness, I have the abomination in my presence as you've commanded. There were... complications." He bowed meekly, hoping to soften whatever blow came next.

She brushed a raven colored lock from her lips and smiled. "Complications?"

The fiery silhouette softened, relieved by the smile. Malachai started to explain. The Liche Queen was on her feet in a second, running down the staircase of skulls. She seized Malachai's blazing image by the throat, impervious to the scorching heat. "Complications like burning one of my villages to the ground? Fool! You may be Captain, but I am Queen! *Queen*, Malachai! Do you understand? Or has that Wakeful brain of yours rotted to nothing?"

Across the void, she knew Malachai's lungs burned as she tightened her grasp on the illusion's throat.

"Your majesty is unquestioned, Highness," Malachai's illusion gurgled,

"I thought only to honor you by destroying the coven of heathens."

Won over by the expected flattery, the Liche Queen released her grasp. "You will bring the girl to me, Captain. You will not delay. You will not assume. You will do as commanded."

"Of course, your Highness," Malachai muttered. "Always as commanded."

The silhouette retreated back into the Echo, massaging its throat.

"And Captain... You are being followed."

Pandora waved her hand, severing the mystical connection. The Echo went cold and fell from the hooks, crashing into the depths. The water's mirror-like surface rippled once and then was still. The walls cringed with mortal dread as the Liche Queen's furious scream rattled the throne room. Blasted Malachai had once again overstepped his boundaries and required punishment. She would deal with him later; a fact he should count on. Still, that she had been unable to sense the petulant Captain's whereabouts disturbed her. Perhaps it had nothing to do with the child after all? *Had he found a way to obscure the tie? A place to hide?*

The twisted branches of the floor circled up and encapsulated the seething Queen. The chamber's large branches spiraled away, allowing her descending passage into the heart of the dark castle. The Hollow.

Pandora dismissed the branch-lift with a wave. The cradle separated into singular pieces and rejoined the chaotic tangle of the wall. From floor to ceiling, a sophisticated layout of breakneck walkways and narrow tunnels crisscrossed the Hollow. The armory, barracks, throne room, and even her private chambers were all within reach. She threw open the heavy door to her War Room, smashing it into an unfortunate goblin slave. The frail creature, who looked on the brink of starvation, tumbled head first into a shelf, dumping stacks of parchments and dusty tomes to the floor. The goblin picked itself up, eyes bulging, certain its life was to be gruesomely interrupted.

The Liche Queen said nothing and walked by the trembling slave without so much as a customary backhand. She stepped over the scattered mess, taking a place by General Thraal's side at a monstrous triangular table. The goblin sighed all the relief it dared and began returning the shelf's contents.

"Out."

Slaves and minor members of the War Council hastily filed out. Few spoke, none established eye contact. All knew the penalty for dawdling. The clumsy goblin was the last in line. Until the Liche Queen commanded the contrary, freezing the creature in place. The goblin's knobby knees knocked, echoing the chatter of its teeth. The Liche Queen sliced at her throat with a pale bony finger. She regarded the doomed creature with a mask of stone as a thin, oily line seeped free of his scrawny throat. She blew a kiss...

Its head tumbled free.

The goblin's eyes bulged as his head bounced, smearing blood onto the fallen parchments. Its body twitched once and slumped to the floor. A coil of branches peeled away from the floor, wrapping around the corpse like the tentacles of a squid, claiming the carcass for the Nekropolis. The Liche Queen turned to her top advisor and the strange artifact recently delivered on the table.

She beamed like an excited child. "Now, where were we?"

Thraal drummed his fingers on the table's edge, pounding like miniature hammers. The grizzled veteran cut an imposing figure at over six feet tall. Dressed in casual garb, evidence of a lean body hardened by decades of combat and discipline were abundant. Thraal's dark hair was touched with gray and cropped close to the scalp. Two ghostly scars carved jagged ravines up from his throat clutching at his temple. Thraal gestured to the strange object centering the table. "Your Highness, our scouts bring word of triumph."

Two twisted dowels of petrified wood were secured to a simple base, an arm's length apart. A simple spiral of spider's web connecting the dowels swayed on a cold draft.

"Show her majesty," Thraal said.

On command, a nightmarish horde of tiny spiders crept up from between the floor's spaces. They scaled the table's legs and swarmed the cobweb. Immediately they went to work, crisscrossing, jumping, spinning thousands of silk threads. A moment's worth of feverish effort passed. The spiders disappeared back into the dark gaps, leaving the Liche Queen astonished.

Try though she may, she could not help but to be impressed. A corner of her mouth curled. "Remind me to thank Arak'Jai."

"Indeed. It is as the Prince of Stingers promised." The old general's eyes narrowed. "The spun web shows no lies."

The intricate detail of the spiders' tapestry was undoubtedly infallible. The detail, from individual trees to the subtle shifts in elevation had been spun between the dowels. Her excitement peaked, leaving her breathless. The anger over Malachai's insolence melted away. Anticipation gripped at her, twisting barbs of pleasure through her body.

The fountain had finally been found.

***

Followed. Hunted.

How could he have been so foolish? Of course someone would come for the girl.

Malachai swung a bladed gauntlet, cleaving a wrist-thick branch free in a storm of splinters. Slipping into the Gloom had been a choice born of necessity. The little abomination's power required limits. What better way than to bring her to a place where her magic simply could not follow? No matter, arrangements would be made to ensure his success.

The Gloom was his oasis, long providing precious safe haven from his telepathic link to the Liche Queen and her constant nagging. He was grateful the Dark Lord had permitted him access to the realm between realms.

Here in the Gloom, Malachai reigned.

Here in the Gloom, Malachai was free.

Chapter 14

Lia startled from a fragile slumber. The Gloom's grey replaced a burning nightmare of Sensheeri's final moments. She wasn't immediately sure which was worse.

"Back to sleep little abomination. When I wake we ride without rest to her Majesty's throne."

Lia sensed a rare note of resignation in her captor's voice. She watched the black rider slump against a savaged tree trunk and fall instantly asleep. His words hung overhead like a dark cloud. Weariness was etched around Malachai's slumbering eyes, pained testimony of his eternal servitude. Those same eyes would soon blaze to life, consumed by the Liche Queen's Blight. Yes, she quite pitied the Wakeful captain.

Pitied him, but was no fool.

Memory of the whispering voice warmed Lia and encouraged her first movement since waking. She crept from the campsite, holding her breath in a deep gulp as she tip toed by Malachai's sleeping mount. She looked over her shoulder and then slipped away into a veil of ashy trees. Soon after wicked Malachai was lost far behind a dense wall of forest. Lia ran, arms pumping, blissfully ignorant of the scratching twigs. The daring escape was aided by an unseen draw that willed her little legs faster through the snow.

Far from Malachai's grasp, Lia tumbled into the snow. She rolled about, giggling at nothing in particular. She rolled onto her back and carved a jubilant angel into the Gloom's lurid snow.

A lonely star's persistent gleam caught her eye. She wrinkled her nose. *Well, hello there.* She did not remember seeing any stars upon her arrival. Lia pushed herself onto her elbows. She giggled again, happy to have a friend.

"I don't belong here, you know," Lia said matter-of-factly, the way a person would chat with an old friend.

The star's sapphire shine flashed its agreement. "No, star-shine, you do not."

Lia sprang up, eyes widened. The star was speaking to her! *To her!* Her excitement piqued. Cedrik had spoken often of the Aether and magic and how they were born of starlight. His fairy tales had teased her to sleep all her life. Her face flushed as she desperately clung to the memory of his soft voice.

"Please, I want to go home." The words barely squeezed by the lump in her throat. Deep sadness washed away her briefly re-kindled joy and settled around her heart. Even if she could escape the Gloom, where would she go? There could be no home without her *pafaa*.

Lia dropped to her knees, pressing a sucking sound from the oily snow. Tears filled her eyes, but she shed them not. A promise reminded her to be brave. In her heart of hearts she wept anyway. She had escaped nothing but Malachai's torment. Slipping free of the Gloom would see her banished to a different prison. One without gates, built by Malachai's dark deeds. She would languish alone there. Branded.

Orphan.

The star brightened and the ashen forest cringed in the lambent glory. "Never alone, starshine."

The words were faint and, for a crushing moment, Lia thought the voice had sped off to wherever stars came from. How she wished she was a star herself that she may fly away too. The star pulsed a ghostly blue, quickening with each kiss upon the earth. With every rhythmic beat the star stretched and grew... Lia's mouth fell open. The surging star was bigger than any moon or sun in memory. The light warmed her skin, soothing away the gooseflesh.

The starlight demanded a retreat from the greasy snow. Inch by inch, a widening circle of grey grass sprouted between her feet. A fierce wind gushed from the giant star, battering back the lifeless trees with rippling energy. Lia remained upright, unaffected by the pulsing energy.

A woman, beautiful and slender, descended from the sky-filling star. She waved with a delicate twist of her wrist and the puzzled child returned a mittened wave of her own. The star poured like wine from a carafe into the woman's outstretched palm. She smiled at the cupped starlight; a cherished gift. She knelt in front of the awestruck child, taking in the familiar eyes she feared lost long ago. She brushed the chocolate locks from Lia's dirty face with a translucent hand. To her surprise, the child made no attempt to shy away.

Lia was grinning daybreak. "You are Polaris, the North Star."

Polaris's eyes twinkled her namesake. She pinched the child's chin. "And you are most wise, star-shine. And pretty besides."

Lia's lips pursed, still baffled by the use of the private name. "How do you know my name is star-shine?" Her heart dropped through the forest floor. "Only Cedrik called me that."

Polaris countered with a flashing wink of stardust. "Who do you suppose taught Cedrik that name?"

Confused tears streamed down Lia's face. She hid behind dirty mittens.

"Cry not little one," Polaris said gently, "your tears pain the very stars watching over you."

Lia blurted through her mitten shield. "But it's all my fault. My fault Malachai came. My fault Cedrik... *pafaa...*"

Polaris pulled Lia tight to her breast, banishing the red-eyed demon who had destroyed their worlds from her thoughts. "No, the fault is my own." She combed her fingers through Lia's hair, determined to absorb the child's guilt.

"Were it in my power I would spare you all of this ugliness."

Lia dabbed at her eyes. The North Star's warm embrace was comforting, but she could bear not a moment more in the Gloom's terrible malaise. "Please take me with you. I don't want to stay here anymore."

Polaris shook her head. "The Gloom is a funny place. If brought here as prisoner, one can only leave as prisoner. Ahriman declared it so when he forged the realm from the pitch of midnight. Such was his hatred for magic's potential in the hands of mortals that he constructed this ugly place. A perverted reflection of the vibrant beauty of the Mortal Realm where their magic was forbidden."

Lia had heard the name 'Ahriman' before, in another of Cedrik's stories. Her head tilted to one side and Polaris continued.

"Ahriman longed to steal magic from the hearts of mortals but possessed no enchantment powerful enough. After centuries of trying, he created this empty place and drained it of Breath and Blight. If he could not forcefully remove magic from the mortals, he would remove the mortals themselves and imprison them here."

The story flowed like a dream. Lia snuggled deeper into Polaris's star warmed chest, feeling the celestial heart beating softly like a distant drum.

"We Guardians struggled, but Ahriman's dark power was vast. His forces swept through the Mortal Realm, razing entire kingdoms to oblivion. Hope was all but forgotten. Many honorable friends were lost." Polaris paused reverently before beginning again. "It was decided that in order to save the realm, magic itself needed limitation. The realms' patron guardians each sacrificed a piece of their immortal soul-shines and combined them into the most powerful enchantment ever conjured."

The North Star sighed. She hadn't the heart to continue and further burden the child with such sorrow. Polaris hugged her tighter, closing Lia off in a moment both wished would last forever. A shimmering veil of violet mist spiraled around them as a bond lost was remade. A blissful eternity later, Lia stirred. She was confused by the tale's ending. How could magic be so most powerful in the hands of fragile mortals? Polaris had only just shrunk a star down into a waiting palm!

"But magic has no limit!" Lia cried, fearful that Cedrik was lost for always. Polaris immediately plucked Lia's fear away.

"Star-shine, beautiful star-shine, magic's bounds are indeed finite. But restricted only to the single enchantment Ahriman needed." Polaris hesitated for a breath. " 'Wish'..." Lia sensed the gravity of Polaris's shifting tone. That 'Wish' granted dominion over reality's book of magical laws was known by every lonely soul who sought shooting stars. It was a leap of faith near to Lia's own heart. Not a single star had ever raced by without finding her eyes squeezed tight.

The eyes of Lia's new found guardian welled with tears of glittery moisture, sparkling of twilight. It was the saddest, most beautiful sight Lia had ever known. "Your friends banished 'Wish' didn't they? So Ahriman couldn't take everyone away." Her words rang of the beautiful innocence that only children spoke.

A pair of starlit tears fell from Polaris's eyes. "The Mortal Realm was mine to protect above the others. I alone cast the enchantment." Guilt for banishing magic's most splendid wonder crushed the North Star under an avalanche.

Lia dabbed a delicate fingertip, drying Polaris's tears. "Oh, it's not your fault. It was Ahriman! It's not fair for you to be sad. People needed you, you had to be bra--". The lesson had finally set in. The same lesson Cedrik had taught at bed times and summer picnics. The one he had given his life for. The same basic truth was woven in Polaris's sorrowful tale.

Lia's intonation was a perfect mimic of her beloved *pafaa*, words brimming with proud defiance. "Sometimes you must be brave, especially when you're most afraid." Polaris's heart swelled. Such bravery in one so small. If only all mortals could be counted upon for such valor. Things would have been much different. Lia fidgeted with the front of her coat. "Are wishes gone forever then, Polaris?"

"Of course not, little one. Echoes of 'Wish' are the heart of every good deed. It is the single most powerful bond between us. Every kind word and every noble sacrifice is part of its promise."

Lia climbed free of Polaris's lap. She did not know it then, but that small ember deep within her began to glow... She took a few play skips, watching the grey snow flee. She varied her path, trying to catch the snow off guard. Each time the muck managed to escape her feet like a repelled magnet.

She retreated to Polaris's protective aura. The ash colored snow quickly swallowed the patch of exposed grey grass. "The Gloom is afraid of us," Lia stated flatly," it hates us."

Polaris levitated to a nearby tree, reaching for its brittle bark. The tree groaned in protest and leaned away from the glowing sapphire finger tips. The Gloom's eerie response was not unexpected. It behaved exactly as Ahriman's blue print had called for. Still, the North Star was saddened to see any being so frightened of starlight.

"It is a sad watch-dog, fearful of disappointing its master," Polaris countered," but one that can yet learn new tricks."

Polaris beckoned for Lia to join her by the cowering tree, now bent at a ridiculous angle. Lia moved quickly, wondering why the snow had not feared her upon her arrival. Polaris motioned for Lia to place her hands on the twisting tree trunk. Lia reached tentatively, saddened that it continued to struggle.

"You must first remove your gloves."

Lia tossed her mittens aside as instructed and laid her bare hands on the brittle surface. The tree lurched, then froze in place, paralyzed by Lia's touch. Lia furled her brow, not understanding. Polaris glided to a spot behind her, hovering inches above the ground. The North Star covered Lia's hands with her own, pressing them deeper into the tree. She hummed a melody of enchanting notes. To her surprise, Lia picked up the melody after only a few bars.

"Cedrik used to play this on his lute when I couldn't fall asleep," Lia said with a smile.

Polaris smiled and encouraged Lia to join the melody. The notes sounded a haunting stir of echoes as the pair worked the enchantment. Carefully, they weaved the musical fibers through the grimness of the Gloom. Small ripples of energy distorted the air by the platinum locks dressing Polaris's bare shoulders. The power surged down her pale arms and through Lia's hands.

The anguishing tree vibrated against the magical current, and then shot straight up from its painful crooking, shaking loose what snow remained on its spindly branches. A tempest of bright light burst from the tree's top into the starless sky and then swirled down to the roots. The howling winds rattled the surrounding trees, leaving them trembling in panic.

Polaris pulled Lia's hands free, allowing the enchantment to run its course. Lia shielded her eyes against the bright light, but Polaris's firm hand on her shoulder insisted she watch. Lia obeyed, immediately glad for doing so.

The sight would be precious forever.

Color, beautiful life-affirming color, had seeped back into the Gloom. Shade by shade, the wretched tree came alive, gorging on magic's prismatic elixir. Several reborn branches reached for Polaris's hand. The North Star clasped a spindly branch, pressed it to her forehead and then kissed the chestnut bark. "You are most welcome."

For the second time since meeting, Lia stared agape at Polaris's humble display of grace. The North Star merely smiled back at the little girl. "Life always begins with something small, but never insignificant.

Then love, more powerful than Breath and Blight, takes hold and nurtures the seedling. Shaping it, preparing it."

Lia's eyes sparkled. "Preparing it for what?" Polaris winked a flicker of stardust.

"Destiny, starshine."

Chapter 15

The Beast propped his paws on his knees and marveled at the panorama. The journey from the Troll's Breath had done little to strain his wind, but the view stole it away with ease. An endless ocean blue glittered in the setting sun shine, painting a canvas that made envious the coming stars. Fresh salt air wafted from the valley's floor. The unusual smell rolled his snout in sniffs and scrunches. The Beast had never before laid eyes on the sea. On Sensheeri's Lake Tamahl one could see the score of sister villages dotting the coastline. At Meridian's border, faced with the vastness... he finally felt smaller than.

Nestled comfortably between the rolling woods and the ocean beyond was the sprawling expanse of Meridian: Home of the largest fleet of sailing vessels and several legendary families of sailors. *Pirates.*

The rolling tides stretched into forever, curving slightly upon the horizon's blade. The Beast stared at the thin cerulean line, wondering if anyone had ever voyaged to its end. What had they found? Treasure? Strange cities?

Home...

The sunset fell like a stage curtain, dropping a cascade of rusts and lavenders from the darkening sky. Beneath the magnificent mural, Meridian prepared for another night of lapping tides and the harmony of whale song. Heavy chains wrapped around the Beast's chest, squeezing breath from his lungs. The seaport's sprawling network of cobbled stone and muddy roads looked like the scribbled handiwork of a mad man. Alleyways disappeared into dead ends, side streets emptied into two and three places on the same artery. *Total chaos...* The crowd's scurrying buzz clamored to pick the market clean before the City Watch called an end to business.

Must I really go there?

The Beast had less than an inkling how to navigate such a nightmare of crowded twists and turns. The tangled web of humanity would likely see him jailed by night's end, or worse, find his head mounted on a wall.

The medallion spread a warm wave through the Beast's chest, gently nudging him forward. His paw rose as if tugged by an over-excited child. To his dismay the amulet did not offer guidance on top of the welcomed encouragement. The whispering wind said Malachai had traveled to Meridian. A familiar tone caressed the wind's words. He trusted them without understanding how or why. With no other leads, he had little choice.

Lia is down there.

The leary Beast studied Meridian's landmarks, hoping to gain some semblance of orientation, plotting his obligatory escape route. It was an old habit, but one that had served him well. The shipyard was a collection of open air warehouses filled with a mountain range of stacked wooden crates and barrels. Nearby a dry dock freed newly finished vessels into the sea, surrendering them to the pull of sister ships. Dozens of tiny shops dotted the outer edge of the district. Craftsmen and their apprentices hurried to shutter them for the night. Surrounding the merchant's enclave was a sprawl of homes, some hovels and some much grander, puffing wisps of grey smoke into the evening air.

Ten barnacled piers jutted into the ocean blue for, what seemed to the Beast, no less than a mile. Scores of ships, dinghies to schooners, had taken moorings for the night. Their crews disappeared into Meridian for the promise of adventure. Speckles of lantern light, like frozen fireflies, illuminated the wooden highways with an aura of mystery. Beyond the fishing vessels, the silhouettes of Meridian's navy patrolled the harbor and sea lanes. The Beast had never seen such massive ships. He knew that their toy sized appearances on the horizon made for an impressive illusion.

Meridian's main gate waited impatiently, covered by murky shadows. The giant grid of wrought iron fit snugly into a fifteen foot high, equally thick, sun bleached stone wall. Braziers were ignited by the City's Watch as the sun plunged into its watery cradle. The Beast favored caution on approach, hoping to avoid a nervous arrow from one of the many watchmen patrolling the battlements. Meridian's City Watch was a collection of venerable soldiers and gruff men who had seen their share of the world's dangers. They would not hesitate to answer any threat.

The patrolling guards were clad in tanned leather armor, armed with parings of bow and short blades. It was the armament of peace time, but the Beast harbored no illusion that these men were anything less than capable. It was showcased by the precise pattern and timing of their movements, down to the subtle shift of their positioning. Every few moments, a watchman leaned between crenellations, inspecting a shadow or imagined movement. A brief flash of hand code in the brazier light signaled a silent 'all's well' soon after.

Twenty paces from the gate the Beast halted. Experience preached caution when dealing with members of a usually frightened constabulary. Gaining entrance typically required the cursory attention of someone in charge. He hailed the nearest watchman, ready to issue a formal declaration. The guard waved a torch in the Beast's direction and waved him through the open gate. Disappointment mixed with surprise. Surely Meridian, despite its magnificence, had never before seen his like?

The Beast offered a parting salute and marched through Meridian's fluttering blue-grey banners. The doors were heavy, nearly as thick as the wall. The sharp points of a portcullis caught his eye, each tip thick as a man's thigh. He flipped up his hood, saddened by a fresh tear in the battered garment. He eased through the thinning crowd, taking great care to avoid any unwanted attention. The movement came easier than he expected.

Meridian's promenade failed to notice its giant newcomer and he preferred to keep it so. He scanned dozens of banners and chipped wooden signs hanging from closed shops and rowdy taverns, hoping to pick up Malachai's wretched scent. The streets remained alive with risqué catcalls of the nocturnal. Vendors pushed rickety wagons into shadowy side streets, emptying the marketplace. The changing energy prickled at the Beast's skin. He sensed a growing danger lurking unseen.

Meridian after dark...

Lamp posts, hidden by day, breached the surface with a grinding vibration that rattled the Beast's spine. They flashed to life, filling the dark spaces, coloring the city in the grey-blues and gold of Meridian's banner. The Beast scanned the crowd. No one seemed to notice the sudden intrusion. Parings of men and women, arms interlocked, threaded their way through companies of pirates and peddlers, seeking their entertainment in Meridian's score of taverns. More than once, they brushed the flap of his cloak. The Beast held his breath, anticipating the inevitable scream.

But none came. Men and women alike passed by, paying no mind to the horned gargoyle newly affixed to the shop's wall. He did not understand this Meridian at all. How could he possibly find his way?

A shard of glass cut through the Beast's memory. *Patience. Discipline.* He was on his back, propped onto an elbow. A man with a blurry face and silvery hair, wearing polished armor loomed over. The man's blade hovered just beneath his chin. An armored hand appeared, deflecting the blade away. The man extended his hand and jerked the Beast to his feet.

The man clasped his shoulder *Patience, Discipline...*

The memory vanished and the Beast shook free the temporary trance. Remnants of magical current prickled beneath his thick fur, tracing to the amulet. The Beast kept moving, one foot in front of the other, certain a member of the City Watch would soon stop for a friendly word. He looked over each shoulder in turn, searching for their approach. Once more, confusion reigned.

Such a strange place, he thought. He had entered without incident. He was twice the size of Meridian's most robust inhabitant. And now he had almost assuredly created a spectacle with his magical delusion. And no one had bothered batting an eye.

Perhaps here I am invisible.

A fat man, beard soaked of suds, stumbled out of a tavern, stabbing a sweaty shirt into his trousers. He stumbled a few steps, careening between harsh stares and stiff shoves. After a few slurred apologies, the man tugged on his shirt a second time and broke into a pub song. The drunkard staggered face first into the Beast's chest, falling away like he had walked into a wall. He looked up, glossy eyed, face ruddied.

The Beast said nothing. Waited.

The man flashed a toothless grin, then staggered away, picking up the tuneless song where he had left it. A trio of City Watchmen approached, hands resting on their swords. The middle watchman took the lead. "Stay where you are."

The Beast froze. This was the moment he had expected. Tension surged to his shoulders. His eyes darted for the best escape route. The watchmen closed to an arm's length. The Beast shifted his weight, readying to explode into an alley.

"Mermaid's bollocks, it's just Tram, drunk as usual," said a wiry watchman.

His comrades chuckled, relaxed their readied weapons, and broke into a trot. The City Watch caught up to the drunk, hoisting him upright. The lead watchman patted Tram on the back, dusting him off. "Gone off and found the bottle's end again, have you?"

"No worries, old boy. We'll see you home to the missus."

Tram stuttered his gratitude. His body slackened soon after. The watchmen gathered him up, laughing alongside the inebriated fool while leading him off.

How odd that the man, an obvious miscreant, was treated with such kindness. The Beast quickly chided himself for the notion, knowing his own callous philosophy was responsible for such a thought. Perhaps in Meridian, full of light and shadow, room for mercy existed.

"He'll be fine. They'll even feed the lucky bastard," said a man with a square jaw shaded by a day's stubble. He pulled a shop's door closed behind him and stepped down into the street. The Beast looked down at him, stunned that someone finally acknowledged his existence.

The man brushed wavy dark hair behind his ears. A fine cutlass with a twisting hand guard was pinned behind a thick leather belt. At his other hip, a dagger with a grip carved in the image of a grim reaper, resided in easy reach. The man's wrists were adorned by the traditional bracers worn by the freest of the free.

Pirate.

"You can see me?" the Beast asked.

The man snickered. He donned a thin cloak, concealing his armaments. "Of course I can see you, you dolt. Did you really think something as big and, well, as fuzzy as you would go unnoticed?"

The Beast's muscles tensed and he loosed a low growl. Locking a penetrating gaze onto the soon-to-be-pummeled man, he balled two fists of iron and squared off.

More laughter. The pirate dared to even slap at a knee. He wiped away a phony tear and rubbed a spasm in his side. "My friend, I meant no offense. An off-colored joke, in poor taste at your expense. Come, let us share stories of adventure and glory! What is your name?"

The tension in the Beast's shoulders twitched. "I do not have one."

"Ah, no worries. We shall find one for you by night's end!" The pirate brushed at his cloak and made for the adjacent tavern. The Beast had never before met a man so free with his tongue. The urge to flatten the pirate's rudeness was undeniable, but his gruff honesty stayed the Beast's hand. "What are you called, pirate?"

The man shoved the Rusty Rudder's door open, inviting the Beast in with a sweeping bow. A devilish grin painted his face from ear to ear.

"Captain Poogs, at your service."

Chapter 16

Malachai's fiery wrath threatened to consume all of creation. How the little abomination had managed to do it was unclear. Such a thing was impossible. He had been guaranteed as much. Yet the evidence to the contrary, though beyond belief, was equally beyond reproach.

The girl had breathed life into the Gloom.

That was hours ago. Malachai had slung his prisoner like baggage over the saddle, taking the road to Meridian in a fury. Now, returned from the Gloom, the mocking obsession of 'how' remained. Malachai glared at the door across the room.

"The Gloom is my realm. Mine," Malachai spat, anger steadily rising with each breath, like a volcano. The words crashed inside his skull like falling rocks, so deafening the black rider struggled to keep focus on the road. His jaw clenched. "I will have my answers."

He stormed to the door, knocking aside the table and chairs. The two officers of the City Watch wisely stepped aside. Malachai obliterated the door with a savage kick, leaving little more than a pair of rusted hinges. He stepped through the splintery wreckage, quaking like a rabid dog with bared teeth. The armored plates of his gauntlets screeched as black steel awakened at his side.

Lia sat cross-legged on the damp planks of the cell's floor. With delicate grace she gently wove slivers of warm light into a luminous fabric. The bundle floated above her lap, slowly spinning as she worked her hands back and forth on an invisible loom. Her button nose scrunched, further tightening her concentration. Through pursed lips she puffed a lock of hair from her squinting eyes. She beamed at her latest attempt. "Almost finished."

"How dare you," Malachai droned.

He swung his wicked sword high overhead. The sword flashed like an obsidian lightning strike, slicing within an inch of Lia's face, close enough that she felt the malice of its hateful hunger. The vicious slash cut through Lia's handicraft, banishing the light back to shadow. Malachai twisted the muscles of his pale face into a grin. *Look at her*, he thought, *sitting there alone on the floor. Pathetic. Defeated.* He sheathed his sword, certain that the little abomination's rebellious spirit was crushed once and for all.

Lia regarded the fading remnants of spell craft in her lap. She plucked a strand of light like it was yarn, watching it waver in the drafty room. The light dimmed and then died into nothingness. She sighed a child's sigh. Malachai turned for the demolished entrance, savoring his victory.

"Oh well. Looks like I'll have to start over."

Malachai froze dead in his tracks, snared by Lia's gleeful defiance. He pivoted on a heel to face the challenging taunt. Searching for bluster, Malachai found his tongue felled. All he could do was stare. Lia was already fast at work, mending and shaping new fibers of light. The colors were brighter than before, fuller. *Alive.* The dark of the empty room was aglow in shifting pigments as she worked, crafting the strands into ribbons. Then ribbons into patches...

Malachai's sword instantly flashed back to life, tearing at the fabric, cutting the deviant heresy to pieces. Lia only smiled and began again. Another fabric of light formed, this time bearing shape: A flower, petals blossoming in a violet that had only before existed in Lia's imagination. Malachai's drone burned at his throat and lifted to a roar. He slashed at the flower with sword and dagger alike in a flurry of wild strikes. Unfamiliar fatigue burned at the Wakeful Captain's shoulders as he hacked away. What was the strange power this girl had to defy him?

Lia climbed from the dank floor, hands weaving wildly. Her fingers, too stubby to learn Cedrik's lute had found an instrument all her own. She hummed Polaris's tune, *Cedrik's tune.* She threw her shoulders back and chin up, increasing her pace to match Malachai's slashing. A dozen swathes of luminous fabric appeared, each larger, more magnificent than the previous. Sweat trickled from Lia's brow as she directed the pieces into fusion. The patches stitched together in shades of Lia's violet. A pattern emerged; a wondrous design born of the child's dreams.

The patchwork unicorn reared majestically, filling the room with the intense blast of dawn's light. It scraped at the floor, lowering its spiraled horn. Malachai's pale head tilted to one side. He could not believe the sight. Would not believe. It could not be...

Malachai lunged into a twin strike of sword and dagger shaped like an X at the illusion's throat. The majestic beast parried the strikes and Malachai's blades clanged harmlessly away. It neighed and reared, nearly connecting a pair of trampling hooves to Malachai's skull. He dodged swiftly aside, then retreated for the safety of the doorway. He snatched a halberd from a wall rack and leveled it at the gaping door, hoping to impale the charging beast. A tense moment passed. The Wakeful captain approached cautiously, halberd raised. Malachai leaned around the doorway, finding darkness had reclaimed ownership of the small room. Slowly he peered inside.

The unicorn had vanished. All that remained was a sleeping girl, curled into a ball, murmuring a lullaby.

Malachai stared through the bars of emerald flame cast onto the empty door. His shoulders ached and his head pounded. That he fatigued at all was cause for concern. Did the little abomination's blasphemy know no limit? How could this have happened? Doubt started seeping into his mind through a tiny crack threatening to burst. *I should feel nothing at all. Not soreness, not fatigue. Certainly not fear.* Yet the child's blasphemy chipped away at the Wakeful Curse, robbing him of strength.

Malachai felt a sudden charge of rage. He regarded the green flame once more, then conjured additional cross bars for good measure. The wooden frame hissed wisps of grey smoke. He stepped back, armored boots clunking, pleased with his work.

The City Watchmen pressed against the jailhouse wall, watching Malachai's every move. Castiel was more than slightly unnerved. His thick fingers cramped around his sword's hilt: they had been wrapped around it the moment Malachai had splintered the door. In all honestly, he knew little could be done if Malachai turned the wrath of his crimson eyes onto him. Nothing in Castiel's meager experience with the City Watch had prepared him for such dealings. He snuck a look to his sergeant for reassurance, but found no aid.

Dacian joined Malachai with a lingering sneer of his own. His rat like face, pockmarked and picked at, was devoid of compassion. He knew Malachai's Queen would honor the arrangement as brokered. He gestured to the newly resettled chairs.

"Captain, forgive me but there is much to discuss, preparations to make. The dauntless men of our City Watch stand at the ready to apprehend your fugitive," Dacian continued with a sardonic grin. He hated the City Watch, thought his comrades less than rubes. If not for the opportunities wearing the uniform provided, he would have abandoned the post long ago.

Castiel levied a disgusted look. When he had joined the Watch a summer ago he could have never have imagined such corruption. *Paid to detain a child?*

Malachai gave no reply. He twisted in the chair, drawn again to the darkness behind the emerald blaze. *How had she made the tree blossom?* Dacian boldly tapped Malachai's forearm. "Captain..."

Malachai's dagger sang out, slicing through the tip of Dacian's index finger. He howled and jumped from his chair, cradling the wounded digit to his chest. Castiel quickly wrapped the shortened finger, tying the bandage tight. Both men knew Wakeful swords were often enchanted to cleave wounds unable to cease hemorrhaging. Dacian hope their daggers were neglected in that regard.

Malachai finally regarded the frightened pair. His dagger dripped a pitter patter of Dacian's warm blood. He wiped the blade at the flimsy, yellowed table cloth and sheathed it. He gestured to the chairs, commanding more than requesting. "Come, we have much to discuss and many preparations to make." The watchmen nervously lowered themselves into chairs at the table's far end.

"And you, you diseased pizzle," Malachai said to Dacian, "If you touch me again, more than a fingertip will roll."

Neither watchman dared to move, let alone speak. Or breathe. Dacian clutched at his bandaged wound grateful that the bleeding had stopped. Both men stared at the table's center. Malachai drummed his fingers. The clawed gauntlet gouged away flecks of wood with each impatient strike. Soon, the table looked like a savage pet's used play thing.

"I do not know what manner of fool pursues me. I presume they mean to claim the abomination for their own," Malachai said, gesturing to the cell. "Someone on a fool's quest destined for a fool's painful end."

The last of Malachai's cold words froze the room like winter's frost. The watchmen knew of the Liche Queen's proclamation and ban of magical practice. Few in Meridian were foolish enough to dabble in even the smallest of magical feats. Indeed there was little desire to do so. Meridian was well served by the technocratic alliance fostered by the grand twin cities of Neverdawn and Dayscape. Simply put, Meridian had no need for magic.

"Your men are stationed? Well-armed?" Malachai asked.

"As you've ordered, captain," Dacian blurted. The weasley watchman's gaze bored a hole through the battered table top. "They are quite capable, equipped to handle any opposition."

The hollowness of Malachai's voice returned. "We shall see about that."

"It would be the City Watch's great honor if the Captain would allow us the pleasure of apprehending this criminal antagonist on her Majesty's behalf," Dacian said, flourishing a wide bow.

The watchman's shameless ploy at currying favor went unnoticed. Malachai neither wanted nor required his ego stroked. He needed an end to this fool's errand, an end to the heresy. His Queen would see to it. And if she did not...

***

Lia stirred from her slumber, chilled by a sudden draft. She sat up in a panic, forgetting where she had fallen asleep. It was a small room, even for her. The glow of night time trickled in from a single barred window. Her stomach soured at the sight of Malachai's ugly barricade. Its roiling emerald flames offered no warmth and familiarity with the terrible blaze encouraged her distance.

Nightmares had plagued her short nap, leaving her restless. Houses obliterated by malachite stars crashing from the skies and people crying out. She shook the images free and began exploring her meager accommodations. A small stained cot occupied a corner. Next to it sat a foul looking bucket. She stretched to the tips of her toes and just barely managed to peek between the window's rusty bars.

The glow of lamp posts dazzled the thoroughfares and water front of Meridian. Lia had never seen such a spectacle. The 'city' below was as foreign a place as the Gloom. *It was like having stars close enough to reach out and catch like fireflies,* she thought. She suddenly longed to be sitting in Polaris's lap underneath their tree.

"Get down from there, before you fall out," Castiel called.

Lia hopped down, searching through the fiery door for the voice's owner.

"Cripes, imagine that. You fallin' out the window and Malachai tossin' me out on after you. Would be just my lot."

Lia knelt by the door, careful to avoid the bars, finding a spot to peer through. Castiel sat at the table, feet up, rocking back. He toyed with a dagger, spinning its tip on the pad of his thumb. Castiel stared back, contorting his face into a twisted mockup of Malachai's stare.

"It's bad manners to put your feet on the table, you know," Lia said candidly. "My *pafaa* said so."

Castiel's dagger took an errant spin. He bobbled it twice and let it clang to the floor. He stretched to retrieve it and slipped, breaking his fall with a bulbous chin.

Lia stifled a giggle with a swift hand. And then couldn't help herself. She laughed at the heap of Castiel still collecting himself, straightening his tunic and rubbing his scraped chin. Castiel heard the laughter and followed Lia's eyes to the stain on his stomach. He laughed, grateful for the break in tension Malachai had provided.

"Are you alright?" Lia asked through a cupped hand.

Castiel carefully extended his hand through the fiery barrier. "I'm fine. Clumsy as an ox, I am. Name's Castiel."

Lia shook Castiel's hand and introduced herself. He withdrew, frantically rubbing at his hand. She chanted, summoning the Breath, pleased to find it came easier now. Her hands gathered up the misty white light. It pulsed in the air around her fingers, rippling like a disturbed pond. She brandished the light at the bars. "I can help."

"I'm sure you can little one, but I am fine," Castiel said, presenting the unharmed hand for inspection. "I needed see for myself if you burned with the unholy blasphemy and heresy, blah, blah, blah." Castiel's sarcastic smile broadened as he delivered his best Malachai parody.

Lia giggled at the impression and let the Breath's power fade. She shrugged free of her thick over coat, rolled it into a cushiony ball and plunked down in front of the bars. "When we left it was winter, but when I looked outside there wasn't any snow," Lia stated flatly, hoping Castiel would elaborate.

Castiel remembered vividly his amazement with Meridian's marvels when he had first arrived.

"The Dreamers of Neverdawn have given Meridian many gifts in the name of friendship. Our very streets capture the sun's warmth and use it to resist the snow. Some of Meridian's buildings are lined with the same type of stone. That's why you're sweating through your clothes."

With grave concern she sidled tight to the burning gate. "But if there's no snow, how can there be a Winter Festival?"

Castiel chuckled. "Not to worry. Our Elders disable the warmth when it suits our needs. We have no need for warm buildings in the summer do we?" Castiel sliced a few pieces of crusty bread and mashed a bitter smelling cheese between them. He half-offered the morsel and then quickly pulled away, with a curious eye brow arched high.

"Promise not to tell anyone?"

Lia's stomach lurched and grumbled. She couldn't remember the last time she had eaten. She nodded enthusiastically. "Promise!" Castiel passed the offering through the green flame, making sure Lia did not come close enough to be burned. Lia warbled through a mouthful. "Thank you."

Small acts, she recalled Polaris saying. *Small acts of kindness and courage.*

Chapter 17

The Liche Queen was unaccompanied on this particular visit to her favorite chamber. She could not recall the last time she wandered the drab pathway, filling the last decaying remnants of her mortal lungs with the stale odor of her labors beyond. Perhaps it had been when she had called upon Malachai to serve. The Garrison awaited its queen from behind a veil of black satin. It was the only guard needed.

No one dared enter uninvited.

Nothing stirred within: there was nothing alive to do so. The deepest level of the Nekropolis was restricted to the Liche Queen and her revered guests. It was a sprawling marvel of cavernous recess. Massive slabs of stone were anchored into a morbid cathedral by interlocking twists of petrified branch. The Liche Queen herself had designed the castle's fusion of wood and stone. It was Pandora's favorite place in all of her domain. Just inside the veil, a hovering pathway of stone tiles spiraled up to a broad platform. An altar, a similar fusion of wood and stone, resided at the end. An arbour carved in the cardinal runes of the Blight stretched over the altar's basin of unhewn stone.

Pandora paused, taking in the beautiful symphony of deathly silence. It was a perfect moment in the deep dark. She tilted her head back, straining for any sound at all. Nothing. Not even a draft from the passage was admitted without her consent. She regarded her altar, carved from the Nekropolis by her own hand and birthed into being by her own blood. She circled it, tracing frigid fingertips lovingly up and over the arch, reveling in the devilish magnificence. It was at this very altar she had first conceived the end of Adella's cursed reign.

The runes flashed to life, excited by the presence of their mistress. One by one they glowed a feverish lava shade. Pandora counted off the thirteen runes in the order they were inscribed, each one burning brighter at its mention. The combined sheen bathed the macabre altar in the light of hellfire. The Liche Queen stroked the altar's rough surface. "I'm sorry, my love, but it is not you I have come to visit."

Her fingers fell away and she peered into the pit of darkness beyond the reach of the altar's jealous light. The disappointed runes faded quickly at their neglect, but returned to slumber confident their hunger would be seen to in due time. The Liche Queen raised her arms high and wide, embracing the dark.

"My children! Your mother has arrived!"

Her greeting shook the Garrison, echo reverberating far and fast, earning a moan from the black castle. A league away in the darkness, a pair of emerald specks began to shine. A second pair. And then a third. Pandora's icy heart fluttered; it always did when *they* were awakened. A wave of green orbs spread through the pit. Uniform lines stared back at the Liche Queen as the surge rushed to the Garrison's entrance, consuming the darkness in its path. And leaving behind something much worse.

The Liche Queen watched as her favorites heeded her call. The glowing Wakeful eyes reflected harshly on the sea of surrounding armors. The legion stood at perfect attention, grasping obsidian swords at eye level in salute to the queen who had gifted them with life eternal. Shoulder to shoulder they ranked ten thousand strong, clad in the suits of jagged plates and spikes that had become a symbol of terror across the land.

How Pandora loved to gaze upon her loyal Wakeful. With a thought she could teleport them to the castle's gate, unleashing them upon the world at her whim. What a glorious sight to behold: a plague of Wakeful locusts cleansing the world of Adella's memory. How would have loved to remain in the Garrison forever. But the duties of Her Majesty beckoned.

It pained her greatly to leave the Garrison. Thraal awaited, probably with another tepid lecture on logistics or some other foolish thing. *Why did he not simply advise me to unleash the Wakeful's full might? Why not send the legions to crush and burn all that opposed her will?*

The branch-lift creaked as rolling branches returned the Liche Queen to the Hollow. Servants scurried to make way, forever fearful of blocking the Liche Queen's path. She took to the wide flight of petrified stairs leading to the war room. She admired her handiwork, every so often stopping to telepathically re-mould an errant branch until the shape pleased her. The door closed behind her with a heavy thud. "General."

"My Queen," Thraal replied, with the enthusiasm of wet mop.

Thraal's emotionless nature was legendary. It was said that no one had ever see him raise his voice in anger. Nor had anyone ever seen him smile. Thraal just 'was'; a stoic force with little use for anything less than absolute victory. The General had shed his daily attire of dull gray tunic and britches, having instead donned his armor. The Liche Queen was instantly excited. Perhaps Thraal's summons was meant to announce that the time had come to claim what was rightfully hers from the mountains.

The impressive onyx cuirass was a gift from a grateful Pandora and the only piece of Wakeful armor not bearing the sigil of the Pierced Skull. At his request, his own sigil had been emblazoned in its place. Pandora was all too pleased to see the crest of a fallen dragon impaled on three serrated lances. The mockery of her parent's own Rearing Dragon was the only motivation needed for her to allow the cruel substitute.

Thraal retrieved Pandora from her ghoulish daydream with a cough. He pulled a high-backed chair from the only table. Pandora's eyes flared. She did not typically permit such gross insolence. General Thraal was the only man alive afforded the luxury of such daring. She understood the general's great importance to her campaign. But there were limits.

Impulsive ones...

"Malachai has reached Meridian with the child. Arrangements with the more ambitious men of the City Watch to apprehend his pursuer have been made."

"Excellent," Pandora said. "We take the fountain upon his return. I will summon the Legion at once."

Pandora pushed away from the table in a flourish of cape and whipping raven's locks. The general caught her by the wrist and guided her back to the chair. "There is to be some delay, your Highness. I have given Captain Malachai leave to remain in Meridian until the creature is in custody."

A gust of rot scented wind swelled at Pandora's sudden temper, snuffing the small candelabras and braziers scattered through the room. Pandora's face contorted. The beautifying enchantment echoing her human beauty fell away, revealing her true features.

The grim kiss of Undeath.

The left side of her face and jaws were little more than bone and scant tatters of desiccated skin. A scattered jigsaw of teeth, jagged of rot and molding, were all that remained beneath the vanished pair of pouty lips.

Thraal was familiar with the indigo fire of Pandora's, the Liche Queen's, eyes. He searched the face of the demon for hints of the princess he had helped to raise. What remained of her lustrous mane of curls was nothing more than sparse tufts clinging to a cracked skull. He bit the inside of his cheek, staunching his pleasure at the grim sight. Princess Pandora of the Once Kingdom truly was no more.

The fury of screaming voices in the Liche Queen's head surrendered to the silence. Gradually, her focus returned. The beautifying enchantment restored itself, filling in the decayed reality of her appearance, restoring the pale-skinned beauty the Nekropolis called Queen. Thraal hesitated, giving Pandora a moment to breathe. "I thought it wise to investigate a creature strong enough to disable a band of your Wakeful. Unarmed. Not to mention one cunning enough to hunt the Captain without his knowledge."

"Very well, general," the Liche Queen said curtly. The sudden swell of rage had left tight chains around her chest, threatening to crush what little breath remained in her decaying lungs. She forced herself to focus, shattering her bonds. She ached to fully unleash the fury of the Blight but Thraal had consistently warned against it. *The masterful warrior is cunning above all else, always keeping his true strength hidden.*

Lessons be damned, she thought, *one day I shall let him gaze upon the truest of horrors...*

"Let Malachai play his game," Pandora said. Her eyes sparkled in the returned flicker of candle light. "The child will be mine."

She burst through the war room's door and disappeared into the Hollow. Thraal heard the echo of clicking heels fade away into nothing. It was a wise decision to let her leave. Even the general was not willing to press his luck.

***

Pandora twisted the skeleton key, locking the door behind her. A satisfying click sounded as the tumblers fell into place. For good measure she lowered a heavy wooden brace into waiting brackets; additional protection against untimely interruption. One could never be too sure.

The suite of chambers comprising her private quarters was unlike any other in the Nekropolis. Billowing tapestries hung from the vaulted ceiling. A roaring fire cast dancing shadows onto the walls of mortared stone. Pandora retrieved a torch from beside a grand fire place. She walked the room's perimeter, igniting the baker's dozen sconces positioned to shed optimal light on the treasured collection of tapestries.

She regarded each piece in turn, letting tattered fabric slide between her bony finger tips, remembering fondly the circumstances of their acquisitions. *Banners from fallen kingdoms and routed keeps.* She could still taste the acrid smoke from the scorched battlefields, hear the echoes of wailing men as the Blight purged them from the mortal realm.

Glorious.

Pandora returned the torch and drew a dagger from a display case. It was the simplest of blades, unassuming, yet razor sharp. She sliced at her palm, watching as the thin red line wept blood. The act no longer troubled her for so much as a flinch. In truth she looked forward to it now. She slung the handful of blood into the waiting fire. The liquid sizzled, filling the room with a foul metallic odor. In a somber tone she called out to a place beyond the flames.

"Master, your servant awaits. Your will, my hands."

The fire swirled like a cyclone and was sucked away through the flue. An indigo fire mirroring her eyes replaced the orange and scarlets, arranging into the angled features of a face. The demon god Ahriman stared back from the fire. A single gigantic eye pierced the veil between realms, penetrating into Pandora's mind. A jeweled horn crowned Ahriman's head, protruding from above the glaring eye. The demon-lord twisted his three jaws, grumbling.

The penetrating stare brought Pandora to her knees. She pressed her forehead to cold stone, arms extended in homage. The blissful feeling of Ahriman probing her mind reeked of palpable dread and dripped with pending doom. It was the only fear Pandora had ever known. It was her great reward. Ahriman scoured the newly formed memories in her mind, searching for news of the captured child and the statuses of his other agent's. Her vision blackened. A thin trickle of blood dripped from her nose, spattering the stones. Pressure built between her ears. She winced as it built, laughing, wondering if this time her head were to explode.

The demon god's inspection concluded with a lurch. Dark fire flared in the hearth and then blinked away, blanketing the room in near darkness. Pandora struggled to her feet, found the wide stone block of her bed and flopped onto it. Every cell in her body ached of Ahriman's lingering traces. It was a price she was more than willing to pay. She was grateful the dark god had found her. They were of the same wretched soul, possessing the same cynical view of the world. In Ahriman, Pandora had found the means to destroy all she hated. Likewise, Ahriman had found a champion avatar in the realm from which he was barred trespass. One who required little effort to control.

Magic's abhorrent contamination by the mortals would be ended once and for all.

Pandora sprawled across the stone bed, drifting into the waiting shadows that always followed Ahriman's visit. She wondered if the dreadful feeling would ever abate as the sleep demons claimed her.

She hoped with every fiber of her being that it never did.

Chapter 18

The walls of Meridian's most notorious tavern were covered in joyous homage to life at sea. A burnt auburn rudder hung proudly above the bar. For generations Meridian's sailors saluted the rudder with their last drink of the night. It was a humble gesture that sought safe journey in the morning and respite for friends lost the night before. The Rusty Rudder's patronage was a spirited collage of sailors and locals. A spattering of wealthier merchants shared in the festive mood, shielded by a phalanx of guards wearing scowl and sword. A lonely musician sat on a modest stage, shouting more than singing into air rife of salt water and spilled spirits.

The half-drunk pirate tossed a handful of coins into the air. "Another round!" Poogs cheered.

A dense crowd echoed the jubilant cheer with shouts of bawdy gratitude. The patrons closest to the bar immediately turned to the bar keep, shouting drink orders over the din. The fair skinned man shouted into the kitchen for extra hands. Two lads looking every bit his progeny quickly punched through a sheepskin covered doorway. They hurried to work, deftly serving drinks without a single spill, slinging flagons down the bar to grubby hands. The barkeep filled a flagon of his own and then downed the foamy ale in a single pull. He smashed the cup into the floor and raised his arms in victory to the crowd's roar.

Poogs slipped from the bar with four steins dangling from his fingers. A sailor with a crooked nose and a thick mask of stubble slapped Poogs on the back, spilling a waterfall of foam. Poogs saluted the kindness with a fistful of raised drinks. After nudging aside a few more fans, he slid into a booth across from the Beast, proudly slapping the drinks down. The pirate laughed into the crook of his elbow. The Beast flashed a suspicious eye.

"I miss something?"

Poogs lifted his head, the last of a chuckle falling from his mouth. "It'll be weeks before..." The pirate slumped back into his arm, seized by a laughing fit.

"Before what?"

"Before they realize those coins were false," Poogs whispered with a wry grin. He pulled a coin from his purse, bent it between his teeth and flicked it away into the sea of people.

The Beast panned the room. "Won't they come looking for you?"

Poogs sucked down a refreshing quaff. "How would they know? Besides, I'll have reached fairer port by then." Poogs finished his ale, wiping his mouth with an exaggerated flourish.

"And even if they did, I'd think of something. I always do."

Pirate or not, Poogs played the part of host well. Every man present seemed to know him. A constant stream of faces dropped by their booth, sharing sea stories and laughs at the other's expense. A bevy of women did likewise, but the Beast averted his ears when they arrived. He was quite certain those tales were best left unheard. A pretty brunette fell into Poogs's lap to the annoyance of a second lass who stormed away in a huff. Poogs shouted a few names into her wake. None were correct.

The pirate shrugged his shoulders. "Oh well," he sighed with a broad smile. And then buried his muzzle into the brunette's neck.

Maybe it was Poogs's infectious charm. Maybe it was Meridian's twilight shine. But in the scant hours since his arrival the Beast had transformed from wraith to right hand man. He even managed to tell a joke of his own. Maybe he had been wrong about people. These folk seemed more than amiable once Poogs provided introduction. He finished his drink and set the empty stein down.

Then again maybe it was the ale.

A lumpy skulled man watched the reveling pair from the bar's far end, salivating at the prospect of turning in his bounty. He lifted an arm from under a brown cloak, signaling to an unseen associate. Just a simple, unassuming rub of the right eye, code amongst his guild for 'he's here, with company'. Outside, Tavril nodded and silently flashed a signal of his own into the alley. He hopped down from the crate, cursing his dwarfish stature under his breath. He squinted at the shadows, searching for his men. Men who were supposed to be watching for the signal. A moment later, the alley remained silent as an abandoned graveyard. Tavril sighed.

Idiots.

He whistled through stubby fingers. A crash answered. Then a curse. A slapping sound and then a second curse. A mumbled apology followed. Two men chased the racket out of the alley, one rubbing at a sore spot on his head.

"You two are gonna be the death of me. Of all the muscle the boss could have sent," Tavril said, flaring his arms wide in mock embrace, "he gives me you."

The men mounted a protest, but were immediately stifled by Tavril's stubby fingers. If only the dwarf had come unaided. The job would have gone quick and clean, seen everyone paid and sent home. He regarded his associates. Both were twice his height and bulkier than a team of oxen. *They would have to do. What the boss says goes.*

***

Hours later the pleasant throng spilled into the night, arms draped over shoulders, singing of mermaids. An inebriated Poogs had babbled the night away with fantastic tales of forgotten temples and heart stalling escapes, each tale more outlandish than the last. As an orator, Poogs had no equal. The Beast cocked his head to the side, finding it sloshed with every subtle move. Keeping up with Poogs's autobiography had fast become a herculean undertaking. His snout tingled, his tongue felt too wide and he was quite certain that a cloud had leaked into his skull. The room lurched to the opposite tilt.

"...and that, my friend, is how I came to captain the Reaper's Song."

Poogs's lips were moving. But his words were distorted echoes. The Beast tossed his head, trying to clear away the cobwebs.

"...changed my name when I left..."

Poogs's garbled stories overlapped into one sordid diatribe. The Beast wavered in his seat, trying to manage the litany of details.

"Enough about me," Poogs said, "What glorious tales of adventure has the fabled Beast of Briarburn brought to my humble table?" Poogs had matched the Beast drink for foolish drink all night, showing no signs of slowing.

A pirate's life...

"I have no glory to share. There is not a single moment I wish to relive." The Beast's tone hardened. "You said you knew where I could find the Wakeful filth. Do you?"

"In good time, my savage friend, in good time. Malachai is indeed in Meridian. But one does not simply demand an audience with the good captain. Tell me of your past, surely there is something more than the desire to feel the sting of Wakeful steel."

The Beast fumbled under his cloak, snagging the medallion after a few errant gropes. He pulled the chain taut, yanking his head forward.

"This is the only tale worth telling, pirate," the Beast slurred, "and I haven't a clue what it is. The amulet drew an intrigued look from Poogs whose hand slowly reached out. The Beast, suddenly sober, snarled and jerked the medallion away.

"That's close enough," the Beast rumbled, "any closer and you will not get it back."

Poogs fell back in a drunken slump, sulking like a disappointed child. "Oh, I was only after a look-see."

The Beast tucked the medallion away and swiped up the last of his tepid ale. Poogs grinned. "Was it a gift? From a fair lady-friend perhaps?" The Beast shifted uncomfortably, unwilling to discuss the details of the medallion. Instead, he spoke briefly of life on the Great Road. Something about Poogs labelled the pirate trustworthy. He recognized a shadow of sorrow behind the charismatic glint in his eye. Something he had lost, perhaps. *Or something taken.*

Poogs pointed at the firestone. "I have heard of such stones." He leaned over the table, shielding his mouth from eavesdroppers. "Your medallion is of the Aether, crafted of the stars themselves."

The Beast lunged, grabbing a fistful of Poogs's shirt, lifting the pirate from his seat. "Have you seen this stone before? I must know."

A lingering crew of rough looking longshoremen abandoned their drinks and cast Poogs a sympathetic glance. None were interested in being caught up in the scuffle despite his exuberant hospitality. Only Tavril's lumpy skulled associate remained at the bar. Janten hadn't even flinched when the Beast's roaring interrogation had begun. His orders were clear:

take Poogs by any means necessary.

Poogs felt the warmth of the Beast's ale laced breath on his face. Glowering amber orbs stared back at him over a pair of ivory white fangs. For the first time since their meeting, Poogs panicked. He knew struggling was out of the question. The Beast could likely crush his skull with a thought. He had to keep him talking. Poogs raised his hands in mock surrender, willing his grin to re-appear.

"If you'd kindly put me down..."

The Beast pulled Poogs in closer till they were nose to snout, close enough for Poogs to be brushed by coarse fur. *A warning.* The Beast released Poogs who immediately set about repairing his disheveled appearance. The Beast towered over the preening pirate, awaiting his answer. He growled a guttural rumble. Poogs shot the Beast an annoyed expression.

"Well it's your fault I look of riffraff! Would you have me cowering in such disarray? What if, oh, what's her name with the mole were to come back? Hmm? What then?" The pirate finished his tirade and seated himself gently, like a Lord holding court. "Now, if you would be so kind as to join me in a more civilized fashion."

Poogs rambled a lengthy prologue to the medallion's origins, but the Beast only heard a portion of it. He had finally noticed the Rusty Rudder's lone remaining patron. The lumpy skulled man sat motionless like he was part of the decor. The Beast's suspicion was tripped, but he was inclined to give the man a pass. *Probably a regular, allowed to stay on late,* he thought. Poogs's voice melted into babble. The Beast tapped a claw on the table, impatience preparing its coup. Poogs was arriving at some semblance of point when Janten finally stirred at the bar.

Janten flashed two fingers up and across his throat. At first the Beast thought it an itch being scratched, but a second gesture caught his attention. He recognized the combination for what they were: signals. A silent code used throughout the criminal underworld of thieves guilds. Code for 'take them both'. The Beast quickly scanned the bar room without moving his head, checking reflections in windows and hanging coats of arms. He had to maintain a pretense of oblivion, but the situation was plain.

Malachai had set a trap...

Chapter 19

The Beast exploded from his seat. He grabbed Poogs around the waist and hurled a stool at Janten, then barreled through a maze of tables. Janten dove from his seat, dodging the missile by inches. The bar-keep ducked behind the bar, covering against the storm of flying furniture. The Rusty Rudder's doors exploded open and the Beast darted off into the night.

The Beast sprinted down Meridian's main street, knocking aside a group of sailors. The men cursed as they picked themselves up, but quickly thought better of pushing the issue. A confused Poogs jostled atop the Beast's shoulder, cloak flapping at his face. As the world bounced, he caught a glimpse of the familiar dwarfish features of an old colleague. It appeared the guild had caught up to him. He would have to move on once more.

After he collected his bounty...

"Faster! Run faster!" Poogs yelled to his improvised mount. "At the fountain turn left and then immediately right into the alley."

The Beast grunted acknowledgment, lowered his shoulder and bolted on. The shallow fountain grew larger with each stride. A life-sized brass statue of a woman poured water back into the pool. The Beast rushed past, cutting left at the intersection, earning a sharp slap on the back as he blew by the next turn.

"No, no! Go back, go back!"

The Beast twisted at the waist, skidding to halt. Poogs flew from his perch, innate athleticism flashing to life. He landed on a shoulder, tucked his limbs and rolled. He sprang up from the tumble like a lithe acrobat bored of a rusty routine. Poogs brushed his coat clean and then raced for the missed turn. "This way. Come quickly!"

The Beast hesitated. How much better than a few drinks did he know the pirate? The side street Poogs indicated disappeared into a nest of tightly knit buildings that blocked the moonlight.

Poogs gestured for the Beast to hurry. "Come on then! Those fools will be along any minute." The pirate's concern appeared to be rooted in the genuine. He hadn't resisted when he was snatched up and kidnapped and he knew more of the medallion, that much was clear. The Beast hurried to weigh the facts against the dangers.

"Silence your braying nag," the Beast grumbled. He ducked into the side street, catching up to Poogs in a half dozen strides.

The pirate navigated the twisting streets of the merchant's enclave, periodically turning back, checking for signs of Tavril's men. He pulled up in front of a nondescript shop bearing no signage. Its windows were dark and yellowed by a layer of grime. The Beast snorted. "I don't think they're open."

Poogs produced a key from a coat pocket, brandishing it in a column of pale moon. He inserted it, turning a half-twist before abruptly stopping. His eyes glinted, privy to a private humor.

"You might not want to stand there."

The Beast shrugged and trundled a few steps back. Poogs turned the key home. A sharp click was followed by the thud of a falling counterweight. A square of road, wide as the door frame, dropped away into blackness.

A trap door, hidden in plain sight...

Poogs chuckled at the clever security system. He invited the Beast to peer over the side. The Beast declined with a shake of his horned head.

"Suit yourself. In that case, welcome to my humble workshop." The pirate nudged the door open, ushered the Beast inside, then reset the trap.

The Beast spit shined a peephole on the grimy window and peered outside. The trap's outline was gone, vanished into the street. The workshop was dark save for a few sickly traces of moonlight penetrating the windows' filth. Acrid fumes from the forge were tinged with hints of alien scents the Beast could not identify. Rows of crude shelving filled with chipped beakers and other equipment were stationed around the open floor. The Beast nodded at the general disarray. "Too busy to tidy up for company?"

Poogs answered from behind a wall of shadow. "Company is typically reserved for my ship. The Reaper's Song is much more accommodating."

Ceiling chains dangled broad canvases, obscuring several large structures on the workshop's floor. The Beast counted a dozen rust-stained coverings. Some were spotted with mold, others bore the singe of forge work. The unseen mysteries lurking beneath poked at their shrouds. A draft gently rippled the canvases, giving them the illusion of ghosts at play. Poogs confidently wove through the junk laden shelves, boots crunching on layers of saw dust and discarded parchment. The sounds of burrowing rustled through the silent workshop. The pirate grunted then cursed in the dark, kicking at something. "Damned contraption is stuck."

A moment later, grinding gear works clanked to life. Wall mounted metallic rings of a varying sizes flooded the workshop with a sterile white glow. Enormous sprawls of hand drawn sketches and architectural schematics filled the spaces between the rings. The three largest rings, a man's arm length in diameter, were mounted onto wheeled bases.

The Beast marveled at the brilliance of the pirate's ink blotted renderings. Seeing Poogs's work, his attention to detail, the scope, was every bit as impressive as Urda's sky writing. The voice from the woods whispered softly in his head. *The world was much grander than the Road had revealed. It is out there, waiting for you...* Perhaps rescuing the girl was as important as the old ghost claimed. Perhaps this was his chance to matter.

Poogs worked one of the dangling chains. The ratcheting clicks stirred a few critters from hiding. A rust colored mouse streaked from underneath a canvas, then disappeared into a wall crack. The tiny critter reminded the Beast of his wintergreen home. A mere three days had passed since stirring from his mossy bed. Much had happened since then. The world was getting larger and larger with each step; an exciting and terrifying prospect. He wondered if he'd ever see his green cushioned bed again.

Poogs released the chain, clapping dust free from his hands, snapping the Beast's daydream. He awoke to find one of the canvas coverings had revealed their secret. Astonishment was understatement. The sprawling schematics had been impressive. The item on display stole the very breath from the room. The Beast's jaw dropped like a boulder. Poogs circled a display, waving for the Beast to join him. Inside the shell of light an odd looking device rested on iron prongs.

A weapon... the Beast thought. The device's wooden stock was familiar enough, but beyond that... A long metal tube was fastened to the device's top, a trigger below. *What had Poogs conjured up?*

Poogs puffed his chest. "Blunderbuss."

The Beast was speechless. He reached for the strange device, but Poogs froze him with a terse warning.

"Careful, she's loaded."

The Beast stepped away. *No quarrel, no sign of magical charge.* "Loaded with what?"

Poogs hoisted the blunderbuss free. He thumbed a switch near the trigger. The weapon's barrel broke apart, tilting forward. Poogs tapped a metallic projectile free, catching it in his unoccupied hand. He pinched the smooth object between his fingers and then flipped it nonchalantly to his guest. The Beast plucked the projectile from flight. He regarded the curious weapon, unsure how such a simple device could hurl something fast enough to damage a target. He tossed the projectile back to Poogs who deftly reloaded the shell and snapped the weapon shut.

"Some years ago, the winds carried my ship to a walled city far to the East. There I saw a child, a boy, no more than six, playing with a black powder. He was snapping pinches of it against the city's roads." Poogs threw a snap of imaginary powder.

"The powder ignited and then... boom!" Poogs puffed into a closed fist, blowing it open. "I purchased a pouch from the boy. The possibilities seemed endless. I've been working with it, refining it. It will change everything we know of armed combat. No longer would a man need years of training to learn to fight. The meekest among us could defend his family with the simple pull of a trigger."

The Beast caught a flare of anger in the pirate's eye. The flash burnt strong for a heartbeat and was gone, swallowed up by Poogs's natural swagger.

Poogs racked the blunderbuss and lowered the covering. He tossed another cover aside, revealing a modest work bench well stocked with worn hand tools. The bench was a perfect microcosm of the shop:

plastered in schematics, buried under discarded junk. The Beast regarded the messy scene. How the pirate got any work done at all, he did not know.

Poogs cleared a space on the bench with a cavalier swipe. Clutter crashed and fluttered in an avalanche of refuse. The pirate moved a strange looking device to the bench's center. It was of better quality than anything else the Beast had seen in the shop. He manipulated the stack of seven affixed lenses. "This was a gift from the stuffiest professor I have ever had the privilege of being expelled by."

Poogs invited the Beast to place the medallion beneath the lowest looking glass. The Beast responded with a look to kill. Separation from the medallion occurred on exactly one occasion since his awakening. The consequences had been dire for all.

Never again will the chains bind...

"If you wish to know more..." Poogs gestured again to the work bench. "Where would I run you big fool? You'd have me in two steps."

The Beast hesitated and then lifted the medallion free. The firestone's iridescence battled the workshop's sterile light in dazzling shards of copper and crimson, protesting the separation with pin pricks of energy into his paw. Poogs manipulated the individual glasses, searching for perfect magnification. His fingers worked the device the way a master musician would play his favorite piece. Poogs adjusted the medallion and the Beast moved a fast step forward out of reflex.

"Extraordinary, truly extraordinary," Poogs said with hushed excitement. "The inscription is flawless, absolutely perfect. I cannot translate most of the glyphs." Poogs removed the medallion and pointed to a collection of symbols.

"But this one assuredly says '*wynisahil*.'"

The Beast shrugged. Never had he made the claim that he was a great scholar of magical tongues. Poogs snickered at the Beast's ignorance until a flared nostril interrupted his fun. "I have heard this word. This '*wynisahil*' is an ancient word. A root word from which all magic flows. The word has not been purposefully uttered by mortals for ages."

The Beast lunged at the pirate, pleading. "How do you-- Where did hear that? Is there more? Speak fast, pirate, I have little patience and you have little time."

The gleam in Poogs's eye reflected in the medallion. "My friend, its meaning is as simple as it is elegant." Poogs's flashy grin spread over his face.

"It means wish."

Chapter 20

Beads of sweat dotted Tavril's sloping forehead. The dwarf yanked a monographed handkerchief from a pocket and dabbed at the salty droplets. After his mark had escaped the ambush at the Rusty Rudder, Tavril had the good sense to summon more muscle from the guild. A dozen men now convened on the fountain outside the merchant's enclave. Tavril split his swelled ranks which included a few on loan from the City Watch.

Tavril's legs dangled from his seat at the fountain's edge. He would remain behind with his personal guard. The other teams would storm the workshop, front and rear. They would tighten the noose and squeeze. A basic enough strategy. Or so he hoped.

He stroked absentmindedly at a lengthy beard while the last of his men disappeared into the merchant's enclave. Now, he need only wait.

***

The Beast was hunched over the looking glass when a crash rattled the workshop.

"Our guests have arrived. Quickly, to the back--" A second boom muffled Poogs's instruction. The workshop's doors exploded, flew into the shop and smashed into the canvased pedestals. Several bizarre displays sent their contents sliding across the floor. The blunderbuss skittered behind a pile of scrap metal.

A pack of masked men, clad in leather armor, stormed inside crossbows raised. A staccato retort of twangs echoed. Quarrels ripped through the canvases, pinning shreds of fabric into the walls. The assault was fast and furious, meant to shock the wanted men within into surrender. Captain Poogs of the Reaper's Song harbored no such intention. He dove to his side and smashed a hidden wall panel with a palm, dousing the array of ring-lights, blanketing the shop in blackness.

The Beast dodged a swarm of quarrels, tumbling behind a large brass globe. He peered over the model, flinching at a ricocheting quarrel. He quickly retreated and scanned around for options. He found Poogs on the move. The pirate had slipped undetected around the room, nearly reaching the wrecked entrance. Poogs crept along, crouched low, hugging the wall. The pirate reached into a pocket retrieving two small objects. The Beast's keen vision strained but he was able to see the contents of the pirate's hand.

The shop key and a small metal ring.

The crossbowmen held their formation just inside the door, less than thrilled at the prospect of advancing into the darkness. "Profit over peril" was their mantra. Poogs was one thing, the monstrous demon with him, another thing entirely. Instead, strings were re-drawn, quarrels reloaded.

It was exactly the reprieve the pirate needed.

Poogs sprung from the shadows, slamming the metal ring against the floor. He shielded his face, bracing an arm tightly against his eyes. The ring exploded a second later in a blinding flash and a thunderstorm's boom. The guild assassins cried out, deafened and blinded. Crossbows piled onto the floor as the intruders stumbled over one another, fighting for the exit. Poogs appeared from behind a rack of shelves with his wide grin painted in place. He strolled to the door's frame and inserted the key. The pirate whistled as the last of the guild stumbled from his ruined workshop.

"I'd like to thank you all for coming, but most regrettably I must bid you good-night and farewell," Poogs said with a low, flourishing bow. He twisted the key, activating the trapdoor. He spun back to the shop, arms raised in victory. "All is well, my friend. They are gone, you may quit cowering now."

The Beast stood from behind the globe. Only muffled shouts remained of the intruders. "The trap?"

Poogs winked.

"And that flash? Do you meddle in sorcery as well?"

"Tis not sorcery, my savage friend, but science. A power all may claim regardless of lineage," Poogs replied. The pirate brandished a second ring before slipping it over a blackened fingernail. "But no time for lessons now. There are more waiting outside to be sure."

The fur of the Beast's golden brown mane quivered as his jaw set. He started for the door. "Then let us take the battle to the cowards who would shoot us down like dogs."

It took Poogs both hands and two braced boots to slow him, sliding a full two feet backwards before the Beast relented. "The guild will shoot us down indoors or out. It matters not to them." Poogs pat the Beast on the chest. He pointed to a rack of cluttered shelves. "Have no fear. There is yet another way out."

The Beast pushed hard against the wall, tensing as the wall stood its ground. "We are to walk through it I suppose?"

Poogs sighed. "How sad it must be to possess such shoddy vision." The pirate tugged on a hunk of scrap lying waist high on a shelf. Dust puffed from the outline of the hidden door. He swung the shelving away while the false panel slowly slid into the wall.

The proud pirate turned his back on the passage, preparing another grandiose quip. A quarrel fired from within the newly exposed exit grazed Poogs's shoulder. He staggered a step, caught off guard by the sudden pain. Warm blood trickled down his arm. He grabbed at the wound, trying to squeeze away the spreading sting.

Three men filled the short passage to the alley. The man at center dropped to a knee for a reload, ordering the others to advance. The pair fired into the workshop as they closed in. Poogs smiled and tilted his face away from the inevitable.

The Beast flew through the darkness with a roar, knocking Poogs from his fate. A quarrel ripped a fresh hole in the Beast's tattered cloak. He rolled to his feet, grasping for a suitable weapon. His paws brushed something curved and cool. And heavy.

The globe.

The Beast heaved the gigantic brass sphere at the assassins, battering the pair into their comrade and back into the night. The globe wedged into the hidden doorway that now restricted admission to only slivers of moonlight that cast an eerie glow over the brass. Poogs picked himself up with a groan, still clutching at his wound. He uttered a gratitude and then a curse before slipping to his hands and knees.

The Beast thought the pirate to have feinted at the sight of his blood. He knelt to pick Poogs up and was greeted with a laugh. The pirate stood, clutching the blunderbuss, winking with an air of defiant confidence. "It will take more than a scratch."

The Beast sidled next to the wall and peered out the window. "What now? Too many out front." He regarded the brass globe. "And I broke your secret door."

Poogs smirked at the heavy handed renovation and tapped the blunderbuss against the brass barricade. "It would seem so."

The clanging of heavy armor intensified near the door. Poogs pointed to a staircase behind his work station and shouted for the Beast to move. The pirate retreated to the base of the stairs, blunderbuss raised. The

Beast snatched up the medallion and took the stairs by three. He found a loft full of stacked shipping crates at the top. At the far end, moonlight painted a wide window in a welcoming silver hue.

The Beast snaked his way through the wooden maze of crates stamped in tongues he did not recognize. It seemed that Poogs's stories of wonder had been truthful. The tight labyrinth's splintery edges snagged and tore at his cloak. Halfway to freedom the sad sound of ripping cloth tore the cloak free. The Beast doubled back, but Poogs's shout warned him off. "Keep going!"

A dozen men in heavy chain armor veered around the open trap door and stormed the workshop. The time for crossbows was over: The new arrivals brandished swords and battle axes and were eager to avenge their comrades in the pit. But fortune smiled upon the pirate for a third time. The pirate squeezed the trigger and the blunderbuss' muzzle flashed with a sharp crack.

The shell struck a mercenary square in the chest plate, knocking him from his feet. The man went down hard, winded into unconsciousness.

"You're gonna' need more 'en one of those," snarled a man near the pack's front. He clapped a chipped battle axe against his chest.

Poogs rested the smoking blunderbuss on his shoulder. "No, I believe one shall suffice."

The projectile exploded into crackling arcs of blueish-purple lightning. They danced from the fallen man, claiming his closest comrades. A second pulsing arc claimed the rest. The tight formation was fast reduced to a quivering mass of limbs and rolling eyes.

"See?" Poogs taunted. "Only one." The pirate sprinted up the remaining stairs. He reloaded the blunderbuss as he navigated the forest of crates.

At the other end of the loft, the Beast tore at the barred window objecting to their escape. He paid the objection no mind and rent the rusty iron free. Behind him came the sounds of toppling crates. The Beast snapped back to the racket, ready for battle and was relieved by the sight of Poogs fast on his way. The Beast looked behind the pirate shimmying his way through the rows of crates, raising a brow at the mess. The small pile would have failed to block a curious child. The Beast dropped the mangled handful of barred window. "I don't think that will slow them."

"It wasn't meant to," Poogs replied. The pirate dangled the remains of the Beast's hunter green cloak and then tossed it home.

***

Tavril's brow was sheeted in perspiration. The dwarf knew that another failure was out of the question. The code allowed for no more leniency than a single second chance. Poogs must be brought in, dead or alive.

Preferably dead.

"Where is that blasted Janten? I should be parading that pirate scum's body by now."

Neither of Tavril's body guards answered the dwarf. Sergeant Dacian of the City Watch joined the pursuit to protect his deal with the Wakeful captain. He cared nothing for the pirate or the dwarf's guild. All that mattered was keeping Malachai happy and paying.

Drawing slender blades, Dacian and his City Watch lackeys moved in unison to the workshop. He gestured for Tavril to remain close behind. The crossbowmen still groaned from the pit's bottom. Tavril's cheeks flushed beneath his thick beard. The dwarf kicked at the street, cursing Poogs's name. He stopped for a breath, and his nose filled with the acrid smell of burning chemicals.

That damned pirate...

Tavril turned to run, but was too late. The loft exploded, ripping away part of the roof and most of the store front. An avalanche of burning crates rained down, flattening the shelves and covered projects. Fire greedily rolled over the walls, fueled by the endless expanse of schematics. Tavril pushed the smoking body of a mercenary away and struggled to his feet. His head was a vibrating mess. A carpet of writhing watchmen decorated the street. The workshop was little more than debris.

A grim smile slowly crawled over the dwarf's chiseled face. *No one could have escaped the fireball.*

***

The Beast fled through the maze of blind alleys with Poogs trailing close behind. "Ahead, next right and we should be clear."

The Beast reached the intersection and stopped. The pirate's judgement back at the workshop had been correct. A stand up brawl would not have ended well. Not for Poogs. Not for himself. *Not for Lia.*

Poogs finally caught up and joined the Beast in a moment's rest. He bent, bracing a hand on a knee, chest heaving.

"Thank you, captain," the Beast said. He pat the medallion beneath his cloak. "My quest continues with purpose. Now I need only find Malachai and the child."

Poogs stretched his back. "Who is this child you seek, why does she mean so much to you?"

"Her grandfather said she was special, that she could heal your world. The old man offered his assistance with this." The Beast tapped the medallion. "I've had visions of her, heard her voice."

"It is truly the most terrible of things when a child is lost."

"She is no child of mine and yet we are connected somehow. It is as though I know her without ever having met her. She is..."

"What?"

The Beast hesitated, unsure of the words. "...mine to protect." He was sure that a zinging quip would be the price paid for his sentiment, but none came. Instead, Poogs merely gestured to the intersection.

"We must go."

The pair ran deeper into the Merchant's Enclave. On all sides, store fronts full of dark and shuttered windows pressed together into a narrowing, dense nest. The Beast stumbled through a switchback as the pirate spoke once more.

"She would have been lucky to have you. As my son would have been to have me."

The Beast heard a familiar click. He turned to find an expressionless Poogs raising the blunderbuss.

"I am truly sorry, my friend."

The projectile thumped into the Beast's chest, knocking him back a step. Disbelief was fast replaced by a sudden burst of white-hot rage. *Betrayal. As expected.* He lurched forward, picturing a headless pirate. An arc of lightning surged from the metallic shell, piercing the Beast's breast. His muscles spasmed and he stumbled to a knee. Fury carried him through a wobbling stride into the blunderbuss's wafting smoke.

The Beast swung at the pirate, claws begging for the soft flesh of his throat. Poogs stood motionless as the claws raked down, missing by inches. The Beast reached up from the ground, willing his arm to another strike. Vengeance would be his.

And then he fell into oblivion.

<u>Chapter 21</u>

The prow of the Reaper's Song cut through the rolling waves of Meridian's coast. Her trio of main sails caught sweeping currents of wind, speeding the massive vessel true. She was a constant fixture of the seafaring world. The buxom figurehead with the skeletal face had haunted nightmares since the dawn of time. Clutching her lyre to her chest, she pierced the morning mists with an out-stretched sword.

The majestic ship had slipped away unnoticed by the City Watch, courtesy of her captain's considerable influence. Poogs knew intimately the power of a coin laden purse. He tapped his own laden purse, jingling its fresh contents, pleased by the heft. Satisfied for the moment, the pirate returned his attention to his beloved vessel, lazily guiding the helm with one hand.

Sergeant Dacian of the City Watch was not faring as well. His left eye was swollen shut, blood poured from his bludgeoned mouth. The corrupt watchman faced the dawn bound and kneeling on the main deck. Malachai paced a short path in front of the bloodied man, spiked boots gouging the deck. "You were warned." He stomped Dacian's chest, sending him reeling. Mercy was a wholly unknown concept to the black rider. Kicking a downed opponent was a central tenet of Wakeful combat doctrine and one he particularly enjoyed.

Shivers climbed the spines of Poogs's crew as a second savage kick curled Dacian into a ball. Blood spurt from his mouth. He rolled onto his back, pleading for mercy. Lia met Dacian's panicked gaze as he panted beneath his tormentor. Terror stared back from a single teary orb. She wracked her mind for a way to help. She looked to the seas, blue like a hummingbird, but found no answers. She considered calling out to Polaris, but a memory of her *pafaa* stirred. *Bravery no matter the odds.*

Malachai hoisted Dacian to his feet. His fiery gaze scorched Dacian's face. He contorted his slit-like mouth into a half smile while wisps of smoke peeled from Dacian's cheeks. "You were warned. And you knew the penalty." The Wakeful Captain seized shivering Dacian into a tight bear hug. The condemned man cried out in agony, torn by the blades and barbs of Malachai's armor.

Lia screamed to her lungs limit. Malachai dropped the bloody mess, kicking him again for good measure before gesturing to the crew. The crewmen looked wide eyed at each other, then to their captain. A dour Poogs grimaced, then nodded once. He would not share in Dacian's mistakes. He would not fail the Wakeful. The doomed City Watchman begged for mercy as the crew lifted him overhead and tossed him over the rail. His final cry stretched over the waves as he fell.

Lia rushed to the railing and peered over the gilded woodwork. A single bobbing arm stuck up from the waves. A moment later, Dacian was gone.

"Bring me the other," Malachai commanded.

Lia's heart plunged into her stomach. Across the deck, a door opened. Her lip quivered as Castiel was shoved stumbling forward to Malachai's judgment. His hands were bound behind his back and cold sweat pasted his shirt to his blanched skin. Malachai swatted his victim with a stiff backhand. Castiel's head swiveled, his face torn by the jagged gauntlet's kiss. It was more than Lia could take. She rushed down from the helm, throwing herself up as Castiel's shield. "Stop!"

Malachai raised his fist, deciding between victims. Salty air rushed over the Reaper's Song, tussling Lia's rich curls. Malachai lowered his hand, cautioned both by the wind's sudden intrusion and fresh memory of Lia's strength. The child reached for Castiel's wounded face. She muttered a secret word and the Breath came, wrapping her hands in healing orbs of white light. Castiel's jailors hastily retreated to the safety of their shipmates.

The deep cuts warmed under Lia's gentle touch. Slowly, the Breath seeped into Castiel's wounds, sealing them with light. Jaws slackened down the line of Poogs and company. Most knew of magic only in old seafaring tales. Poogs, for all of the grand sights he'd seen, had encountered magic only once before, on the day he had acquired the Reaper's Song. Lia removed her hands and the Breath disappeared. A moment later the collection of grievous lacerations were no more than faint traces of thinning scars.

"Blasphemy!" Malachai swatted the child aside. He seized Castiel by the throat with an iron grip. "His fate is of *your* doing, little abomination."

Castiel struggled, but Malachai tightened the iron noose of fingers. The railing grew closer. Castiel's eyes rolled into his skull. Malachai dangled the watchman effortlessly over the side, relishing in his torment. That he possessed the means to punish the little abomination fueled the hell in his eyes. He flinched, letting Castiel slip a few inches.

The orbs returned instantly to Lia's hands. "No!"

Poogs laid a steadying hand on Lia's shoulder. Her head snapped around, finding the silent plea in his steel grey eyes.

No.

Lia carefully regarded the tall pirate, then let the glow fade.

"Captain Malachai, perhaps an arrangement could be made?" Poogs thumbed the heavy purse from his belt, and flipped it across the deck to the Wakeful captain.

An eternity passed and Malachai finally dumped a limp Castiel to the deck. He stepped over the unconscious watchman, meeting Poogs nose to nose. The pirate instinctively scooped Lia behind him. A foolish gesture, but one he had to make. Malachai flung the pouch from the Reaper's Song. "Her majesty has no need for your currency."

Malachai regarded the fast spreading mass of island forming on the horizon. A dozen private docks reached out into the open waters. He shouted to the gathered crew of the Reaper's song.

"But I yet have use for you."

***

A piercing scream abducted the Beast from the dream world. His body wrenched from the wooden floor as he tried to quickly scramble to his feet. Thick manacles chained him doubly to the wall and to a floor mounted ring. He tugged at against his restraints, but soon understand the dire nature of his situation. *Trapped.*

Long buried memories flooded his mind. Panic spread through the Beast's veins like icy poison. Every freezing moment brought agonizing, day-long visions of the chains. He shivered, struggled against the chains. He slumped back to the floor, burdened by the crushing weight of memory. *Shame. Fear... Anger.* The Beast remembered the prison camp, the year he had spent there. Chained and beaten. Abandoned and left to answer for the crimes of his band. Drop by drop, the torment returned to him.

But there was more...

He remembered the child in Urda's skies. He remembered the stone walls and suffocating darkness. He remembered Arak Jai and the stinging legion of his venomous pets. Turn by twisting turn the kaleidoscope shifted. A scarred figure lead him into the dungeon and without a word, chained him to the wall. The man left with no pity, abandoning the boy to Arak Jai's torments. The dungeon's door slammed shut. The man's muffled voice called back with promises that punishment would make him strong.

The Beast snapped from the memory and braced against the chains. The iron links were as thick as a blacksmith's wrists and showed little sign of distress. Still, he had to try. If not for himself than for the crying child left alone in the dark. He squat with a handful of chain, then drove hard against the bracket.

Nothing.

He tore instead into the wall, prying at the mooring.

Nothing.

The Beast tugged at the little slack he had, fighting for a view from a nearby porthole. The horizon rose and fell, each undulation tying a knot in his stomach. The cargo hold swayed, dancing with the Reaper's Song over the waves. The Beast skulked from the porthole: the sure footing of the Great Road was all he knew. Wherever the destination, he hoped it remained unmoving.

He rested his broad back against the wall and found the familiar lump of his pack was missing. His hands flew hopefully to his neck. *The medallion was gone.* His hackles jumped to attention, newly fired blood pumped hard. Nausea melted away, forced out by a thirst for vengeance.

He would find a way out. He would tear the blasted ship apart plank by plank if need be. Experience dictated that escape was always possible. *Patience and discipline...* The sunrise provided ample light, pouring in from portholes dotting the walls. There were no other chains, no other bars to be found. *This was no prison cell*, he thought. He looked at the bindings on the wall and floor. *Freshly bored.* This was no prison at all.

An advantage to him.

That blasted Poogs had probably collected quite the windfall at my expense. The Beast seethed at his foolishness. Of course the chains had caught up with him. He had been played for a fool once more by a would-be ally. He swore a silent oath that he would turn his back on the mortal realm forever.

After I mangle the pirate of course.

The Beast reigned himself in from the vengeful fantasy, coaxing the gears to turn. Escape was never a foregone conclusion. It was only a matter of divination. First, the chains. Then the door. Then...

The manacles dug through fur, biting into flesh. Their touch was more than he could stand. Chained too long and the sensation would spread driving him to madness. Suddenly the hold's lone door opened, flooding the planked stairs with daybreak. The Beast retreated, allowing the chains to slacken. Surprise and maneuverability were his only allies. He regarded the portholes, cursing their spears of light. Darkness would have proven a valuable asset.

Armored boots stomped into the hold, sounding a menacing tone the Wakeful Captain was notorious for. Malachai took the last step, grinding to a halt. He gestured an invitation back up into the morning. Lia crept down the steep stairs, one at a time, lowering each foot in turn. The Beast's head tilted. *Did Malachai's arrogance know no limits?* He drew himself tall, until his horns scraped the ceiling and then took a pair of measured steps into the pool of daybreak.

Malachai clutched Lia's shoulder and stroked the girl's hair. Her wide eyes pleaded to the massive stranger. The Beast's jaw clenched. He stormed forward, stopped by chains snapping taut.

"Release her, and I may decide against crushing you into dust."

The Wakeful's broken laugh fell from the slit of his mouth. He grabbed a handful of Lia's hair. "An interesting proposition. Unfortunately, Her Majesty yet has need for the little abomination.

Malachai wrenched his handful, twisting until Lia yelped. The gnashing sting snatched at the girl's tears, pulling them from the corners of her eyes and down her cheeks. Her amber eyes flashed, meeting the Beast's as she openly wailed. Her cry pierced his heart like a barbed lance. The frustrating shrouds concealing his memory melted away. He was not sure how, but he remembered.

He remembered that cry.

It had once been the most beautiful sound in his world. A challenge had been issued by the Breath. On that day, as the midwife placed the tiny bundle in his arms, he knew there was no limit to how far he would go, no danger he would not face, no fire he would not brave. All to protect her, to spare her any harm. The newborn wrapped her pink fingers around his. It was the smallest of gestures with the most magnificent of meanings.

The Beast peered down at his clawed paws, slowly turning them over. The long obsidian talons and brown fur did not fit the memory. They were cruel deceptions, punishment for a crime he could not recall. He looked again to the sobbing child in Malachai's grasp, struggling to understand the word slowly forming in his mind. He remembered her amber orbs reflecting in his own like-colored eyes.

There was no doubt. The word settled onto his heart where it had always belonged.

Daughter.

Wells of forgotten strength, primal and unyielding, surged. He tore at the chains, shearing the manacles free. Severed steel clanged into a pile. Malachai released his grip, stunned. He pushed the girl into the stairs and swept his arm, summoning a wall of emerald magic. The enchantment rolled into teaming bars shaped like wrought iron. Green fire slammed into the floor like a portcullis just in time to cut off the Beast's furious advance.

The Beast's claws flailed through the bars. Malachai's mouth twisted into a sneer. Satisfied, Malachai turned to reach for another handful of

Lia's hair. A crackling sound grew behind his back. Malachai spun to the Beast. What little remained of his mortal heart froze in his breast.

The Beast seized the bars, light intensifying where flesh met magic. Smoke poured from his paws as the magical flames burned. He grimaced at the searing pain, but refused to let go. The corded muscles in his forearms tensed, bolstered by his massive barrel chest. He squeezed tighter and then pulled at the bars blocking his way. Malachai reached a cautious hand to his sword. The bars were holding fast, but the Wakeful's arrogance had abandoned him.

The Beast's jaw tensed and he pulled harder. The bars' unholy magic burned brighter, gathering more dark power from Malachai's enchantment. The emerald light began to test the limits of his strength. Pain burned through his paws, then gnawed at his wrists. He looked to Lia, to his daughter. *All those years stolen.* He had missed their entire life together but now, someone would pay. Growling, he yanked harder at the bars, twisting their enchantment nearer their breaking point.

Malachai waved his hand, tapping his magical reserves. The emerald bars flashed with new life and pulled against the Beast's crushing grip. The bars resisted, little by little bending back to their original shape. Smoke filled the cargo hold joined by the growing reek of singed fur. The green fire seared through the thick pads of the Beast's palms. Pain surged past his elbows. His knees weakened.

The Beast's lips curled back over grinding teeth. Sweat traced through deep creases around his eyes. His right knee buckled and gave way. He fought to maintain his grasp, but his strength was ebbing.

"Pitiful creature. What good is your brawn against Her Majesty's will? By nightfall the little abomination will be gracing the Nekropolis."

"Never..." The Beast's chin snapped up, will resolved in full. He rent the bars in a frenzy and with a mighty roar the Beast tore the enchanted portcullis down.

Malachai shoved Lia aside and retreated to the stairs. Something caught his ankle and dragged him crashing down. He snapped his head around. A length of chain was wrapped tightly around his boot, snagged by its bladed edges. He followed the chain back into the cargo hold. The crimson energy of his eyes wavered.

The Beast held the chain's end.

Salivating.

Chapter 22

Poogs brought the Reaper's Song to port at the island's eastern end. The private landmass belonged to a venerable family of merchants whose influence maintained a powerful grasp on Meridian's politics. Poogs himself was no stranger to their sphere of influence. They had, from time to time, solicited his services in moving 'parcels of interest' beyond notice of the meddlesome City Watch.

And they always paid well.

Taking Malachai's bounty on the Beast of Briarburn was all he had intended. Truth be told, Poogs hated the Wakeful and their accursed queen. The Liche Queen's quest to rid the world of magical effects had indeed placed his career as smuggler in perilous waters. He was inclined to rebuke Malachai's request for the use of his ship, but granting the Wakeful his berth had saved an innocent life in Castiel and that was worth the cost.

Poogs manned the helm, watching the crew offload a freshly re-shackled Beast of Briarburn. The massive brute required two shots from the blunderbuss to put down and two coils of anchor chain to subdue. He regretted use of the painful weapon, but it appeared his only option. There was no doubt in that moment the Beast would have torn Malachai limb from limb. The price of which would have been a never ending supply of black armored thugs in his wake.

The pirate fidgeted with the coral charm on his necklace, remembering the beach he had found it on long ago. He had been a different man then: lost, frightened and alone. He rolled the star shaped piece between his fingers. As captain, he had always placed his faith in the simple totem. If he wanted to be rid of Malachai he would have to trust in it now. It was trust easily placed, for the North Star had yet to forsake him.

***

The island's interior was a dense blanket of tropical trees with fronds heavy of dew. Like Meridian, the island had been provided the gifts necessary to maintain perpetual summer. The dull buzzing sound of insects droned constant in the humid air. Malachai, flanked by two dozen mercenaries supplied by the island's owner, lead the Beast over the beach's soft sand and into the trees. Lia followed at Malachai's heels, sneaking frequent glances at the hulking prisoner with the familiar eyes.

On the Reaper's Song Lia had shared in the connection. Her heart swore they were bonded despite never having met. Though the Beast's savage strength nearly tore the cargo hold apart, Lia had remained unafraid. She knew the Beast would never hurt her. She just knew.

Lia wished she was back on the Reaper's Song. The corsair had vanished into the mists as soon as the landing party had crossed the beach. She thought of Castiel falling from his chair and dared to smile. She stumbled over a log, falling to her knees with a splat. Malachai glared at her, but said nothing. Lia brushed off a bit of mud and pressed on. Poogs had assured her with a wink that he would look after Castiel. Lia liked the handsome pirate. She saw good in him, lurking just beneath the surface. She hoped to see him again.

Branches jabbed at Malachai's company like greedy, skeletal fingers. The Wakeful tirelessly lead the way, hacking at the netting of leathery vines with his serrated blade. Hours later, a break in the fading path appeared. An enormous crater bored into the surface just beyond the tree line's constant insectoid buzz. Malachai droned a command and the Beast was prodded by a phalanx of spear tips to the crater's side. A trio of mercenaries stalked behind them at the rim, crossbows notched and ready. There would be no second escape.

Malachai grabbed Lia by the scruff and half-lead, half-dragged her up the jagged incline of a stout crag guarding the crater. He kept a strenuous pace and it wasn't long before her legs burned of soreness.

"Where are we going?" Lia dared to ask, quickly tiring at the exertion. Drawing upon the Breath to heal Castiel had left her drained. She hoped the magic came back soon. She had a feeling that the Beast would need her help.

Malachai offered no reply, save for the flash of hellfire in his eyes. He reached down and hoisted Lia up to the crowning steppe that leveled into a sand covered plateau presiding over the island. The view stole Lia's breath. It was like nothing she had ever imagined. A sprawling lake of waving green tree tops was framed all around by an edge of blue-grey sea. Carrion birds circled the crater's mouth; foul scavengers biding time.

An old tale of Cedrik's popped into her mind about just such a crater, one that had been carved when the first falling star crashed down from the heavens. *How terrible*, she thought, *that stars could fall. How wrong that they could be denied their rightful place shining in the night sky.*

The ground suddenly shook, throwing Lia to her backside. Fine fissures spider webbed like shattered glass beneath the trembling ground. She struggled for footing as the ground jostled her from foot to foot. Then, the rumbling stopped as abruptly as it had begun. She looked to Malachai, hoping for an explanation, but he merely nodded to the edge. She hesitated, but curiosity won the moment. She crawled to the plateau's edge, certain she would dislike what she found.

A rising cloud of brownish dust lifted from the crater, glimmering in the morning sun. Lia watched for a moment, then two. She rubbed at her eyes. *The crater was expanding.*

And getting closer.

Lia stepped away, expecting the hole to swallow her up. A frightful heartbeat passed. Not eaten, Lia inched daringly close and peered over. A dusty cyclone rushed around the crater's wide perimeter, magnifying the scene underneath like a stormy looking glass. The surreal image made Lia feel as though she were standing at the bottom of the crater herself. She glanced at Malachai, finally understanding: He had brought her along to bear witness...

She watched as the Beast teetered his way down the crater's rocky face, freeing an avalanche of small stones. The rocks clattered their way to the bottom, finally clacking to a stop against a tall stalagmite. An ear-splitting shriek pierced the morning. Lia clapped her hands tightly over her ears. "What is that?"

Malachai toed the ledge. "Those, little abomination, are my pets."

The taunt stung her like a swarm of bees. The Beast was trundling downward. *Towards the awful sound.* He looked close enough to touch. Lia's hand twitched by her side. She wanted to reach out and touch the illusion, but was intent on denying Malachai the pleasure of seeing her do so.

A wall of readied spears glistened at the crater's lip. The cabal of hired thugs remained silhouetted against the cloudless sky. A spear-man centering the phalanx gruffly called out for the Beast to keep moving. Lia read fear on their faces. *Malachai must have mentioned his pets.*

She held her breath as she watched the Beast stumble to a motionless halt at the crater's bottom. He too, was scanning the pit, searching for the source of the agonizing shrieking. He circled right, trying to keep his back to the rocky wall. The ground ahead was broken by dozens of razor sharp stalagmites. Like a dragon's fangs, the stone teeth pointed skyward hoping for prey. Rays of sun light filtered through the bony forest, encouraging unnerving shadows to dance.

Lia saw the Beast's slow crawl to the crater's far side. She knew he meant to escape the pit and flee to the safety of the jungle. The coils of anchor chain binding his arms rendered him defenseless. *He's going to need my help.* She focused her thoughts, reached deep down and plucked the little ember from her spirit.

***

The Beast stalked his way around the nest of stalagmites, building a much needed buffer against the mercenary spears. A league away, the incline leveled into a gentler grade. *Escapable.* A strange sensation tingled at his elbows. His mane prickled and fluffed for a moment, charged by the magical static. Then a warming aura settled over his chest and arms. A child's voice carried by a humid breeze spoke to him. "You are free."

The Beast flinched at the unexpected whisper, but was quickly relieved to hear the sweet voice. He strained at the chain's embrace, wrestling his arms against his sides. The warming sensation continued to grow, nudging him to greater effort.

"Be free," Lia's tiny voice commanded.

The Beast flexed at the knees. He drew strength from the earth itself, channeling power into his core. And then...

He threw his arms apart, shattering the chains and shucking them away with a heavy grunt. The Beast smiled broadly, hoping Lia sensed his gratitude. He stared up at the mercenaries above, letting his grin fade into a snarl.

"Why not come down and join me?"

A caterwaul sent the mercenaries scurrying back. The Beast dropped instinctively into a crouch. Movement ahead twisted a shadow. He squinted against the glare. Another shadow darted behind a stalagmite. This time the Beast locked in on the motion. He shifted his center even lower. Unlike the feeling of being overwhelmed in Meridian, the Beast was quite familiar with this type of tension.

He was being hunted...

A stalagmite crumbled, confirming his suspicion. A snake-like head bobbed back and forth at the end of whip-like neck emerged from the dusty cloud of rubble. The hideous creature's body followed soon after. The Beast froze stone solid and studied his new threat. The monster looked like a man-sized, wingless dragon. Leathery skin stretched over an emaciated body the color of mottled flesh. The Beast made to move, but a shiver in his spine screamed 'ambush'.

The shrieker reared back and peered over the tallest stalagmites. Gill-like slits behind its jaw flared out, blasted free by a splitting shrill. Four more shriekers appeared from stalagmite burrows. The new arrivals were smaller than the first, with shorter necks and stout tusks protruding along their lower jaws.

The Beast tensed, ready for battle. Lia's voice pleaded for caution.

"They're dangerous. Malachai put them there for you."

Lia's voice stayed the Beast's instinct and he relaxed his shoulders. So far the shriekers had failed to detect him. Maybe escape was preferable to fighting. He sidestepped around the crater, gaze shifting from foe to foe. The shriekers scouted the stalagmites, lowering their leathery heads to sniff at the crumbled stalagmites. He was nearly to crater's gentler slope when a loose stone tumbled into the crater. It crackled down the side and rolled to the Beast's paw. Five shrieker heads whipped around to track the intrusion.

And then the Beast understood. He knew of other predators that relied on senses beyond sight to stay fed. These foul things hadn't found him, because they couldn't *see* him.

The foursome of smaller shriekers reared and deafened the island with a shrill chorus. A dozen stalagmites trembled under the blast and then crumbled away revealing their denizens. The nest of shriekers scrambled closer to the 'queen'. The long-necked shrieker screeched a short burst of calls. The nest retorted with a staccato of piercing whistles. Heads low, they surged past the remains of their burrows.

The Beast launched from his crouch into a mad sprint, then flung himself at the nearest shrieker. The vicious tackle carried a blur of fur and leather careening through a stalagmite. He rolled through the rocky rubble and jumped to his feet, ready for the next attack. Beneath him lay the stunned shrieker, twitching from the impact. Twenty feet away, a dull hum combined with a rapid-fire clicking emanated from the shrieker pack. Arcs of purplish-blue current sparked between their mandibles.

He glanced to the crater's looming face, tall and imposing. Despite being a gentle route than the one he had followed down, there was no way he could make the climb, not while being hunted.

He would have to fight.

The Beast scooped up the shrieker at his feet and hurled it. The living projectile crashed home, momentarily scattering the tight group. The flung shrieker slammed into the rock wall and twitched a final time.

He had to remain on the offensive.

The Beast tore a stalagmite free. Club in hand, he rushed the shriekers, swinging in wild, sweeping arcs. The makeshift weapon crashed into leathery bodies and snake-like skulls. Shriekers fell by the side, broken and stunned. One of the more daring creatures hopped over a battered body, electricity crackling along its mandible. It reared up and darted forward, jaws wide. The Beast's club whooshed downward, cracking its skull with a satisfying thud. The arc of current flickered and then disappeared.

A pair of shriekers suddenly appeared from his left. The first snapped at his leg, just missing a mouthful of flesh and fur. It hopped away after the miss, narrowly avoiding a club to its spine. The swing carried the Beast off balance, dragging him into an awkward stumble. He braced for the inevitable.

A fiery sting punctured his shoulder. For an agonizing eternity, the Beast's muscles spasmed. From the corner of his eye he caught a glimpse of his assailant. The shrieker's mouth was spattered with clumps of bloody fur. It circled left, trying to remain at the Beast's back.

The Beast willed the spasms away and spun. Both shriekers lunged, jaws snapping. He thrust the stalagmite club outward, bashing the creatures away. The queen caterwauled her frustration and clawed into the fray, smashing the remaining stalagmites in her path. She stopped ten feet shy of the Beast's sky high club.

The gill-like slits vibrated on the queen's neck. It sucked in a massive breath and then blasted it through the slits, stretching them to their limits, emitting a shriek pitched to shatter glass. The ground shook. An excruciating pressure built in the Beast's skull. He dropped his club and crushed his ears into his head. The sonic blast reverberated against the crater, shoving him back. White stars flashed over his eyes. The pain worsened, blackening his vision. Finally, it stopped. The entire cluster of stalagmites had crumbled to sand. All that remained were previously dormant inhabitants.

Hundreds of them...

The Beast's heart pounded like a war-hammer pummeling a gong. He scrambled for his club. But it was too late. The horde crashed into him like a ravenous tide. A wall of snapping jaws knocked him over, battering away his breath. His every limb flailed, battering away the shrieker's relentless surge. For a fleeting second, a speck of hope flickered. The Beast's haymaker blows flew like a storm of hurricanes. His fists smashed the onslaught to the nauseating symphony of cracking bones and the bloody reek of iron.

The odds finally caught up to the battling Beast of Briarburn. A shrieker clamped down on his muscled forearm, fangs penetrating deep. The burn of current jolted his arm from his body, painfully spasming. A second shrieker seized the advantage and sunk its teeth through the tough sinew of the Beast's leg.

Fire spread through his nerves. The world was fast melting away into smears of black and grey as he fell to the ground. The Beast writhed in agony. A horde of surrounding shadows worked themselves into a frenzy. The shriekers clawed over each other like crabs in a bail, snapping and rending, angling for a chance at their fallen prey. The burning pain in his limbs gave in to an icy numbness. The toll of the bites had enacted the highest of prices, robbing him not only of his strength, but of his will to fight. His head lolled. He soon was only vaguely aware of pressure and tugging...

Blackness pushed the scant remaining light from his eyes. He thought of Lia and a deep sadness settled over his heart. A massive shadow of darkness descended upon the crater, blocking out the morning sun.

So this is how it finally ends?

A mighty wind gusted from the shadow's tail and the horde was blown back from their tortured prey. Through glossy eyes, the Beast watched a blurry shape fall from the sky. The crunch of fast approaching footsteps hurried towards him. The Beast was rolled to his side as something cinched tightly around his waist. A tug came next and the Beast was lifted high from the pit of rock and sand. Soon he was drifting over the crater, gently swaying in the island breeze.

Below, flashes of steel glinted in the sun. The dazzling display swept through the horde of shriekers, pirouetting and slashing through the foul creatures. The queen answered the dancing blades with a screech that rattled the Beast's failing senses. A staccato of *bangs* cut the cry short. A twirl of dual glints sliced clean through the shrieker's lengthy neck. The queen's head rolled sloppily from her twitching body, coming to a rest against a pile of cleaved shrieker corpses.

Scores of shriekers lay dead, filling the crater's gullet with a thick layer of mottled flesh. The Beast grinned at the sight before slipping away.

Maybe the dancing light would save Lia.

Chapter 23

So this is the World After? How bizarre...

The Beast was stretched out, flat on his back, looking up at a velvety purple sky. A splash of unblinking stars returned his stare. He first tested his legs and then his arms, and finally his neck. Something rustled during the flexion of aching muscles. He tore his gaze away from the lifeless canopy. A spate of ridiculous laughter fit for a fool erupted from deep within his belly. His blanket gently rippled and then thrashed as his amusement shook the bed.

The room was richly appointed; more luxurious than any the Beast had ever seen. Plush carpets like stormy seas stretched corner to corner. A pair of walls was covered floor to ceiling by leather-bound books, stacked neatly on gilded shelves. An oaken desk dominated the corner of bookshelves.

Golden light poured into the room through a wide window of pristine glass. The light called out to the Beast, compelling him to rise. Thick carpet squished between his clawed toes. Jasmine perfumed the air, growing stronger as the Beast crossed the grand room. He ducked to avoid a swaying chandelier laden with candles. The floor seemed to share the gentle roll. The window was within arm's reach when, abruptly, he stopped.

Maybe I don't want to see...

A million thoughts invaded. His woodland home... The medallion... Lia... A well of sorrow filled the pit of his stomach. His thoughts swirled and settled upon his daughter.

Malachai must pay.

The Beast stepped to the window, closing his eyes. He pressed his palms against the cool glass and inhaled deeply before taking his first glimpse. Masses of fluffy white rushed at the window, vanishing on impact. It took a moment, but the Beast soon realized they were clouds. Which meant...?

He was flying!

The Beast pressed his snout to the glass, eyes darting in all directions, fighting to understand. Far, far below, an endless expanse of glistening water stretched into the horizon. He couldn't believe it. The world rushed by below in a blur as he was carried above it like a song on the wind.

The loud click of a door closing spun the Beast around like a top. Poogs. The pirate's face was a blank slate. Unarmed, he stood his ground, arms by his sides. Rage flashed a scarlet veil over the Beast's eyes and he growled. Quivering with fury, he charged the doomed pirate. He seized Poogs by the throat with a crushing paw and smashed him into the decorative door. The Beast squeezed tighter, salivating at the color draining from the traitor's face. The pirate did not struggle, did not beg.

His arrogant lack of resistance stoked the Beast's ire further, pushing it dangerously close to the edge.

How could a man deal in such betrayal and have nothing to say for himself?

The Beast squeezed tighter still. He leaned in closer until his snout was a hair's breadth from Poogs's blood-shot eyes. A thin rivulet of crimson dripped from the pirate's nose. The Beast smelt the sweat beading on Poogs's forehead.

"Do not fear, Malachai will join you soon enough," the Beast said through a clenched jaw full of bared fangs.

Poogs fished into a pocket as he dangled, inching closer to his fate. The Beast's words were the frigid breath of icy winter. "A little late for one of your toys, pirate."

The pirate struggled to raise his arm with the last of his breath. Something glimmered beyond the corner of the Beast's eye. He felt a warming pulse on his face and dropped Poogs to the floor. The pirate gasped and gagged for breath, but kept his hand high and steady.

The firestone glinted from deep within its golden setting.

"Take it, it is yours after all."

The Beast snatched the medallion, holding it to his eyes, stunned. It was like a piece of his soul had been returned. He looped the golden chain over his horns. Relief coursed through his veins when the treasure came to rest over his thumping heart. He hoisted Poogs to his feet by a fistful of cloth. "Explain yourself. If I think for a second you're lying you won't witness another dawn."

Poogs rubbed at his throat then primped his shirt, trying to reclaim his usual semblance of charismatic bluster. A quick shift of the Beast's weight shattered any illusions and the pirate plead his case. He regarded the door with the hint of a grin. "Malachai made the mistake of leaving his quarters unsecured." The Beast's skin crawled at the thought having shared a room with the black rider. He arched a wary eye brow, encouraging Poogs to continue.

"I don't deny that I took the bounty on you. But it called for your detention only, to prevent you from following, I swear." The words flowed from the condemned like a river un-damned. "The Wakeful scum altered the deal upon your capture."

The Beast said nothing. A touch of sorrow in Poogs's eyes validated his words. There appeared no deceit, but he had wrong about the pirate before. He beckoned for more with an impatient gesture.

"Malachai demanded that I turn you over to him and bring the lot of you to the island." The pirate stared down at his boots. "I saw the way you looked at the child in the cargo hold. She is your daughter, isn't she?"

The Beast tensed slightly, but recovered. "I don't remember having a child or her mother. Somehow I just know. How did you--"

"My friend, I have sailed the world's seas from dusk till dawn. I have seen wonders to tantalize the passions and horrors to haunt the soul,"

Poogs said. His words softened to little more than whisper. "The emerald flames have razed more cities to the ground than I care to count and somehow you seized them in your very palms and tore them apart."

Poogs, looked at his own hands, burying an old pain. "Only a father's love... I could not abandon father and daughter to such a cruel fate."

The Beast's demand for vengeance grew silent. It was Poogs that had cut the creatures down in the crater, at risk to his own life. And the price of defying Malachai was no laughing matter. His tongue stumbled for a moment but eventually found footing.

"You have my thanks for pulling me from that pit."

"We can never be even, Beast of Briarburn, but one day I hope you can forgive me." Poogs opened the door. "Come, there is much to be done."

The Beast followed Poogs down a narrow hallway filled with brass accents. A thick door with a heavy ring marked the exit. A thin slice of golden light filled the space and then grew to a flood as Poogs pulled the door in. The Beast shielded his eyes from the sudden sting. The pirate's tall silhouette chuckled in the sun. "Come on then, it's only a bit of light."

Wind whistled through the doorway as the Beast breached the light. He climbed onto the Reaper's Song's main deck, disbelieving every step as he followed Poogs to the helm. Poogs noted the Beast's slackened jaw and reverently took the wheel. "Every time I take her helm my heart flutters like a school-boy with a secret crush."

The Beast felt a faint tinge of jealousy. He would gladly have given anything to feel as at home as the pirate did. It had taken him only a glance to see it: Poogs was truly lost in his moment. He was free.

The speeding seascape transitioned beneath the soaring Reaper's Song into streaks of flowing greens and browns. The Beast felt a gentle roll in the balls of his feet, adding to his trepidation.

"That feeling shall pass soon enough."

"It had better," the Beast replied. The Beast tentatively grasped the handrail. "How is this possible? You built a flying ship?"

Laughter rolled as Poogs cut the wheel. The Reaper's Song banked sharply and drifted to a silent halt. Only the Beast's keen reflexes saved him. He shifted his weight into a low crouch and avoided being thrown to the deck. He flashed Poogs a knowing grin of his own.

"Did you hear nothing I said in the tavern?" Poogs's voice carried a note of disappointment. "I won my lady from the Death's own agent in a game of chance. She was none too pleased, I assure you. But fair was fair and the ship was her wager." He laughed at the memory and the Beast thought it bizarre that one could be so cavalier at having bested the Grim Reaper. The pirate was either fearless or the most reckless man alive. Probably both.

"You stole Death's ship?"

"Won Death's ship. *Won!*" Poogs replied, "She truly is a remarkable vessel; fast as falling darkness, nigh unsinkable, terror inspiring." He joyfully counted off the ship's finer points on his fingers. "And upon her deadly wings, we shall see your daughter to safety. And end Malachai's treachery."

The Beast clenched a fist until his arm trembled. "Malachai will pay with his life a thousand times over if he has but drawn a single tear. I will see to it with my last breath."

A feminine voice spoke from amidships. "You shall need more than pomposity to survive the Nekropolis." An iridescent blue sphere floated down from the center mast, landing on the deck between the startled onlookers. A grand light flashed and a woman clad in a flowing dress of the same iridescent blue appeared in the orb's lingering glow. She bowed formally, but before she could introduce herself Poogs fell to a knee. The pirate covered his heart with a trembling hand and stammered.

"May the North Star always brighten the darkest night," he said quickly as though he may forget the greeting. "Lady Polaris, welcome to my humble vessel."

Polaris brushed her platinum blond hair over her shoulder. She smiled at the Beast and rested a hand on the pirate's bowed head.

"Thank you, captain. May the light always see you home."

Polaris invited the awestruck pirate to rise and then regarded the Beast. She stretched to the tips of her toes and stroked a slender hand from an ear to the tip of his snout. She levitated until their eyes met and gave him a quick peck on the forehead. A trail of sparkling light fell away from her lips. She wrapped her delicate arms around the Beast's waist and buried a warm cheek into his chest. A tear fell from a crystal blue eye. Voice wavering, the North Star spoke. "It's been too long, Donovan."

The Beast's arms hung over Polaris like a pair of oaken branches. He looked uncomfortably to Poogs. "I, err--," the Beast stammered. He knew he looked like an awkward fool holding his arms up, but he couldn't help it. He hadn't the faintest idea who was clutching at his waist. He twisted his mind, trying to force free the memory he wanted more than anything to believe was buried in inside. It had to be there. The woman's obvious gentle affection indicated as much.

Polaris pulled away from the mountain of muscle and fur and stroked the Beast's face a second time. All the while her eyes were misted.

"My sweet, sweet, boy," Polaris sighed, "you do not remember." She closed her eyes and whispered into the wind that was sweeping through the flapping sails. She swung her arms high, stretching a wavy dome of starlight between her fingertips. The waves climbed high over the Reaper's Song, painting the sky in dark shades of violet. The enchantment blotted away the sun, leaving behind a tapestry of shimmering ripples.

"I will help you remember."

The Beast grasped for a handhold, uneasy at being unable to see the deck. Moving too far in any given direction would send him plummeting to the World After. He heard only the thump of his heart beating. The whistling wind, the flapping sound of the sails... gone. His unseen footing lurched. He threw up a paw as he began to fall.

And found the rough texture of cool, hewed stone that should not have been there. In between eye-blinks the world had filled itself back in. It was a world he hadn't expected.

The Beast stood alone in a wide corridor that stretched fifty yards in both directions. A pair of tall wooden doors stood guard at each end. Poogs and the woman in sapphire were nowhere to be found. Along the walls, incensed torches lit the dark with traces of myrrh.

"Follow my voice, Donovan," Polaris called. "Remember..."

The Beast roared into the darkness. "That is not my name!" His head sunk.

"I have no name."

Polaris's voice charmed him forward. "Walk the path. Be so named once more."

The weight of too many lonely winters haunted his footsteps. Had his entire life since reawakening truly been no more than a cruel trick of fate? No. There had been no deception. Someone had stolen his name. Someone had stolen a father from an innocent child who needed him. Someone had stolen his life. He would see them returned.

Now.

The Beast dropped one paw in front of the other and trundled for doors emblazoned with a six-point star of solid gold. The Beast immediately recognized the icon: he had seen it dangling from Poogs's neck. But how could that be?

Between the flickering torches, framed portraits of a hundred sizes came to life as he passed by. *They seem so real.* He could not help himself. He reached a curious claw to a canvas. A swirl of memory coursed from the painting, up his arm and straight into his deepest of hearts.

A young man with messy, chocolate hair proudly stood in a castle's courtyard. He was clad head to toe in armor of polished chain. A magnificent sun effortlessly lit a perfect spring afternoon. Hushed murmurs circulated through an excited crowd. Atop a sprawling dais of white oak, a distinguished looking older man in formal military garb held a glistening sabre. He spoke in words the Beast could not, at first, decipher.

The Beast walked through the crowd and approached the dais. He passed through the spectral image of commoners and nobility, reaching the stairs at the same moment as the young knight. The young man climbed three short stairs and knelt in front of his commander. The sabre flashed in the sun and then touched the knight's shoulder.

"Donovan, you have served your queen as a beacon of honor and defended justice throughout the distant reaches of the Once Kingdom. Rise, and join your brothers… Captain."

The Beast shook his head. The commander's words had become crystal clear. He looked behind the grizzled veteran and saw a formation of knights extending from the flanks of a modest throne. The Beast blinked hard in disbelief when he saw the throne's occupant. Polaris rose from the throne and invited Donovan to join her Guard. The Beast finally realized the truth. He rose and solemnly walked to the Queen he had forgotten, the Queen stolen from him, and took his place by her side.

The Beast snapped out of the memory to a warming glow radiating from within. It felt like an eternity since Urda's crystalline orbs had begun chipping away the prison of his memory. This was more potent. He could feel the elixir of memory seeping back into his blood.

It would never be stolen from him again.

The glow of the star-adorned door brightened. The Beast took anxious steps towards it, thoughts racing at the truth aligning in his mind's eye. The portraits spoke in whispers, begging him to stop and listen. The door's magnetic pull was too strong, allowing for only furtive glances as he neared the hall's end. Each portrait told a story like a miniaturized theatre, chronicling his stolen life: a triumphant return from bloody battle, a muddy prank played on an old headmaster, the first time he took up a blade.

The star now blazed in the dark hallway, illuminating all of the portraits at once. A storm of memories flooded the Beast all at once; the dam was finally broken and swept away.

A daring jump on horseback over a burning, broken bridge...

Celebration with his Knight brothers at autumn festival...

A beautiful girl with shining obsidian hair. A secret kiss under a droopy willow...

Out of habit, the Beast raised a meaty fist to knock on the door. Before he could strike, his eye caught one last portrait. He let his hand fall gently to his side, leaving the star temporarily undisturbed.

The picture was framed in twisted vines of silvery ivy. The dark haired lass was of age now and featured prominently in the center. She was dressed in frilly white linens and sitting up in a luxurious poster bed, covered in thick emerald drapes. Though her hair was matted, tussled, her tears rang joyous. She was cradling something close to her breast.

Someone.

He did not need to touch the gleaming portrait of silver. The memory exploded all on its own.

The Beast remembered that day, its traces now a solid stream of emotion. Warm globs swelled at his eyes. He had just walked into the sprawling bed chamber the first time he had heard the sound. In the corner, a fireplace crackled behind frantically scurrying hand maidens. One woman alone maintained her composure at the bedside. She was much older than the others and had presided over many such occasions.

"Patience, Pandora, patience," Urda said as she stroked the princess's forehead. "Only moments and she will be back." The gypsy delivered the hidden bundle to a hand maiden.

Urda's eyes twinkled. "Have you decided on a name?"

"Lia," Pandora replied, "Lia, after Donovan's mother." The princess stretched her hands to the midwives swaddling the infant. Her perfect smile warmed the room more sweetly than any fire could ever hope.

The Beast bowed his head. Twin tears fell heavily to the floor. When he looked back up, the portraits were still and the great corridor restored to darkness. The only light came crawling from underneath the door, inviting him in. He grasped one of the golden rings... and pushed.

Chapter 24

A second blast of searing energy slammed into Malachai's pale abdomen. The former Wakeful captain collapsed to his hands and knees, eagerly greeted by the cold floor of the Garrison. His lungs were fiery sacks ready to burst. A river of ice cold terror dripped down his back. He spat up a glob of hot blood as pain's forgotten sensation was restored. He stared at the clot, wondering how much of his blood the Liche Queen would exact as the price of failure. He shivered; another forgotten feature of humanity creeping back into his body.

Dragon steps thundered in his chest, crushing his black heart. He could not recall the last time he felt the terrible growth spreading within, but its name was plastered vividly in his racing stream of thoughts. *Terror.*

Tapping his fleeting strength, Malachai shoved himself away from the floor and onto a knee.

Crack.

A blast struck him squarely in the face, knocking him flat onto his back. Malachai's vision blurred and doubled. The vaulted dome spanning the Barracks began a slow spin. Pandora paced back and forth. Icy venom bathed each word in fury. "If I wished for you to stand, slave, I would have commanded you so."

She nodded and a pair of Wakeful soldiers hauled their former captain upright. He had never before experienced the Liche Queen's wrath so intimately. Three savage blows were all it had taken to sap his strength. Malachai knew the very minutes of his life were counting down. That blasted pirate had double crossed him, ruined his grand designed. Despite the betrayal, he had successfully delivered the little abomination as commanded. But the Beast of Briarburn had escaped.

And that transgression Her Majesty would never allow to go unpunished.

Malachai, Captain of the Wakeful, Her Majesty's Highest Champion, the Black Rider himself was now stripped of title and armor, though his punishment did not end there. At the height of her rage, the Liche Queen had stripped away Malachai's Wakeful curse, allowing the agonizing futility of mortality to reclaim his body. The crimson flames of his eyes were extinguished, replaced by a rotten bloodshot yellow.

Now, his final punishment loomed. The Wakeful guards hooked Malachai under the arms and dragged him to the dark altar, his toes scraping the floor. Pandora playfully stroked the runic archway spanning the altar. One by one they came to glowing, lava colored life. *Hungry.*

The guards bowed their heads in unison to their queen and then roughly shoved Malachai back to his knees. He fell into the altar's stone basin with a grunt.

"Rise, Malachai, and accept your fate." The Liche Queen grasped the spiraled hilt of a ceremonial dagger edged with a sliver of obsidian. Pandora dragged the blade across the stone, charging the cruel weapon with the Garrison's foul tension. The sickly dagger whispered Malachai's name into the cavernous chamber. Malachai grasped at the altar and pulled himself up. His voice cracked and trembled, gone any sense of bravado. "Your Majesty, please! I have only ever wished to serve you!"

"Turn and face your judgment."

Malachai pressed his back into the hard stone. His fingers clenched the jeering altar and he counted down his breaths, certain each was his last.

"Highness--"

Malachai's words were severed by the flash of the slicing blade. He choked down a last gulp of air as the cool edge pressed into his throat's alabaster lump. He gasped as blood trickled from under the blade. He closed his eyes, content to depart his wretched existence in darkness. An eon later, the dagger's kiss was severed and Malachai dared to steal a breath. Pandora placed the weapon gently down on the altar and reached overhead to the arbour. A sneer crept over her mouth, curling back her lips, freeing two rows of gleaming porcelain teeth. A menacing silence deafened the Garrison. "Perhaps you can yet be of use to me."

Pandora touched the highest rune, siphoning out the powerful magic she had inscribed long ago. A surge of florid orange coiled down her cold fingertips like a serpent stalking prey. Drained, the rune went lifeless. Malachai stared long and hard at the magic crawling around the Liche

Queen's arm. He had no heart left to speak of, but had he, it would have sunk deep into the bedrock. The high-point rune was the thirteenth and final mark carved into the arbour. And Her Majesty's favorite.

Malachai sank to his knees. Life as he had known it as both man and Wakeful was over. He was to become something more. Something evil and twisted, born of the haunted depths of the Liche Queen's own hateful dreams. Something never before seen in the waking world.

Something wicked...

"Resist and you will die," Pandora cautioned. With no further warning she pressed her glowing palm into Malachai's pale forehead. The blaze of the rune's Wicked curse consumed Malachai like a wild-fire, spreading over his body in seconds. His muscles spasmed, contorting his limbs into a snapping tangle of flesh and bone. He tried to scream but the curse burned away the air from his ruined lungs.

Pandora's warning was Malachai's sole thought as he burned. He spasmed again, severing the tip of his tongue and grinding teeth into bloody dust. Pungent sulfur mists wafted from Malachai's writhing body. The Blight worked quickly, efficiently. The death force ate at Malachai's corpse a layer at a time, rotting away skin and tissue. Soon, all that remained was a pile of trembling bones.

"Arise, my dark champion," Pandora whispered, "Your Queen has need of you."

The pile of bones began to shake and then exploded violently into a tempest of jagged, skeletal debris. Pandora snapped her fingers and the cloud collapsed, interlocking its broken pieces like a child's puzzle. Malachai's jaw stretched into an exaggerated equine shape. Two rows of empty eye sockets climbed the muzzle's surface into its brow line. A mane of greasy black sprouted forth, covering the new face. Deep crimson light flickered in the vacant spaces until their blaze split the Garrison's gloom. Veins and muscle covered the horrid new skeleton as the spine contorted and stretched. The morphing vertebra creaked like a crypt door as it split into two snapping tails covered in thorn-like barbs.

The creature shook the slate grey fur covering the new born muscles of its rippled chest. It rocked on its haunches and licked the leathery scales of its hind quarters with a forked tongue. Malachai's new jaws stretched into a yawn, revealing a maw filled with razor sharp teeth. The wicked thing trundled to the Liche Queen, its steps punctuated by clicking talons. Twin tails curled around her leg like a loving pet's.

Pandora scratched the behemoth under its jaw, when it suddenly reared back and howled, rattling the Garrison, shaking dust and splinters free from the dome. The cadre of Wakeful drew their blades but was halted by a girlish laugh and the stay of her hand.

The Liche Queen admired her handiwork with an evil grin. "Now that's more like it."

***

The door closed behind him with a satisfying thump. The throne room was exactly as the Beast remembered: regal but never an ivory tower. The familiar sound of trickling water invited him to approach the dais. The fearsome stallions of warm marble maintained their staunch posture, but happily received the overdue visitor.

The Beast humbly trod the maroon stretch of carpet to the throne. The walls of the great chamber were still covered by thousands of tiny white candles. Their flames danced in cool breezes siphoned in by slit-like windows stretching from floor to ceiling. As a child he had felt like the windows were the tallest things in all the land. He regarded them once more as he reached the dais, happy to see they retained their grandeur.

Polaris sat on the simple throne, beaming at the Beast's timely arrival. He bowed respectfully and then bent to kneel. She gestured for the Beast to stand. "Welcome home, Captain. I've never understood the need for such formality."

The Beast kept his amber orbs affixed to the floor and shook his head. His knee remained firmly planted on carpet covered stone. "I kneel not of law or tradition." He approached the throne and embraced the petite figure with the out-stretched arms.

"I kneel of gratitude and love…" the Beast said softly, "Lady Adella."

Polaris squeezed tighter around the Beast's broad neck. "You remember," she whispered.

"I am ashamed to have ever forgotten, my Queen."

"My son, you forgot nothing. The memory was stolen from you."

The Beast's heart warmed. Despite the genuine love of their bond, Polaris had never before used the word 'son'. As if reading his mind, Polaris tilted his chin up firmly meeting his sheepish gaze.

"You *are* my son."

The Beast was grateful beyond measure to finally feel a semblance of belonging in the world. The revelations of the Corridor of Chronicles had restored the pieces of his forgotten memory; Polaris's motherly love restored his forgotten heart. The Beast cocked his head. "Why did you never tell me? Surely, you could have confided in me you true name."

"The Aether used to walk with mortals with no pretense of disguise. Sadly, mankind has allowed its love for magic to fade and have turned their backs on the Once Ways. Having abandoned our guidance a cloak of anonymity became necessary," The North Star sighed heavily. "How I wish it were not so."

The throne room vanished upon Polaris's last word. The helm of the Reaper's Song and a stunned Poogs filled itself in around them. A blustering wind tugged at Polaris's sapphire dress, rippling it like one of the ship's sails. The Beast moved to shield her; fearful the gusts may sweep her away, leaving him alone once more. The pirate did his best to collect himself. He fidgeted with his cuffs, hiked up his trousers. "You truly keep the highest of company, Beast of Briarburn. The light of the

North Star has watched over my ship on many perilous nights."

He pumped an excited fist. "And now that she has joined our noble cause defeat will surely flee at the sight of our approach."

"As I've said, we shall need more than bravado and brute strength. Pandora's power has grown vast and terrible since I departed this world." Polaris's face grew dour. "She has an army of sleepless soldiers, her own dark champion, and a madness that will consume the world should we fail."

The Beast studied Polaris's face, finding he did not like the sorrowful mask of her expression. It was beneath her somehow, as though she did not deserve to be troubled so. "I will see to Malachai and his traitorous Queen," the Beast said growling. He remembered the last time he saw the Liche Queen: the day Lady Adella's castle fell by her daughter's own hand. The Liche Queen had been named Pandora then he remembered, back before the crystal blue of her eyes was claimed by the darkness.

How could she leave? How could she have chosen to abandon her kingdom, her people? The Beast was suddenly aware of Polaris's presence. Embarrassed, he let the fanged scowl fall from his face. "How do I get inside? How will I know where they are holding my Lia?"

"Leave the first part to me, my friend," Poogs said. He swept his arms open in a wide arc. "The Reaper's Song is, of course, at your service."

Polaris tapped the Beast's medallion, charging it with a touch of her star-born essence. The firestone began to cast an iridescent shine.

"The medallion is all that remains of many dear friends. Long ago, they sacrificed themselves in a desperate attempt to concentrate their magical essence to battle Ahriman's conquest. Entire kingdoms of the bravest souls were lost standing in defiance of his tyranny. In the end, the highest court of Aether sacrificed their soul-shines to banish the brightest magic, '*Wynisahil*', from the world before it could be used to destroy all of creation," Polaris said looking suddenly sullen, "And I was its bearer."

The Beast pinched the ball of light between his fingers. *That something so small could be so powerful.* He thought immediately of Lia, how she had demonstrated on multiple occasions that very same thing. He inspected the medallion closely, for this, the millionth time. All of the years, all of the countless miles walked in solitude through the cruelest of elements. All of the sleepless, endless nights crushed by the burden of nothingness. If only he could have heard the soft call of the fiery gem's cradled souls.

"The medallion will be drawn to the aura of other Aether souls," Polaris continued, "Pandora's has long since fallen away to darkness."

"Leaving only the light of my daughter's."

"Precisely," Polaris replied.

"Pandora..." the Beast started with a sigh, "What cruel trick of Fate could have twisted her heart to such blackness? She is your daughter! She is the mother of my child! Is there nothing left of the Princess I loved?"

"Pandora's fate was sealed long ago. Even as a child she could be cruel. You remember, do you not? I had hoped your influence would prove enough to turn her away from the dark, but some paths are chosen by their bearers despite our hopes. Polaris rested a re-assuring palm on his chest. "My grand-daughter will not share in Pandora's fate."

Polaris covered her heart with a translucent hand. "Lia's birth was my last hope for my daughter's soul. It wasn't long before I knew the hope had been misplaced. Pandora knew, as I did, that Lia was special, that the essence of star-light, the source of all magic, flowed through her. The baby was a living conduit for all of the magic that would sustain the world for her generation. It was Pandora's own misguided dabbling in the Blight that attracted Ahriman, 'The Banished'. It was through his guidance that she learned of the Fountain of Starlight and how it could be used to banish magic from the mortal realm. Shortly after Lia's birth I shrouded the fountain from detection, hoping to keep it hidden away from prying eyes. If they bring Lia to the fountain..."

The Beast struggled with a painful memory. "I remember now. I remember the night you told me we had to send Lia away. I was supposed to find Cedrik at the throne room's hidden passage." A forgotten pain burned through his flank. He reached around, rubbing at it absentmindedly. He remembered the piercing sting of the blade.

"I meant to heal your wound and send you to escort your daughter, to raise her in safety somewhere bright and green. Somewhere far from the Liche Queen's wrath. My healing spell combined with Pandora's curse and transformed you into your form as you breached the portal." Polaris stroked the Beast's face, her voice pitched into a plea. "It is my fault you have been shaped into this being. If the power were mine, I would take it all back."

"Lady Adella--" the Beast began.

A lump grew in the North Star's throat, tears glazed her crystal blue eyes. "I searched for you and for Lia. From the Celestial Palace of my people, I searched night and day. But Cedrik, ever the dutiful, disappeared without a trace. And Pandora's curse proved more powerful than any I could have imagined her capable of. There was no trace of my Captain Donovan to be found."

Poogs knelt and wiped at her tears. "Lady Polaris, it breaks my heart to see the North Star endure such sadness. Ask what you would of me and I will follow the mighty Beast of Briarburn to the very end."

The Beast placed a paw on Poogs's shoulder. He fumbled for a moment, having not used the word in so very long. But he knew that the pirate was speaking the truth. "My friend, I would be honored to have you along to face whatever fate has in store... together." He regarded Polaris, fierce determination on proud display. "There must be a way to bring them back," he stated flatly. "There must be something I can do."

"That's my Donovan. Always the knight in shining armor, never accepting defeat." A soft sigh slipped from Polaris's lips. "Alas, my daughter has chosen her fate. She worships at Ahriman's altar freely. She will not be so easily persuaded to abandon the darkness. Lia is another matter entirely. Pandora may be lost, but that does not mean for a moment that Lia will share in her fate."

The Beast clasped his heavy paws around the North Star's delicate shoulders. "If there is a way, *any* way, to bring the princess back to the light, I will find it."

Chapter 25

Many hours had passed since the Liche Queen had locked her away in the crowning spire of the Nekropolis. Lia huddled on the floor, knees to chest. A fell wind sliced through the slits between the petrified branches, filling the cell with icy dread, howling like a pack of hungry wolves. Worse still, the clicking horror of Malachai's talons echoed just beyond the door.

Lia shivered, covered her ears with trembling hands. Malachai's ominous presence did far more to chill her blood than any wind. She rocked gently, wanting nothing more than to be wrapped up in her tattered blanket with the stitched on stars, listening to Cedrik's lullaby. She replayed her island adventure's dazzling climax in her mind. She had watched, in almost as much awe as former Captain Malachai, as the Reaper's Song burst through the cloud cover and descended upon the nightmarish crater. In her wildest dreams she could never have imagined a flying ship, nor its dauntless captain leaping into the monstrous swarm.

Lia paced the cell's jagged perimeter, spurred by the memory's valiant shine, tracing the walls with her fingertips. The tight space offered precious little to inspire imagination. A raised slab of uninviting petrified wood jutted from a corner and beside it, a lonely brazier housed a lifeless green flame. She tip toed to the knotted tangle of a door, doing her best to block out the echoing click of Malachai's pacing. She reached for the handle, but reconsidered it. Instead she pressed her ear to the branches.

Click, Ka-click, click, Ka-click...

Lia scrambled backwards into the narrow alcove behind the bed-slab, certain that Malachai's talons would come gnashing through the door. A long breath passed. She poked her head over the slab, daring a peek.

No Malachai.

There must be another way, she thought as she peered between the tangled walls. The ugly kingdom's sky was thick with the glow of an unseen moon, stars glumly absent. The clicking of talons grew louder and she wondered if they'd ever leave her alone. Slivers of a monstrous shadow stabbed though the door, strengthening the menace of Malachai's threat. The child climbed onto the slab and pulled her knees back into her chest. She sobbed quietly, too frightened to cry out. She was no dauntless rogue. She was no queen of stars.

She had not the blood of a beast.

She buried her face into her kneecaps. "*Pafaa'* I'm scared. I don't want to be alone anymore."

A distant light brightened and filtered into the cell. "You are never alone star-shine." Lia jumped down from the slab and rushed to a gap between branches. She craned her head, searching the skies. And there she was. The North Star blazed proudly, unfazed by the evil lurking beneath her radiance.

"Please..." Lia poked through the narrow gap. Her stubby fingers tingled in the starlight. A peaceful wave rolled over her as it had the first time Polaris found her in the Gloom.

"We are coming, Lia. You need be brave for only a short while more." The light faded and Lia sat back on the slab. *She said 'we'*, Lia thought. That had to mean the giant and Captain Poogs were on their way. It just had to. It dawned on her that despite their connection, she did not know the creature's name. He certainly was every bit a beast: the horns, the claws, the fury. And yet there was more. She had felt it on the Reaper's Song. She knew he was coming for her and that he would not stop until she was safe.

She would be brave as the North Star requested. But that did not mean she need stay in her dreary cell. Lia remembered Polaris's grand appearance, how she had poured the star into her hand. The words slipped free of her subconscious and filled her waking mind. Lia whispered the secret to the howling wind and the magic instantly came to call. A surge prickled her skin and her body fizzled into a miasma of magic that began to rise. It was a peculiar feeling: a spreading tickle and itch combined. Lia willed her cloud-like stream through a gap and into the night. The wind no longer frightened her, now it was more like the gentle whimper of a pet. She asked for its help.

The wind whistled and sent Lia's essence sailing over the Nekropolis's skyline to the highest tower. Her body materialized in a spiraling flourish. She plopped down and dangled her legs as though she were sitting dockside. "I will just wait here," Lia said confidently, hoping that Polaris was still listening. A frozen voice answered, chilling her courage. She spun, nearly tumbling from her perch.

"You are brave, little abomination. Brave, but foolish." The Liche Queen hovered at a mere arm's length, onyx hair dancing on a tempest at her shoulders. Lia's skin shed a thin film of terrified sweat. "Go away!" Lia shouted into the tempest.

The Liche Queen stepped down from the sky, stalking across the angular roof. She surveyed her decaying kingdom, beaming with pride at the macabre landscape. "Where would I go, little one?" the Liche Queen countered. She opened her arms wide. "This is my home."

"I hate it! It's ugly and cold." Lia's voice trembled, but a whisper deep down told her to be strong. "I'll never stay here with you!"

The Liche Queen threw her head back and laughed a terrible laugh. The dreadful sound fell from the tower and rushed over the compound in a deathly echo. Lia was certain it was the most hideous sound in the world. Pandora bunched her flowing cloak, twisted her legs and seated herself. The child was obviously a defiant little thing. She would have to try another tactic.

"I was once like you. Alone. Locked away," the Liche Queen lied quietly, "Taken places I did not wish to go, told to conceal my...gifts."

The wind died to a gentle breeze and the pale moon seemed less sickly in the cloudless sky. Lia was shocked. That someone once gave commands to the sorceress beside her seemed unbelievable.

"The other children didn't like me. They never let me play their games or share their songs. My *'pafaa'* always told me to be careful who saw my magic. He said monsters would come. Lia's eyes widened.

"He told me you would come."

The Liche Queen covered her heart with her hand. A very warm, very human laugh filled the night. "Of course I would take you. You did not belong with the peasants. You have a special destiny, one I am to play a special role in preparing you for. It was wrong of your grandfather to hide you away."

"But, but, you sent Malachai. You burned my home. I don't understand," Lia said. Tiny tears welled up at the fiery memory.

"No. You do not," the Liche Queen said. Her face softened to a rare smile. "But I shall show you."

The Liche Queen waved her hand and a cloud of darkness wrapped around them. Lia smelt something foul, like a swamp on a humid summer's day. The cloud vanished with a 'pop'. A swath of black satin floated on a draft at the end of long corridor. Amber torchlight faded behind them with every footstep. Lia shivered against a slicing draft: the corridor was even colder than the cell. Silence reigned.

The Liche Queen swept the veil it from the lintel. With a servant's bow, she gestured. "Welcome," Pandora said proudly, "welcome to my secret place." The cavernous dark far exceeded any that Lia had ever imagined. She wondered, as the Liche Queen stepped followed at her heels, if it stretched on forever. Orbs of floating Wakeful flame bobbed lazily as they drifted through the Garrison. The Liche Queen led Lia to the altar, waving the orbs into the cavern. Several yards beyond the demonic artifact, emerald light glinted on the slumbering Wakeful.

Lia peered from behind the rune inscribed arbour, nodding her head as she struggled to count the vast Wakeful ranks. There had been only five Wakeful plus Malachai at Sensheeri...

That was all it had taken. *Six.* Six soldiers in ugly barbed armor had managed to destroy an entire village in mere minutes. Here, in the bowels of the Nekropolis, there were more than she could count.

"Do not be afraid. They cannot harm you. I would never allow it," the Liche Queen said. She stepped behind the hiding child, placing her hands protectively on Lia's shoulders. The Liche Queen gestured to the closest battalion. "These are my children."

The front line suddenly came to life. Blazing green flame erupted from their armored face plates. To the man, blades were drawn in unison. They saluted their adoring queen and then drove their blades skyward. The formation stood still as statues. Unquestioning. Loyal. The Liche Queen guided Lia forward. "Please," she offered, "say hello."

Lia crept to the edge, dragging her feet. She thought of the Beast, how he had stood against the shriekers. She too, would show no fear. She straightened her back, set her shoulders.

"Hello..."

On cue, the formations of Wakeful came to life and the Garrison was filled with the scraping sounds of a storm of blades sliding free. The Wakeful offered their salute and the clank of armor striking armor rattled the cavern. The Liche Queen sunk to her knees, stroking the child's back. "They could be yours, little one. All of them. No one would ever dare look down upon you again. You need only seize the power for yourself."

A nagging voice in Lia's head begged her to heed the Liche Queen's advice. It longed to claim the soulless soldiers below, turning frantically desperate as it pleaded its case. It made her think about Sensheeri. And Phillip. If only she had commanded the Wakeful before Malachai came with his own pitiful band. Those pathetic brats would have been sorry! She could have stomped on their drawings. She could have kicked them while they cried out. She could have ruined their games and silenced their songs forever.

The voice hardened. It promised more. Much more. *Why stop at the children*, it asked. All of the adults who turned a blind eye to her torment, who whispered behind her back, they would have been sorry too. Sorry for making her feel like less than nothing when all she wanted was to belong. Lia regarded the Liche Queen. She suddenly felt thirsty, like she swallowed a mouthful of cotton.

"The Wakeful are just toys, my dear. Pawns that we use to achieve our ends," the Liche Queen crooned. She took Lia by the hand and led her back to the altar. The arbour hummed, savoring the delicious scent of the newcomer's burgeoning power. "There is a whole world of magic for you to explore," the Liche Queen said. She pointed at each rune inscribed on the arbour, calling each to life and light. "Your elders have tried to hide you away from the Blight your entire life. They lack understanding, vision. They fear the Blight as they fear their own mortality. They fail to understand its power, instead clinging to the Breath like a crutch. They say its power is unnatural. I say what could be more natural than wanting to keep hold of your loved ones forever."

The Liche Queen gestured for Lia to look beyond. Sheets of tears fell from Lia's eyes like stage curtains when she found him. Cedrik stood no more than ten feet away, his handsome features free of pain. Several orbs hovered above, bathing him in haunting green light. Lia was certain she could hear one of his favorite songs stirring from somewhere within the Garrison. It seemed like an entire lifetime had passed since she had cradled Cedrik's crumpled body back in the village. "*Pafaa!*"

Lia ran and locked her arms around the old man's waist, squeezing with all the strength she could muster from her small frame. She sobbed openly, not caring if the Liche Queen or anyone else saw. Her '*pafaa*' had returned. That was all that mattered. "I thought you were gone," Lia cried, barely controlling the flood. She squeezed again, anticipating Cedrik's arms to banish the terrible memories forever.

But Cedrik remained still.

For the first time, Lia noticed his expression had not changed. In fact, he had not moved a muscle. Something was wrong. "*Pafaa* say something." Lia tugged on his sleeve and searched his emotionless features. The child spun to the Liche Queen.

"His body has been returned from the World After by will of the Blight. His soul is another matter completely." The Liche Queen gestured to Cedrik with an open palm. His body rose, rotating in the stale air with each twist of her wrist. "You see, the body is little more than a vessel. Temporary. Fleeting. From the moment we are born, the Blight has already staked its claim." The Liche Queen gestured again and Cedrik's body aged rapidly. His skin wrinkled and spotted. His hair lengthened into brittle strands.

Lia stepped back, horrified. The Liche Queen stomped the floor. A blast of moldy wind lanced the Garrison, extinguishing the hovering green orbs.

The child stifled a gasp. The Liche Queen's illusion of perfection dissolved in the newborn shadows. Her waves of raven's feather hair melted into a scraggly mess of dusty locks. Her crystal blue orbs rolled over, becoming a sickly mottled silver. She pinched Lia's chin with skeletal fingers, setting the child's teeth to chatter in the frigid grasp. "Typical! You mortals are all alike, incapable of seeing the Blight's beauty."

She released Lia's chin. "The Blight can be reversed. I can show you how. I can show you how to restore him." The wind abated. The illusion restored itself and the Liche Queen was once more the beautiful ruler of the Nekropolis. She offered Lia her hand. But there is something I need first."

Chapter 26

The Reaper's Song sliced through the cloudless night without a trace, thwarting even the moon's keen eye. Her three normally thrashing sails were frozen in place; a trio of hovering shadows. Poogs nervously flexed at the knee while guiding the helm with a steady hand. His skull emblazoned dagger smiled back from its mount at the wheel's center.

Fitting, he thought, *for Death and then a pirate to captain such a vessel.* Poogs brushed the skull with a fingertip. He truly loved the Reaper's Song and the freedom she provided. The fear it inspired was a mere bonus. The ship had been every bit his staunchest companion since the dreary night he rested it from Morgren's cold, dead hands. He wondered how long it would take for the former captain to claim her justice. Poogs rubbed at his eyes, eternally grateful for every thrilling moment he had spent at flight. But the night had drawn long and he knew the worst was yet to come.

A lonesome speck appeared on the moonlit horizon, contorting into a jagged mess of ugly shadows as the Reaper's Song sped to her destination. Though Poogs had never seen it, he knew enough to fear the Nekropolis. Its reputation alone conjured a staggering number of grim tales and breathed a chill down his spine.

The landscape was barren, long ago abandoned by the Breath. A dense barricade of petrified trees blanketed the land for leagues approaching the castle's outer walls. The dark fortress loomed behind the decayed timberline like an angry giant. Poogs nervously tapped his boot to a lingering song in his head. Despite his bluster, he knew the likelihood of success was slim. Still, the North Star had need of him. She was the only patron saint that had ever paid him any mind. He would not fail her.

"We've nearly arrived," the pirate called over his shoulder.

A door opened on the main deck, releasing the Beast and Polaris into the cool night air. The Beast crouched through the man-sized door of the cartography room, then offered a guiding hand to his queen. Polaris somberly took the oaken steps, sadness painting the delicate features of her slender face. Polaris walked past the helm, patting Poogs on the shoulder. The Beast shadowed her steps, unwilling to let her part from sight. They stood in silence at the prow. Their plans had been made and their words exhausted.

The Reaper's Song hovered high over the peak of a twisted tower. Beneath the stalking intruder, a countless number of Wakeful guards patrolled the battlements. The soldiers moved in pairs, probing the darkness, searching for the unexpected. "They have the benefit of her Majesty's unholy blessing, but you could shoot them in the dark for all of the racket," Poogs said, sneering at his mention of the Liche Queen.

The Beast peered over the side, realizing the pirate was right. Though dimly lit by the pale moon, the sinister armor of the guards gave away their movements. It would be difficult, but he was sure he could elude detection.

The Beast enveloped Polaris's hands in the mitt of a paw. "If there is a way—"

Polaris shushed the horned giant with a finger to her lips. "I know you will do what is right. Now go. Find your daughter. Bring her back."

The Beast said not another word. He climbed onto the rail, quickly finding his balance against the gusting winds. He met Poogs's gaze and thanked the pirate with the sincerity of a nod. Poogs winked and returned the sentiment with his trademarked, over-zealous bow. The Beast's lips curled into a half smirk and then he turned to face the night. He embraced the sky and leaned forward.

The air quickly cooled as he plummeted to the castle rushing to greet him. Poogs's skill at the helm was better than advertised: The Beast's landing point would be partially obscured from view by the branching network of interior walls. His incursion would be all but invisible. The Beast spread his arms and then tucked into a roll. He landed on all fours, crouching like a dire wolf ready to explode from shadow. Upon contact the Beast hated the very touch of the Nekropolis. The petrified wood was like the warm wood of his glade. He had assumed the deathly structure would have felt like ice. It was worse. It was numbing and stinging all at once.

Like death...

The decaying power of the Blight reverberated through the Nekropolis like a blasphemous pulse, mocking life with each beat. He scaled down as quickly as he dared, found the darkest shadow, and lunged silently into its depths. Clanking armor drew the Beast's attention. A pair of Wakeful moved in lock step along the battlement, approaching his shadowy sanctuary. Their weapons were sheathed, but pale hands rested on pommels, anxious to unleash violence.

In the darkness, his lips curled back over his fangs. He wished to the Wandering Spirit of the Wood for the Wakeful to cross his path. He crouched low, inching towards the boundary of his concealment, silently daring the Wakeful to come closer. The clanking grew closer. Barbed silhouettes accompanied the nearing din. They were almost close enough to grab.

One more step...

The Wakeful abruptly spun on their heels and reversed direction. A moment later they were a distant clank. He relished the idea of throttling each of the black-armored soldiers, but there was Lia to think about. No harm could come to his daughter. The Beast turned from the departing patrol and trundled for a deeper patch of shadows. The medallion, his oldest companion, danced in the moonlight, bouncing and twisting as he prowled the battlement. He reached for the jewel, pulling the thin chain taut. Polaris said the treasure would guide him to Lia. The Beast regretted not asking for further instruction on the matter. He felt quite the fool, holding the medallion to the moon, knowing detection could come at any moment.

He pivoted on a heel, orienting the medallion in a dozen directions. *Nothing.* He grunted his frustration and rolled the stubborn jewel between his palms. He puffed a warm breath onto its glimmering surface. Still, the medallion slumbered. The treasure fell from his claws. "Stupid trinket."

The castle below was a maddening maze of ramparts and heavy gates. Fire pits dotted the grounds, surrounded by the Liche Queen's legions of human soldiers. The Beast dropped silently from the battlement and then darted behind a stack of crates. He peered around, vying for a better look through tendrils of smoke and steam.at the Nekropolis' denizens. They were a sad-looking lot: hungry, and hopeless. They were men who had proven unworthy of the Wakeful curse, but remained loyal to the Liche Queen all the same.

That will not be Lia's fate.

The Beast clutched again at the medallion. Vivid pictures of Lia and Donovan stoked his mind. "Starshine..."

It was summer. Somewhere warm; safe and far away from the Nekropolis.

Lia stood in her undergarments on top of a cluster of smooth boulders jutting into a lazy river. Donovan waited below, brushing a wet mop of brown hair from his eyes.

"See? Nothing to it!" he called up to the rocks.

The leap was only five feet, but Lia had gotten cold feet at the last second.

"I can't do it, faday!" She huddled her arms over her chest and stepped away from the edge.

"Yes you can, starshine. Hear me now. Fear is but a lonely creature that slumbers within us all. It whispers terrible secrets to your heart and then feeds upon it, that it may grow strong. If you let it, it will consume you."

Donovan let the words hang in the afternoon's warming breeze. He offered his hand up to his daughter. "You mustn't be afraid. I shall protect you always."

"Promise?"

"Promise." Donovan traced a cross over his heart.

Lia put her tiny toes to the boulder's edge and looked wearily down at the babbling river. She swung her arms...

The cool embrace of the river and her father's strong hands enveloped her all at once. The Captain of the Guard lifted his daughter from the water and into the sun. Lia squealed a perfect pairing of innocence and pride.

"I did it!" Her wide hazel eyes sparkled.

"Yes you did!" Donovan replied, "Because you believed in yourself.

And in your old faday."

Lia nuzzled her face into the coarse mask of Donovan's beard. She threw her arms around his scarred shoulders and squeezed. After a moment, the child pushed away, her own face framed with a frown. "I wish you didn't have to shave it off. You're so much more handsome with it... Beastly." Lia beamed and tugged on the scruff at Donovan's chin.

"Aye. I like it too. But I like your mother more," Donovan replied with a wink. He scooped Lia over his head, setting her down on his shoulders. "Ready to go again?"

The memory of what could have been, what should have been, fizzled away. The Beast let the medallion slip from his grasp, grateful for the gift it had imprinted. His head cleared and he felt Lia's presence echoing in the firestone. The medallion pulled him to a supply tent near the edge of the clustered campfires. Fifty paces ahead was a vaulted archway of petrified wood. He dodged the Wakeful patrols, ducking behind horse carts and stacked barrels. He counted a minimum of ten patrolling pairs, each moving in a random pattern. That was only the tip of the sword: The Beast knew full well there would be plenty more.

A quartet of Wakeful guards stood at firm attention beneath the arch. The Beast quickly realized these Wakeful were different. They were taller, almost as tall as he was. And bulkier. From head to toe, the guards were covered in a nightmarish fusion of plated mail and coils of razor wire. Polished skulls of fallen mounts adorned each brute's left shoulder, pierced by long spikes of obsidian. Each soldier grasped a lengthy halberd that burned with the malachite flame of their namesake.

The Beast slunk back behind the tent. He did not doubt that he could defeat the guards. Indeed there was no Wakeful alive that he feared. However, he needed to bypass them without the racket a brawl with four armored foes tended to provide. As he stared past the obstacle, something moist and spongy nudged into his side. The snout of a black boar protruded through the fencing, flaring its nostrils as it sniffed the strange new scent by its pen.

The Beast pet the animal's tusked snout. "You, are no meadow either, ugly." He counted a dozen boar in the circular pen, most of which were rooting lazily in a rusty trough. An idea formed in his head, preposterous to be sure. But worth a try. The Beast nudged a playful knuckle into the boar's snout. "I am going to need your help."

The pen's lone gate was a mess of flimsy wire snagged between wooden poles. Reaching it would be troublesome if the pack spooked too early, but he had to hurry. The Beast dropped as low as he could while maintaining speed. He reached the gate and cast a glance at the brutish sentries. No movement. So far, so good. He carefully opened the simple latch, holding his breath and praying for the gate's silent cooperation. Success. He picked up a large stone and retreated to shadow. Exactly as he had hoped, the Wakeful remained indistinguishable from stone and the gluttonous boars remained feasting.

It was thirty feet or less to the gateway. The Beast needed the guards to completely abandon their posts, only for a moment, for him to gain entry. The North Star blinked reassurance from high up in the lifeless sky. The Beast took a deep breath, took aim, and hurled the stone at the trough. A metallic clang ricocheted from the rusty metal, setting the boars into a squealing frenzy. They stampeded about the pen, butting heads and snapping at tails.

"Come on, come on..." the Beast muttered. Finally, the boars crashed into the gate, trampling the flimsy structure to pieces. They spilled from the pen, squealing in all directions. The Beast quickly snapped to the guards...

They hadn't even flinched.

The Beast's shoulders slumped. He frantically wracked his brain, searching for another option as the medallion pulsed at his chest. A second commotion disturbed the drab night scape.

At first, only a handful of soldiers investigated the din. Minutes later the compound burst to life. Dozens of starving soldiers fell upon the squirming boars, desperate to claim the would-be meat. A heavy rattle of metal rumbled to life shortly thereafter.

The quartet of sentries lowered their flaming halberds and marched into the chaotic fray. The Wakeful drove at the crowd, crashing upon them like a battering ram. The Beast heard the first of the screams as he sprinted to the vacated archway. It loomed high overhead as he passed through its gaping maw. The passage beyond funneled into a small corridor of twisting black branches. Stout doors guarded the castle's entrance at its end.

He hoped beyond hope, as his paw closed around the latch, that his luck yet held. In his haste, the Beast had not considered the possibility that one of the guards may have possessed a key. But there was no time for hindsight. The Beast tightened his grasp and twisted. The latch clicked softly. *Now or never,* the Beast thought. He pressed a bulky shoulder against the door and pushed.

The door accepted his invitation and opened without a sound.

Chapter 27

Navigating the inner sanctum of the Nekropolis proved easier than expected. At every junction and stairway, the firestone whispered a preference for one path over the others. The labyrinth of the Hollow and its never ending cluster of dead ends and switchbacks were little more difficult to manage than a leaf swept forest path. The Beast silently thanked Polaris for having the foresight to entrust him with such an amazing gift.

He soon realized the castle was guarded more by fear than by force. Servants with the same hollow eyes of the Wakeful seemed all too eager to avoid anything but the highest trafficked areas of the upper levels. He didn't blame them. Gods only knew what terrors lurked deep within the shadows of the black castle.

The medallion's pulse guided the Beast into a small round room that stretched twenty paces across. It was Spartan in decor, lacking even the most basic of appointments. He sniffed around the edge, unsure of the medallion's intentions. The same rank musty air was all the answer he received. He trundled the chamber's circumference, pushing against the petrified surface every few steps. He was certain there the medallion hadn't lead him there by error. The tiniest of breezes caressed the Beast's hackles, confirming his suspicions. He approached a tight knit of branches and held a paw to the wall. A second breeze split though his claws and brushed the fur on his face.

A weak point.

The gap was just wide enough to fit his paws through. Bracing a foot against the wall, he pulled at a clutch of branches. At first, the Nekropolis refused to budge. He tensed and pulled harder, driving away from the wall with his powerful legs. The branch strained as his claws dug deeper into the black wood.

Crack!

The clutch of branches snapped under the herculean effort. He stumbled backwards, dropping the fragments to the floor. He flattened against the wall near the door, waiting to pounce on the first poor fool to investigate the disturbance. A minute later there was no clanking of armor, no heavy trampling of boots, not even the light scampering of a curious servant. Satisfied, the Beast returned to his work. A few more tugs opened the gap just wide enough.

Branches clawed at his face and arms as he squeezed his way through. The Beast felt like he had been buried alive within the Nekropolis's walls. Ahead, flickering green light teased freedom. A child's wavering voice echoed from somewhere, defiantly denying an unheard command. *Lia.* He broke free of the gnashing branches and pulled his way to the tunnel's mouth. Beneath him a monstrous space stretched forever into a sea of darkness. Bouncing orbs of emerald cast a ghostly shroud over a floating island of stone. His blood quickly flashed to a boil.

The Liche Queen stood with Lia before a demonic altar, trying to close the child's hand around a dagger. A stone arbour covered in strange symbols he did not recognize stood guard over the devilish stone basin. A column of light shrouded a figure hovering a few feet above the floor. It took a second, but the Beast finally remembered the old man encased in light. Memories of Cedrik stormed home into his head. Cedrik had been more than a commanding officer. He had been Donovan's most trusted supporter and greatest teacher. Cedrik had been the one to fill the gaps of Donovan's military training with a mortar of ethics and strict sense of justice. He hadn't forgotten his old mentor's lessons.

A man should never take more than he was willing to give. A man needed to draw a hard line when dealing with those who took what they pleased.

The Liche Queen had taken plenty. She had abandoned her kingdom and family. She had spawned the scourge of Wakeful and erased magic from the realm. It was her anger that set the plot that saw Cedrik flee with Lia into anonymity into motion. The Liche Queen had burned away everything that opposed her will.

Until now.

The Beast took a single step back and then vaulted from the ledge. He fell like a bolt of lightning flung from the heavens by a vengeful god. His cloak flapped behind him like a ships sail. He made no effort to conceal this descent. He crashed onto the observation pedestal with the impact of a meteor strike. Cracks shattered the stone surface, racing away from his paws like a maze of jagged spider's web.

Lia's hazel eyes opened wide while Pandora's narrowed to the snake-like slits. The child bolted as quickly as her little legs could manage. The Liche Queen snatched at the fleeing girl's hair, but Lia was too fast. The Beast started forward, allowing the child to collide with his leg. Lia squeezed his massive thigh and then looked up into the familiar eyes that she had never seen before. *In this lifetime...*

Lia choked back a sob. "I knew you'd come." The Beast clutched his daughter against his leg. "I will always find you, star-shine."

He maneuvered Lia to his flank and regarded the Liche Queen. A forgotten lifetime's worth of emotions flooded through him, threatening to burst his mind's fragile dam. They had been repressed in silence, locked away for too long, and now demanded their freedom.

And their vengeance.

A million words trampled the Beast's tongue. He raised a black talon and growled pure fury.

"You..."

The deathly still of the Garrison cringed at the Beast's chilling damnation, sending the shadows into hiding. The Liche Queen's jaw all but unhinged as she stepped backwards, colliding with the altar. She reached slowly behind her back for the ceremonial dagger, still dripping with Malachai's blood. Her icy fingers closed around the hilt. The mistake was more than loud enough for the Beast's keen hearing.

"Don't," he growled. "It will take more than that."

Pandora released the dagger and half-hid behind the arbour of blackened stone. She was no fool. Another tactic was in order. She would call upon another skill, one she hoped still applied to such a fearsome creature. The Liche Queen peered around the arch, caressing the runic etchings, regarding the Beast with a curious eye. She flashed a kittenish smile. "Well then," Pandora purred, "aren't you the mighty titan?" She giggled a coy giggle, casually stepping around the arch's base. She abandoned the arbour's safety and dropped her dark robes to the floor. She stepped free of the pile, covered by little more than bands of black silk.

"Not another step." The Beast's roaring command shook the cavern. Lia jumped at the thunderous clap, but remained relieved beyond measure to be standing at her father's side. "If you believe for a moment that the sight of you does anything but boil my blood..."

"Oh come now. Surely the fabled Beast of Briarburn is not without certain appetites." Pandora let her fingers trace the soft skin of a pale thigh. Waves of long, dark locks fell over her shoulders, glistening in the emerald light.

Years before, when they were young and she yet untouched by the

Blight, he would have crossed the deepest seas at Pandora's whim. Indeed, once he had. He had been wrong aboard the Reaper's Song. The craven look in the Liche Queen's eyes told him everything. There was nothing left of the woman he loved, nothing left of his princess. Not even a breath of hope. The Beast snarled at the pitiful advances.

There was no bringing Pandora back.

The Liche Queen's lip quivered. Then her hands and naked arms up to her shoulders. "How dare you!" The Liche Queen rattled the Garrison, clanking the steel of the unseen Wakeful legions slumbering below. Pandora convulsed. "How dare you!" She balled her hands into alabaster clubs, tension chewing her muscles. The air about her shoulders sizzled and warped the darkness. A tempest of black magic forever brewing now boiled over.

The skin around the Liche Queen's eyes melted away, burned by the Blight's unseen flame. Her flesh spoiled, rotting the creamy porcelain into a putrid shell of mottled grays that few had had the terrible privilege of seeing. "How dare you!" The banshee-like wail exploded from the hanging skeletal remnants of Pandora's jaw. Her luxurious raven shaded locks faded to tufts of grey and then crumbled, taking flight on a sinister breeze. The Liche Queen's primal scream rocked the foundation of the Nekropolis, setting the whole of the castle to tremble.

Her neck cracked backwards as she summoned strength from the arbour's incandescent runes before wailing into the unknown.

"Malachai!"

***

The Reaper's Song silently hovered above the Nekropolis, cloaked from view by Death's own magic. Two hours had passed since the Beast disappeared over the side, setting the plan in motion. Poogs hoped it proved better than a fool's errand.

It had only taken ten minutes of those hours to drive the pirate below deck to the calming sanctuary of his work station. Poogs sat at the bench, tinkering with a gadget under the glow of amber lamp-light. He set a prototype model down after a few twists of a hand tool and turned to a half-finished blue-print. Tension gnawed the base of his skull. The loathsome sensation vibrated between his ears. Beads of sweat dampened his temples. He swiped at the blue print with a stylus, leaving rough strikes behind on the parchment.

Not right, not good enough.

Poogs threw the stylus down in disgust and turned back to the model and his tools. "Now where the hell have they gotten off to?" The pirate knocked aside a stack of rolled parchments. "I just had them."

"It does us no good to worry, Captain," Polaris said softly. She held the object of Poogs's obsession in her palm. "And it does you no good to keep getting in your own way."

Polaris playfully tossed the tool to the pirate. She strolled around the sprawling work station, inspecting blue prints, manipulating models. "In all of my lifetimes among mortals I have never seen their equal. You should be proud."

"My lady is far too kind. Apologies for the outburst," Poogs said with a bow.

Polaris returned a tiny model ship to the bench. "The ideas consume you, like any magic consumes its vessel. Your world is only just realizing the natural sciences, yet you speak their languages fluently... when you allow yourself to listen."

"My lady?" The pirate's brow creased, displaying the etched lines of a burdened mind.

Polaris gestured for him to sit. Poogs did as commanded, returning to the simple wooden stool by the bench's side. The North Star stepped behind him and placed her hands on his shoulders. "Now breathe."

Poogs breathed in staggered bursts. They were the breaths of a caged animal: restless and agitated.

"No, no." Polaris shifted her hands to the pirate's chest and back. "With me now. Breathe."

Poogs inhaled, drawing in a steady stream of air as the North Star pressed against his chest wall.

"Out," Polaris commanded, releasing her grip.

The calming exchange repeated for three soothing, centering breaths. At the end of Poogs's final one, Polaris spoke.

"Draw."

Poogs needed no further instruction. He grabbed the discarded stylus, dipped it to ink, and sketched feverishly at the blue-print. Five minutes of scratching later he was finished. He put the stylus aside and pushed away from the work station, inspecting his work.

"When you are ready to listen, the entire world will sing its secrets to you," Polaris said with a smile.

Poogs held the sketch at arm's length, astonished. Aided by the North Star, he had completed in minutes a design that had haunted his dreams for years. He proudly pointed at the various angles and edges of the sketch as he explained his theory. The fervid speech faded away, replaced by a sincere humility. "I hope one day all may enjoy seeing the world as I do. As the stars do. Maybe this design will someday unite us."

Poogs flattened the sketch onto the work bench. "I don't know how you managed to make the voices speak in turn, that I may hear their knowledge," the pirate said, daring to take Polaris's hand, "but I thank you, my lady." The pirate suddenly blushed at his own brazen action. The mere presence of the North Star was an honor to any sailor. But there was more. Her presence stole the words from his lips before he had opportunity to trip over them. He wondered if there was even the slightest chance she felt the same.

"You are welcome, Captain," Polaris said, slipping her hand free.

For a moment his heart sunk, and he thought himself a fool for assuming such a ludicrous idea. She was the North Star: Timeless and constant. She could never see him in the same light. Not in this life. Polaris brushed a lock of hair from the pirate's face and kissed him on the cheek. In that heartbeat, time froze and Poogs was certain that he saw a very human sparkle in the North Star's eyes.

A thunderous boom violently rocked the ship. Parchment and gadgetry crashed from their shelving. The work station, made of solid oak and carrying the weight of Poogs's equipment fared no better and skittered across the floor. Poogs caught the North Star by the arm. "What in the name of the gods?"

A worrisome look crept over Polaris's face. "I believe Donovan and my daughter have been re-united."

Chapter 28

At first the Beast heard naught but his own tepid breath. Then came a rapid click clicking. Somewhere in the darkness, it quickened. And grew louder. Something wicked was fast upon him. *Them.* Lia's safety was paramount; even if it meant sending her away. Again.

The clicking was nearly on top of father and daughter, tapping like angry rain on steel. The Liche Queen levitated and then eased backwards, relishing the surging doom. The menacing storm of clicks built to a terrible crescendo. Lia pressed her palms to her ears and burrowed her face deep into the Beast's side. In a ragged breath he repeated his life's most agonizing decision, tearing his heart in half all over again. The Beast clutched Lia by the shoulders at arm's length. "Run. I will be right behind you."

Lia's mouth opened to protest, but was silenced by a warding paw.

"Go! Now!"

Malachai's twin writhing tails whipped and thrashed behind the hovering Liche Queen, just as Lia bolted for the entrance. She forced herself to focus on the flapping black veil, promising herself she would not look back. A grotesquely lengthened, horse-like skull, glowing with ten fiery orbs reared over the platform's side. Malachai dug in with his hooked claws and pulled his bulk up to his waiting queen. The long talons of his hind legs looked like hand scythes and chewed at the petrified surface for purchase.

Malachai greeted the Beast with a fell howl. It was the call of a rabid wolf on a patch of forgotten tundra. His tails darted back and forth like dueling cobras, dancing above his columns of burning eyes.

"Now this is more like it." The Liche Queen's voice was a hollow cackle. She swept an arm between the two titans, welcoming them to her personal arena. "Do not disappoint me again, Captain."

The Beast had only a second to wonder if that parting barb had been meant for his benefit. *Does she know who I am?* The barbs of Malachai's tails flared and fired towards the Beast from across the platform. He dodged to his right and rolled clear, leaving the twin tails slicing through shadow. Malachai charged in the next breath, jaws snapping open, revealing hundreds of eager teeth. The Beast caught a glimmer of the rotten fangs from the corner of his eye and rolled a second time, treating Malachai to a frustrating meal of empty air.

A flurry of the Beast's battering ram punches pounded wicked Malachai's side and the Liche Queen's dark champion reeled. The Beast grunted, pushed himself upright and dove onto Malachai's back. He hammered an avalanching fist into Malachai's skull, seized the greasy mane and smashed the glowing nest of eyes into the floor. The Beast dismounted the twitching body. His mind's levees cracked further and rage began to freely pour. Around his eyes a red haze crystallized. Three steps to the Liche Queen and the nightmare would finally end.

A barbed tail flashed to life, slashing the Beast across his face, cutting deep into flesh. The savage strike missed an eye by mere inches. He threw an arm up in anticipation. On cue the second tail lashed out from the shadows, coiling around the limb, carving a crisscross of slashes. The Beast jerked away from the sudden sting, rending at the lethal appendage. Malachai pounced on his snared query, pinning the Beast to the floor.

"I grow weary of this," the Liche Queen said, floating to the arbour. Her bony finger danced in the eerie green glow, struggling to select a rune to play with. "Ah, this one shall do." She jabbed a vermillion rune that swirled with the agony of her favorite curse. It was a magic near and dear to her frigid heart; the first of many such curses she had crafted. One she was saving as a special gift.

The Beast struggled under Malachai's weight. One arm was torn and lashed, the other clawed and pinned, leaving precious few options. The rune's power siphoned like syrup into the Liche Queen's hand, charging her cadaverous digits with a ghastly red afterglow. The king of fools himself could understand the need for action. The Beast lurched forward, freeing an arm. He grabbed Malachai by the throat and drove his crown into Malachai's long mandible. Stunned, the wicked creature released the Beast's bloody limb, stumbled backwards and collapsed. His tails twitched like angry snakes and then fell motionless.

"No matter," the Liche Queen said, shoulders slumping ever so slightly. The rune's power set the air to hum as it gnawed at her hand, begging for release. "I will have the girl. I will finish what I began long ago in Adella's cursed ashes. I will burn it all." The Liche Queen's glowing hand reared overhead. The Beast scanned around. No cover, nowhere to run, no weapon in hand. He dug in and squared off his shoulders. The Fated Sorrow soared like a vengeful shooting star, leaving a trail of volcanic reds and coppers.

"No!" A tiny voice shouted. Tiny, but never for a day in her life insignificant to the world. *Or to her father.*

Lia had crept back onto the shadowy platform, undetected by the combatants. With a steady wave, a golden barrier of gusting snowflakes materialized in front of the Beast just before the curse struck. The venomous magic ricocheted from the magical shield and sailed instead for a sweeter target. The Fated Sorrow struck with a branding sizzle.

The Garrison froze. The emerald shadows dancing beneath its dome bit their lower lips and froze.

Lia stood perfectly still. A curious look spread over her round face as the Fated Sorrow claimed its victim and spread through her body. She looked at the Beast, struggling in vain to speak. Her eyes spoke for her paralyzed lips. *Faday...* She clutched her side. Staggered once...

And fell.

The Beast felt it first in his chest; the ripping away of his soul. The red haze swallowed his eyes, tinting the gloomy dark with a lens of crimson. Pure hatred, the very essence of violence finally broke the shackles in his core. He bellowed a horrible sound, one unfit for any but a soul tortured by the most loathsome demon: the sound of parent's infinite torment.

No amount of pain would stop him. Not hellish fire nor the grimmest poison. The Beast stormed at the Liche Queen, leaving spurs of cracked stone underfoot. He grabbed at her, meaning her the very worst of what she deserved.

The Liche Queen vanished from between his swiping claws in a stream of indigo vapor. "A pity, Beast of Briarburn." Her disembodied voice rolled through the Garrison. "A pity you had to interfere. Now she will die most painfully. Alive or dead, either shall suit my needs perfectly." The Beast's teeth ground as he battled to sort grief from fury.

"My children shall see to her," the Liche Queen's fading voice called, "after they see to you of course."

Legions of Wakeful answered their queen's summons, filling the Garrison with an empty drone. Armor and weapon alike clattered as thousands of the Queen's own marched on the spiraling ramps rising from the depths to the altar. A glowing emerald haze climbed the walls, growing closer with each locked step of their approach. The Beast stepped to the platform's edge, ready to render judgment and justice to the whole miserable lot, when the gentlest of murmurs provided distraction.

Lia lay on her side, chest barely rising, life draining away. She straightened an arm, and reached out with trembling fingers. The rage in the Beast's heart fell away. Lia's needs far exceeded his thirst for Wakeful blood. He had to move quickly, had to get her to safety, to Polaris. The first of the Wakeful reached the platform and sealed off the lone egress. The forward row of black-armored drone drew their weapons, challenging the Beast as their ranks yet swelled.

The wall of blades pushed closer to the altar, filling the tier shoulder to shoulder with hooked armor. The vicious wave of obsidian advanced, filling the Garrison with the sounds of echoing war drums. The Beast bound to his daughter, relieved to find her fragile body still clinging to life. There was no doubt in his mind her soul's shine remained ablaze with the Breath; only doubt for the limits of her mortal form. The Beast cradled the child, *his child*, into his arms. How slight she felt. To him she was no bigger than a newborn laying comfortably cradled in his elbow's crook.

The thunder drummed closer, nearing its end. Fury swelled at his temples but failed to silence a whispering question. Scores of Wakeful began to suffocate the modest platform. The passage above was beyond his prowess to reach. A question came from a dark corner of his heart. Maybe it was enough simply to be with her at the end?

"Be still starshine, I am here." The Beast's whisper was unhurried. He brushed Lia's hair from her forehead. The Fated Sorrow was fast spreading its evil. Her brow was drenched of sweat, burning to the touch. Lia shivered and raised her arm into space. For a moment the Beast thought her delirious of fever. To his surprise, Lia summoned strength and spoke, each word growing weaker than the last. "It can hurt... them."

The Beast realized at once her meaning, what Lia had been reaching for. The altar stared back at father and daughter, mocking them with a grisly laugh of silence. In a flash, the Beast hated the Liche Queen's grim artifact more than any despicable thing he had ever laid his weary eyes on.

He swung his evergreen cloak free and swaddled the tattered garment around his daughter. He squeezed her gently and kissed her forehead. "Don't leave me... please." An icy dagger stabbed at his heart. His place was by Lia's side. He wanted nothing more than to hold her, to make up for the stolen moments. Instead, the Beast placed the bundled child upon the floor and lowered his horn crowned head.

And charged.

Chapter 29

The collision was spectacular. The Beast's ram-like horns struck the runic arbour just shy of its waist. A bluish glyph immediately darkened, its energy annihilated on impact. A chunk of stone larger than a wild boar fell free, crumbling to dust as it rolled away.

A serrated blade of obsidian whistled behind his shoulder. The Beast spun, catching the sword's guiding wrist. He slammed a vicious punch into a spiked chest plate, caving it in. Before the Wakeful countered, the Beast heaved him overhead and hurled him back at his comrades.

The quick reflex bought precious time. The Beast swung a heavy fist into the arbour, breaking away another chunk of stone. He cocked his tree trunk arm as far back as it would stretch. He would see the whole of the Nekropolis crumble to dust...

Inches from impact, the familiar sting of Malachai's tail snared his arm, yanking it away. A brutish weight slammed into his back, sending him stumbling. The second tail snapped like a whip, lashing around the thick muscles of the Beast's neck. The barbs lanced like wasps' stingers into his skin, hungry for another taste of blood.

The Beast pivoted, clamping a vice grip around his noose, freeing some slack. It was his turn to feed. Oily sludge poured through the Beast's fangs, splattering onto the floor. He wrenched his neck in a million directions, sawing through Malachai's flesh like the blades of starving saw mill.

Malachai's agonizing howl fell on deaf ears. The wicked creature tried pushing away with a swipe of its hooked claws. Snapped. Flailed.

Failed.

The wounded tail clung together by a slip of flesh. A final rend severed the appendage free with the grotesque sound of tearing skin. Malachai bellowed at the burning pain and released the twin tail's grasp on the Beast's trapped arm. The Beast's movement blurred. He snatched hold of the surviving tail and yanked its caterwauling owner into a crushing bear hug. He flattened Malachai's ghastly face with a savage head-butt, then spun the monster around by a leg like a war hammer.

Malachai crashed into a wave of Wakeful, scattering them like discarded dolls. Metal screeched and grated as the Beast pirouetted with sweeping swings. Scores of Wakeful fell by the wayside and the Beast thought for a moment enough room had been cleared for escape.

The altar.

The Beast dug deep his grip, clutching a pair of Malachai's limp legs. He spun in a tight circle and raised the improvised mace overhead. He swung Malachai downward in a black crescent, determined to return him to whatever hell he had escaped from. Malachai's battered body broke upon the Liche Queen's altar like a tsunami breaking landfall. A splintering fissure erupted through the altar's center, spreading in jagged cracks.

The altar hummed, rattling the carpet of discarded weapons and armored bodies. The arbour's runes drained of life, one by one fading into nothing. *Dying,* the Beast thought. *Good.* The Beast swung his arms backwards and flexed at the knees. He vaulted high, nearly reaching the hidden entrance above; high enough to destroy the castle's vulgar heart. The Beast drove his heels down at the first kiss of stone, spearing the dying altar down the center. A swirling blaze of magical energies exploded, painting the cavern in twisted shades of purplish twilight.

Silence now. The Beast kicked at the rubble, looking up just in time to watch the last rune flicker and die. With grim satisfaction, he stepped down from the steaming pile, hungry for another crack at rending Wakeful bone and steel. Instead, surprise sated him. The Wakeful no longer approached. They no longer did anything. A collection of black suits of armor populated the platform, weapons frozen in place, malachite eyes dimmed to slumber.

The Beast spared not a moment hurrying by the frozen army, scooped Lia up, and sprinted for the black veil. He felt Lia's rising temperature piercing through her swaddle. Her hair was a wet mop of tangled mess. *Still breathing. Still time.*

The corridor raced by as he plunged headlong into the unknown. His horns nicked and scraped at the low ceiling. The sharp branches of the walls came alive, struggling to snare the fleeing juggernaut. He swat them away, not slowing a step, careful to keep his precious cargo cradled close. Dim light from a lone brazier called from the tunnel's center. A section of wall coiled away as the Beast reached the pale torchlight revealing a small chamber; a chamber that gave him a niggling feeling of a prison cell.

"Up, it goes up." Lia's voice was less than a whisper.

The Beast regarded the chamber a second time, hunched his shoulders and squeezed in, certain the wall of branches would seal them in forever. As if reading his mind, the wall twisted itself closed and the floor lurched under his feet. His stomach dropped a foot, realization sinking in soon after.

Up.

The chamber of branches carried the fugitives away from the Garrison to the sick sound of snakes slithering through wet leaves. The Beast's heart pounded and showed little sign of slowing. Surely the Liche Queen had felt the altar's destruction. Surely there would be troops waiting above.

The lift opened to the Hollow and the Beast stepped free. A sweeping expanse of shiny dark surfaces and irregular angles greeted him. Spiraling stair cases offered access to a dozen balconies and a tower of upper floors. Musty wind drifted in from the shady spaces between the wall's crevices. The Beast grunted his frustration. Aided by the medallion, entry had proven much easier. He shifted Lia in his arms and selected a stair case at random. He had no idea which, if any, of the passages would provide an exit. The Reaper's Song was 'up' he reckoned, so 'up' he would go.

The spiral of stairs climbed into the Nekropolis's vacuous towers, burning soreness into the Beast's legs with each stride. It was a maddening climb: for every step taken, the landing seemed further away by two more. *Impossible.*

"The child is mine!" Three daggers of indigo flame slashed by the Beast's head, flung from the floor below. The magical blades *thunked* into the wall behind him, sizzling as they burned out. He peered over the railing. The Liche Queen rode atop a black cloud of surging Blight magic. She would be on top of them in seconds. Three more blades shot through the space with a flick of her wrist.

The landing wasn't getting any closer, but the Liche Queen's daggers were. He cradled Lia tighter, sprung onto the railing and then launched himself through the air, bypassing the endless stretch of stairs. Daggers bit the wall a second later.

The Beast stuck his landing, aided by a clawful of marble statue. The massive effigy depicted a hideous uni-horned demon with a slit-like nose. The Beast shouldered into the sentry, grinding it closer to the edge. *This should slow her down.* A final bump and the statue vanished.

A second later, crashing sounds echoed below. No screams. No more daggers.

The landing opened into a modest space, better appointed than the Beast assumed the Nekropolis had to offer. Towers of bookcases and lecterns were scattered about, some toppled like leaning dominoes. Thick layers of dust and abandoned cobwebs clung to every corner. *Familiar.* Further in, a row of marble busts stood apart from the forgotten tomes. The facial features were gouged from most, part of a skull missing from one. The collection had the air of having been abused by a tantrumming child.

Then it hit him.

He remembered this place. Or rather, a place like it. The Grand Library of Queen Adella's palace had been home to many of Cedrik's lectures. How he would have loved to hear his sagely words now and be free of this horrible place. In Adella's palace, the library was lit by endless sunlight that flowed through a magnificent cathedral of stained glass and danced over neat rows of silver and ivory bookcases. But here...

The Beast reached for a marble bust missing an eye.

"Give her to me now and your death will be slightly less painful." The Liche Queen emerged from a flash of violet light. Blades of dark flame whirling in tight spirals just beyond her putrid fingertips.

"She has not been yours since the day you abandoned her," the Beast said, inching closer to the bust. He looked the Liche Queen square in the eye. "Pandora."

Rage kissed the Liche Queen's melting face. She sneered at the sound of her forbidden name and flung a brace of fiery daggers. The Beast grabbed the eyeless bust and returned fire. The daggers barely missed; a timely dodge doing the trick once more. Moonlight poured in from the freshly ventilated wall, covering the library in a silvery ripple. The Liche Queen did not bother ducking from the heavy projectile. The bust disintegrated upon impact with her decaying face.

"That name is forbidden here," the Liche Queen wailed, levitating between the towers of dusty books. Gusting swells punished the library, knocking over the row of busts and toppling the book cases. Loose paper and parchment flapped in the tempest like a flock of angry gulls. A memory, banished from her fragmented mind, ebbed home.

"How dare you! I abandoned no one! My mother had the chance to save my baby. She stood by and did nothing-- nothing, as the World After claimed my.... daughter." Rage twisted the Liche Queen's face further. "And her bastard orphan of a father held my hand and smiled all the while."

A tower of books exploded into pulp nearby, vaporized by the blur of power sizzling around the Liche Queen's shoulders. The Beast set his jaw and took a defiant step forward. "You've no one to blame but yourself for the deception. You selected a dangerous path long before the child was born. One her father could never allow you to force upon her."

"That was a mistake that fool did not live long to regret." The Liche Queen's energy pulsed, charged by the Beast's honesty.

The Beast held Lia aside, revealing the gleaming medallion at his chest. The firestone split the gloom, adding radiant hues of crimson to the moonlight silver. "Longer than you know... princess." He pulled the cloak away from Lia's flushed face. He shifted her in his arms, permitting the Liche Queen a better look.

"This... is Lia. Your daughter."

The library stilled. The whirling storm of forgotten tomes, torn maps, and yellowed scrolls froze in place like a painted snow storm. The Liche Queen touched down from her hover and regarded the Beast with a curious eye. She stepped into a silvery bath.

The beautiful masking illusion settled over her face. "It cannot be," Pandora said softly, "Donovan?"

The Beast nodded.

"And this, this precious thing," Pandora said, reaching for the fading child, "Lia, my sweet star--"

A portion of wall behind the Beast exploded into the library, rocking the Nekropolis as though an earthquake struck. A second deafening boom brought another explosion. The Beast dove to his side, cradling, shielding. The castle vibrated as a third shock wave pummeled the wall into petrified tinder. The Liche Queen's illusion died away, leaving her true and grim visage. Debris from the wall burned into dust as it neared her. Powerful though she was, the blast stunned her for a moment, drowning her in a hazy netting.

The Beast rolled to his feet, finding the gaping hole in what used to be the wall. On the other side of the monstrous gouge, fifty feet away, the Reaper's Song hovered like a wraith in the night. A row of smoking cannons protruded from the ship's port side. The Beast could not find Poogs amongst the smoke, but Polaris's cerulean beacon was undeniable. The North Star waved frantically for his attention.

The chamber rocked like a ship at sea and his back was on fire, slashed and bitten by the petrified shrapnel. Lia remained his only constant thought. The Beast struggled to keep his footing and staggered a few paces. The Beast steadied himself, then sprint across the debris laden floor. He leapt from the jagged opening into the free air. He landed in a crouch on the vessel's prow and hurried to his only hope.

"Lia... I am losing her," the Beast said.

Polaris took hold of the child, whispering an ancient word under her breath as she pressed a cooling hand into Lia's brow. "Captain, we must leave. Now."

The Reaper's Song rose majestically from the Nekropolis, pivoting on her center. The grinning, buxom figurehead aimed her outstretched sword at the moon. The timeless vessel stretched a bit, an illusion perceived by all mortal eyes who gazed upon the Harbinger's own, and then split the night.

***

The Liche Queen's irate steps melted into the floor, burning deep a permanent reminder of her fury. Straggling remnants of salt and pepper hair threshed like agitated snakes, bolstering the curses she levied against the moon. She wailed into the frigid nothing of the Nekropolis, clinging to the battered fragment of wall. Black spots dotted her vision. Her heart, all but paralyzed by the decay of the Blight coursing through her knotted veins, contracted painfully as the last breath of humanity was flushed away.

"Take flight, my love. Seek out the intruders who scarred my heart and home. Taste the sweet sorrow of my vengeance." The Liche Queen's haunting tone echoed through the Nekropolis' every corner.

The dracoliche vibrated. Old magic settled into older bones as the undead dragon lord was summoned back to the land of the living. Bones creaked and ground into empty joints. Mountains of dust fell free, leaving piles of silt beneath the colossal guardian. Wings spanning a corsair's length unfolded and the great demon leapt into the clouds hanging over the Nekropolis. The ghastly silhouette blotted out the moon, covering the black castle with a blanket of comforting despair.

The Liche Queen's fleshless mouth cracked open in mock smile. The dracoliche flew for its beloved Queen. It was a perfect instrument of her will, crafted from the essence of the Blight itself. It would not be bartered with, reasoned with or escaped. She would have her prize.

Stars and beasts be damned.

Chapter 30

An ocean of sky rushed by the Reaper's Song. Her figurehead grimaced as she slashed through the patchwork of clouds, racing for the fleeing horizon. Poogs's face mirrored his beloved vessel's: a grim mask that sensed approaching destiny. The pirate urged the Reaper's Song to greater speed. *Better to meet that destiny sooner than later.*

Lia shivered in Poogs's wide bed, flanked by a family she had never known. The captain's quarters were luxuriously appointed. His cloud soft bed was covered with thick quilted blankets and plush pillows stuffed with exotic feathers. A heavy silence crushed the room, broken only by the occasional cough of the dying girl. The Beast paced relentlessly, trying in vain to outrun despair. "Is there nothing you can do?"

"The Fated Sorrow was Pandora's special gift. One she had perfected over many years. The fountain is Lia's only hope. Only there sleeps a magic bountiful enough to breathe *wynisahil* back into this world." Polaris lowered herself to the bed. Sitting by Lia's side was all the magic she had to offer. It would have to be enough. The Beast threw himself into a chair designed for two, wedging between the hand carved arms.

Poogs shouted from above. "There's something after us. Something...

large!"

Polaris was the first to the door. The Beast followed fast behind, sparing a breath to caress his daughter's face. Lia curled into a ball and pressed a feverish cheek into a pillow. The vibrant glow of her skin was gone, wasted into a pallor difficult for him to gaze upon. "Hold on, starshine."

It was dark still, the sky colored only by a wash of star-speckled navy blue and purplish black. The Beast scanned the skies. "Where is it?"

Poogs turned from the helm and pointed. "There."

A speck on the horizon's blade grew at a frightening pace, dipping up and down. The faintest pin prick of emerald centered the bobbing shape as it grew. Squinting, the Beast's night vision penetrated the dark and locked in, confirming his fear.

They were being hunted.

The dracoliche's broad wings of chipped bone beat back patches of clouds. The Beast watched in horror as each violent thrash of slender bone appeared to cut the buffering distance in half. The dracoliche stretched its bony neck taut and roared a terrible, warbling roar.

Chills were shared among the passengers of the Reaper's Song who gaped at the decayed creature. The Beast wondered what it had looked like before the Blight had staked its claim. He snapped the train of thought with a shake of his head. The nightmare roared again, this time close enough for his sharp eyes to count the monster's fractured teeth.

"How positively ghastly," Poogs said. "Come on then, let's get a move on." He did not let on, but the pirate sensed the ship had little left to offer.

"An amazingly astute observation, captain," Polaris replied. The North Star drifted a foot above the deck, letting the stern rush closer. Drifting above the ship's rear railing, she raised her palms to the pursuing demon. Her hands glistened with the sparkle of a diamond sea. She swiped a circle into the air.

One by one stars fell from the sky. The streaking storm of vermillion slashes rained down from the heavens, battering the dracoliche, driving it off course. The mass of bones roared its chilling roar, gave a mighty thrash of its fleshless wings and darted higher into the cloud cover.

Poogs grabbed the Beast's arm and dropped it onto the helm. "Hold this." The pirate mantled the railing and hit the ground running.

"You can't leave me to work this-- this-- thing!" The Beast locked his shoulders and elbows, afraid that his slightest movement would break the helm free of its mount. A million sickening feelings boiled in his belly. "Poogs!"

The pirate paid the Beast no mind and rushed to a crank mounted on the main mast. The mechanism clicked as Poogs frantically worked the handle. Beneath the deck a fine vibration rumbled. The Reaper's Song's gunwale slid open. A row of cannons, seven strong, wheeled into position exposing the sheen of polished, tapered barrels. Heavy chains clicked through a complex gear works. Thuds clunked as the heavy weapons locked into place.

"There, that should do it." Poogs dripped with his usual bravado, quite proud of the modification he had made to the ship.

The last of the shooting stars streaked away, abandoning the night to silence. The barren landscape of grey hills and craggy fissures matured into a mountain range tinged of purple peaks. Their destination drew near.

The vessel lurched, threatening to spill her passengers overboard. Poogs hit the deck hard, banging his head on the cannon's crank. The Beast fared better, saved by his quick reflexes. He shouted to Poogs. "Are you alright?"

The pirate rolled to his rump and rubbed a growing egg on his skull. "Been better. Where did that infernal thing get off to?"

The winged horror surged from above, enraged by the sting of burning stars. The emerald flame of its unholy heart roiled over like a forge ready to explode.

"There! Coming in fast!" The Beast shouted over the rushing winds, jabbing a claw at their stalker.

Poogs ran back to the crank, pulled the handle free and reset it as a lever.

"It's almost on top of us!" The Beast shouted.

Each mighty stroke of the dracoliche's wings propelled it closer to the Liche Queen's vengeance. It roared at the fleeing vessel, coating her in a thin layer of frost. Muscles spasmed in the mortal bodies aboard; the foul breath burned at their skin. Still, Poogs hesitated.

"Not yet..." Poogs exhaled a plume of steady steam from between pursed lips. He forced time to slow in his head. He took aim...

The array of cannons fired and a staccato of booms rattled the ship's bones. The cannons recoiled and then slid back into position, reloaded by a feeder of Poogs's own design. The projectiles slammed into their mark. Bones cracked and fractured debris exploded free. The monster roared a sour cocktail of agony and rage. It wobbled in flight for a moment, then resumed a fervid beeline.

The Beast roared his approval and pumped a fist at the successful volley. "Fire again!"

Polaris spoke softly, as though there were no danger at all. "Just a moment. Captain, if you please?" A halting hand accompanied the simple request.

The North Star closed her eyes and recited the words to a nearly forgotten spell with a hushed tongue. The night time sky tore like cloth, allowing daybreak to pour through the breach. The world was suddenly ablaze in the amber hues of morning. The dracoliche struggled against the repelling dawn like a fly caught in a spider's web, thrashing violently and shielding its lifeless eyes.

"You may fire when ready, Captain."

Poogs flashed a flawless porcelain smile and with a low bow threw the lever. Ear-splitting thunder exploded from the Reaper's Song's guns. Barrels flashed with fire and then exhaled wisps of smoke.

Hot iron pounded the stunned dracoliche, smashing away a forelimb and a portion of wing. The creature wailed a sinister howl, loosing a column of malachite shaded Blight from its maw. The blast struck the gun wale, melting the exposed tips of smoking cannons. The battered side of the ancient vessel would heal itself as it always did, but the cannons of the mortal realm were reduced to molten dead weight.

A cheer erupted on the Reaper's Song. "Nicely done, Captain." Polaris said.

The dracoliche's bones pulsed with the green blaze of its fireball heart. Slowly the damaged bones reformed, stretching broken ends into fresh pieces like new. The Beast could not believe the punishment the creature had taken. To be able to regenerate altogether? How could such a foe be defeated? Any battle hardened warship or the mightiest of storm giants would surely have crumbled under the barrage.

Not so the dracoliche.

A jet of malachite blasted through the ship's sails, splitting a mast like a tree trunk. Poogs dove aside, narrowly dodging a mess of ruined rigging and boom. With a final thrash, the dracoliche caught the Reaper's Song, riving through the hand-carved stern. Man sized fragments were sheered free by the demon's fangs and talons and tossed aside like match sticks.

Polaris slipped to safety in a stream of starlight just before the dracoliche pounced. Her liquescent form misted next to the Beast and solidified. A dour mask shrouded her face. "What now?"

The ship rocked under the violent frenzy. Poogs struggled from underneath a pile of fallen sheet and rigging and staggered to the helm. The pirate bumped the Beast aside without a word, reclaiming the spoked wheel. He leaned forward onto the helm, issuing warning with a wink. "Hold on."

The Beast clamped an iron grip on the railing and threw an arm around Polaris's waist. He nodded his readiness. Poogs returned the nod and then leaned hard into the spokes of his pride and joy. The Reaper's Song pitched forward. Hard. Her grim figurehead laughed and aimed her blade at the mountains. Gravity seized Death's vessel and she fell. The Beast's stomach dropped, flipped over and threatened to evacuate. He looked to the back of the ship, hoping to be rid of the nightmare.

But the dracoliche yet gnawed on the Reaper's Song, chewing anything its vacant eyes could claim. A tail of jagged bones bludgeoned the ship's hull, pummeling the masterful craft work into oblivion.

"It's still back there," the Beast shouted.

The dracoliche reared its head, green fire rolling between its jaws.

The Beast cinched his grasp around Polaris. "It's fir--"

Poogs threw the wheel sharply to the side. The Reaper's Song corkscrewed over the speeding terrain, throwing the undead dragon free. Its breath sliced across the hull, rotting a gaping hole into the side. A moment later, dark smoke plumed from the ghastly wound. Poogs righted the ship, sniffing at the acrid cloud. "That bastard must have nicked the powder below. Not good. Another hit..."

"There will not be another hit." The Beast slipped the medallion over his head and pressed the fiery gem into Polaris's hand. "Tell my starshine that I am sorry for leaving her. Tell her that her *faday* loves her very much."

Before the North Star could argue, the Beast mantled the rail and sprinted for the broken mast. He wrapped the thick column in a bear hug and snapped it free with a grunt. The splintered mast stood twice as tall as he and was banded by rings of black iron. The Beast hoped it would be enough.

He scrambled to the aft, wielding the splinter like a great lance. The dracoliche roared its approval of the challenge and dove hellishly from the clouds, wings pinned like a bird of prey.

"Donovan!" Polaris cried.

The Beast did not hear her plea, did not turn, did not stop running. His powerful legs coiled and he leapt from the ship with the makeshift spear readied overhead. Time slowed to a crawl. He soared at his foe like a warding angel, forever vigilant.

The dracoliche bared its fangs, sensing the dangerous morsel ahead. It summoned the emerald fire from the pit of its evil heart. A last moment of harmonious silence passed. The demon's jaws widened. The Beast raised his lance higher.

The Beast smashed the dracoliche's head aside with a sweeping back hand, then quickly grabbed hold of a collar bone. The dracoliche's tail whipped up, slicing the Beast's back as he struggled to maintain his hold. The Beast dug into a cracking rib and then hammered a blow into the monster's spine. The dracoliche reeled from the strike, spiraling and thrashing in a wide corkscrew. The Beast dug in harder, raining down blow after blow. The dracoliche's skull swiveled and fired an emerald jet.

The Beast ducked just in time. The dracoliche wailed in agony at the stinging burn of its misfire. A skeletal wing disintegrated to nothing, shedding a trail of dust. Its flight teetered. The Beast knew he had his chance.

With two hands on the Reaper's Song's mast he drove the splintered weapon into the dracoliche's side. The demon lurched as the spear pierced the pulsing orb of emerald fire in its breast. The blaze of Pandora's gift flickered and died without a whimper. The Beast clung to the plummeting corpse. Together they plunged faster, veering to the forest covered mountains rushing to greet them. In the distance, a thick plume of smoke strangled the sky. *The ship...*

The dracoliche exploded against the landscape, throwing the Beast free. He careened threw the forest, smashing tree trunks into pulp. Something cracked beneath him and a shooting pain raced up his thigh and bored into his brain. He collided with a massive pine that tossed him to the ground like a penniless drunkard. His head swam in the pain and dizziness of the chaotic ride. Blackness swallowed his mind and the edges of his vision faded. He forced himself to hold on to his restored memory.

The smoke... the ship...

My name is Dono--

Lia...

Chapter 31

The Beast stirred. He rubbed at his stomach, hungry as usual. Thick copses of trees shrouded a sky glowing with the hint of dawn. From his back, he regarded the wall of timber. It was unfamiliar, foreign. The trees made him feel unwelcome. *His* grove always felt welcoming and sure. He could name all of the trees, in fact they said he had been the first to do so. These trees were nameless; not a single voice mustered among them.

He had to leave...

The Beast stood, wincing at a sharp pain gnawing his leg. He massaged the wounded limb, his paw coming away with no blood. The unseen wound throbbed nonetheless. *What had happened?*

His first steps seared and the wounded leg threatened to collapse. *A few more moments of rest, perhaps.* The Beast braced his broad back against an equally broad tree and slid to the ground. He rubbed again at the injured limb, still struggling to fill in the blanks. Much appreciated warmth of amber-blond hues seeped through the snow blanketed trees. The sun's kiss felt good on his face. He smiled at the glow, grateful that the king of stars hadn't yet forsaken him.

A sniff of something bitter stole his solace. Wafts of blackness inked the morning's delicate shine. *Smoke.* Memory hit him. The ship, the dracoliche.

Lia.

The Beast clawed at the tree and pulled himself upright. He limped into the woods, heading for the smoke's source. His pulse quickened. There was no way of knowing how badly the ship was damaged. Hopefully Poogs had set her down before the powder keg ignited...

He pushed the morbid thought aside along with a thick tangle of scratching briar. His wounded leg conspired evilly against him. Crawling pain swallowed it whole.

Soon, the trees thinned and the Beast found a great gouge gored into the land. It conjured instantly memories of the island's crater. The Reaper's Song slept on a nest of felled trees, smoke pouring from her side. Two of her masts were split in half and hung limply like broken branches. The Beast dragged his own broken limb, nearly tripping over what debris remained of the ship's proud figurehead. The bust's eyes stared sadly from the mud at her severed body yet mounted to the ship.

"Lia!" The Beast bellowed, "Lia, where are you?" He cleared a path through the rubble, heaving aside the ship's broken bones. He sniffed the acrid cloud and climbed through the smoking breach in the hull.

The ship's tight corridor was thick of swirling black smoke and the stench of Poogs's explosive powder. The Beast pushed a splintered shipping crate aside. The door to the captain's quarters was a dozen steps ahead, swinging from a lone broken hinge.

"No..." The Beast barreled through the door. The blackness shrouded even his sharp vision. He hacked a breath and grasped his way through the room, inching forward until something soft bumped his knee.

The bed.

"Lia!" The Beast scooped his arms down, retrieving an empty armful of soot covered linens.

Lia was gone.

Panic gripped his throat with icy fingers. He dropped to his knees, searching under the bed. Nothing. The Beast flipped the bed over in a fit and then limped back outside.

"Lia!" Grief edged its way into his voice. He shouted her name again, but received only the whispering wind for reply. He hobbled to a nearby stump and gingerly lowered himself. The pain throbbed worse with each stricken heartbeat. He had failed her again.

"The Donovan I know would not give in so easily."

The Beast spun to the trees at his right.

"My queen! You're alive!" The Beast rushed to Polaris and wrapped his arms around her, relieved to no end. "Where's my daughter? And the pirate?"

Polaris gestured behind her. A shroud of shimmering invisibility fell to the forest floor, revealing the hidden pirate. Poogs sat awkwardly, leaning against a snow laden pine. Giant beads of sweat trickled from his brow.

An outstretched arm with trembling fingers clutched the grip of a flint lock pistol. The pirate cradled a bundle of blankets to his chest. Locks of damp chocolate hair flowed over the swaddling.

Forgetting his wound, the Beast scrambled over and knelt by Poogs's side. Carefully, he took hold of the little girl in the pirate's arms. Poogs grimaced but managed a portion of a smile. The Beast placed a paw on Poogs's shoulder. "This is the second time I find myself in your debt."

"Twas nothing my savage friend. Only what any father would've done."

The Beast rocked Lia in his arms. Her breaths labored in little wheezes. She yet clung to life, but none could say for how much longer. He regarded the remains of the fallen ship. The shattered masts, gashed side, and chewed stern painted a picture of grim prospects for flight.

"How much further to the fountain?"

The North Star smiled at Poogs, then pointed through the wall of snowy trees towards the sounds of rushing water. "The masterful skill of our captain friend has all but delivered us."

The Beast jumped to his feet, searching for the fountain, incredulous that they should be so lucky to have survived all they had *and* managed to land on top of their destination.

"If only it were that easy," Polaris said, with an air of sympathy. She motioned for her champion to lower his head. She stretched the chain of the medallion wide, then set it around the Beast's neck. "Much better."

The medallion's ruby warmth caressed Lia's face and she burrowed into the thick of the Beast's mane. He had all he required to see things done. Once and for all.

"Follow the stream through the woods. It shall lead you to the glade the fountain calls home. Let nothing stop you." Polaris's tone firmed and the Beast knew all too well the importance of listening. "The fountain feeds a pool serving as its base. It is within that pool you must unlock the medallion's power."

The Beast nodded his understanding and tested the weight on his leg. It protested with a searing sting, but could not break his will. It would take more than broken bones.

"Donovan, you must remember the fountain's rules. Even a magic as powerful as Wynisahil has limitations. Do not ask for more than you need."

The Beast leveled his brow into a curious expression, but grunted his understanding. Poogs twisted himself upright on a cushion of snowy moss, calling for the Beast to halt. The unlikely friends clasped forearms. He tugged against the Beast's grasp, pulling himself upright.

"I'm coming with you." Poogs propped himself against the tree and checked the pistol's charge.

The Beast wished the pirate could come with him, but one look spoke volumes of Poogs's condition. The pistol was nearly dancing free of his hand. Though he would have appreciated the fearless rogue by his side, the Beast knew Poogs was in no position to fight. This next step was one he had to take alone. He gently pushed the pirate back to the ground.

"Look after her for me," the Beast said.

Poogs sighed his resignation. "With my last breath, my savage friend." Poogs clapped the Beast on the shoulder, then on the hip. "You'd best get a move on then."

Soon after, the woods swallowed father and daughter and the Reaper's Song disappeared amongst the trees. The Beast huddled Lia to his chest as he slogged through the spongy mix of snow and mud. For the first time since losing his memory, he found himself desiring the company of friends. Life was not meant to be a stark voyage mired in solitude. He knew that now.

He thought of Cedrik and their fencing lessons and lectures. He thought of his stern, but reliably guiding words in those dark moments tainted by defeat. Cedrik was always there, always the one to drive him on, to never let him give in. Not to pain. Not to social convention.

Never to fear.

Every trudging step was tribute to his fallen mentor and he took them proudly, adding fuel to his resolve.

A short hike from the crashed ship, the Beast found the murmuring stream. The sparkling water babbled softly to itself as it rushed over stones of muddy brown and soft grays. The fire in the Beast's leg gnawed at muscle and bone, spasming every so often as a reminder. Not too much further...

The Beast trundled his ward up a graciously gentle slope that peaked with a breath taking view of the forest. The woodland mural was painted in frozen, muted tones of mountain winter: slices of sage green pines peeked out from behind a shield of icy bluish snow. A fresh, chilling wind blustered up the slope at his heels, then climbed over his back. It was an invigorating spark that reminded him of his far away home on the Great Road. He inhaled, drawing in as much of the pristine air as he could, then let twin columns of billowing steam jet from his snout.

It was then the Beast saw it.

The fountain waited patiently across the valley's floor. Its pools numbered three and appeared carved from starlight infused ivory. Glowing runoff provided by the twilight's radiant stars poured from finely bored ports at the fountain's precipice and cascaded into the sparkling basins below.

Magic's magnificent provenance shined glory into the world, blessing each gusting wind, every guardian tree. The very earth hummed with the fountain's grace. The Beast understood immediately why Polaris had kept the fountain a secret. Such a thing was too fragile for the mortal world and the dark desires of Man's heart. The wellspring was one of a kind, meant for greater purposes than glory and riches. All that was good and green in the world came from this place. He knew it as sure as he knew the sun would rise after the darkest night.

The Beast no more than lifted a paw for the first step down when a great shadow fell upon the land. A giant blot of indigo swirled within a tempest of black lightning. The storm tore through the wounded sky, leaving a gash of dark space in its wake. He ambled into the valley, taking cover under a canopy of drooping branches. He poked a hole through the snow cover, quickly locating the strange storm. Solid, twisted shapes slowly materialized and emerged from the heart of the storm.

A portal...

Chapter 32

Massive knots of corkscrewing shapes slid through the portal. Shiny, rock solid shards interlocked into walls, broad and tall. A grid of black iron appeared next, then five pointed columns, twisting like the contracted fingers of a skeletal hand.

Towers.

The Beast's jaw dropped past his sinking heart. He knew those towers all too well. He had just fled them. The Nekropolis penetrated the veil between realms, corrupting the fountain's skyline inch by blackened inch. It was as dark a perversion as the Beast had ever born witness. He pulled back the blanket and to his surprise found the opened eyes of his wounded child. She sputtered a cough, then murmured over a furrowed tongue. "*Faday?*"

"I'm here, starshine."

Lia's eyes drooped closed and the Beast choked down a lump. Was that to be her last word?

He bundled Lia back up and willed strength into his leg numb. Haste was paramount now; the Nekropolis all but dominated the sky. The Beast knew that the black castle provided more than a scare. The Liche Queen would not be denied her prize: she would send all she had.

Halfway to the fountain, the Beast craned his head back. The Nekropolis fully breached the tumultuous portal. It loomed like a vengeful plague, darkening the land beneath. That is, all of the land not occupied by the fountain of starlight. The proud reservoir cut the shadow, cleaving the darkness straight down the center.

The Beast quickly limped his way to the path of light. His wounded leg throbbed with each hurried step, but there was more cause for worry than a broken bone. Voices whispered from the swirling drifts of parted darkness. Sneering, sniveling voices, whispered terrible curses in hushed taunts.

"You are forever alone, Beast of Briarburn..."

"She never loved you..."

The whispers sunk into his skin, deep into his blood like poison. His pace slowed. His mind was suddenly abuzz with stinging contemplation. Was it true? *Had Pandora ever truly loved him?*

He slowed to a trot. Had he been wrong? Were all the years spent in service of the princess, teaching her to fight, protecting her every step... falling in love with her every breath... a lie?

"Give us the child," a wraith voice called out, "give her to us and you may return to your grove."

The empty voice stopped the Beast cold in his tracks. It was vaguely familiar.

"What do you care for the mortals? They care nothing for you. You're little more than a monster to them, fit to be chained," the voice hissed.

Cold shivers nipped his hackles. The voice's words, *his* voice's words, echoed in his head. It was a cold, hard truth he struggled to deny. The world of Men had done little to welcome him as friend. Maybe the voices were right. Maybe he should just leave the girl and go home.

He knelt, lowering the bundled child to the ground. Something soft brushed his clawed finger, freezing the Beast in place. Lia's tiny squeezed closed around the digit. In a flash the voices' spell was shattered. He remembered the first time those pink, stubby fingers found his own. The Beast growled at the unseen voice.

The Beast drew himself up to full height, eyes locking onto the shining fountain. The path of light widened around his trundling paws. Shadows reeled at the sudden intrusion of hope's defiance. The voices howled with shrieking rage at their broken deception. They shouted vile obscenities at the Beast's back as he walked away, leaving them arguing amongst themselves.

Seven steps remained. "Hold on, starshine," the Beast said, "almost--"

Something fleshy and sharp strangled the words back into the Beast's throat and jerked him backwards. He fell flat onto his back with an *oomph*, clutching Lia to his chest. He grabbed at his neck, clawing at his attacker. He rolled Lia to the ground just as he was snatched from the path of light. The Beast twisted to his stomach, searching for his assailant.

Malachai.

The barbs of Malachai's infernal tail pierced the Beast's skin, digging deeper into his flesh. Malachai twisted his flank, dragging his flailing prey farther from the fountain. The Beast clawed into the strangling tail, gouging strips of leathery gray flesh. Still Malachai pulled the Beast deeper into the shadows. The Beast wrenched his way to his feet. He grabbed at Malachai's tail with both hands and pulled. The tug of war lasted only a moment: a jet of pain raced up the Beast's leg as he dug into the ground for purchase. He grunted and fell to a knee, his grip loosening on the biting tail. He could not win this fight, not with a hobbled leg.

Malachai reared, howling from the shadows. A monstrous yank of his tail hurled the Beast through the air and crashing down onto his chest. The Beast gasped as breath exploded from his lungs. A fresh pain erupted in his side, vying for dominance over his throbbing leg. Halos of green and red blurred his vision. Malachai charged like an enraged bull, head lowered. The Beast absorbed the crushing blow and swung a heavy clubbed fist. He missed wildly, throwing himself off balance. Malachai kicked his rear legs out, catching the Beast in his wounded side, doubling him over.

A mighty swing warded Malachai away from a quick gnash at the Beast's neck, but only for a moment. Coal black talons raked the Beast's back driving him to a knee for the second time in the short bout. Malachai circled, mocking him with halfhearted feints. The Beast's strength waned. His leg burned. His ribs ached. There was little he could do. He couldn't fight; he could barely stand.

Malachai moved in to claim his victory. He clawed at the Beast's chest, cleaving deep gashes. A heavy, back handed blow struck the Beast's jaw, sending him down in a sprawl.

Triple images distorted the Beast's vision. Warm blood seeped through his fur, rushing to find daylight, staining the mud. He rolled to his side, scrambling to mount a defense. Malachai had no intention of allowing such a thing. He was a monster incapable of mercy. The Liche Queen's transformative 'gift' had only amplified his relentless bloodlust.

Malachi leapt into the air, soaring through the black castle's shadow, and landed squarely on the Beast's damaged limb. His hooked talons dug in and squeezed. The Beast howled and thrashed with all he had left. Malachai smashed a palm into the Beast's snout, then seized his horns. He bashed the Beast's head into the ground once, then again. The third violent blow saw the Beast spasm. And then go limp.

Malachai released his grasp, savoring his victory. The Beast could only lay in the mud, limp limbed, defeated. His head lolled to one side, finding a blurry bundle of blankets. He reached for Lia, but strength abandoned his arm and the limb flopped to his side with a splash.

Malachai marched over his trophy, stepping a single paw onto the Beast's chest, pressing him deeper into the mud. Crimson orbs of fire glared into the Beast, burning with a special hatred that only knights of warring kingdoms could understand. The Beast's paw brushed past his thigh as he awaited passage into the World After, grazing against a hard lump. He fumbled into a hip pocket.

Poogs.

Malachai's jaws all but unhinged, baring rows of terrible teeth, too many to count. Hot putrid breath festering from the monster's gullet erupted from the ghastly maw. The Beast dug deep, willing his fist to close around Poogs's gift. He swung his arm up, closing his eyes in anticipation.

The device ignited on impact. Blinding light exploded between the columns of Malachai's eyes, clouding his vision with a tapestry of swirling color. He hissed and howled, trying to rub the blindness away with the back of a paw.

The Beast found his feet with a grunt, then pushed himself up. He stumbled to blinded Malachai, fists balled by his sides. He snapped into the first earth shattering blow, driving a fist into Malachai's side, cracking ribs like twigs. The Beast lunged again, slamming home another crushing blow.

Malachai fell back, limbs flailing. His tail fired like a scorpion's stinger, searching for the Beast's face. The Beast anticipated the attack, sidestepping to his right. He seized the prehensile limb, then clamped his jaws down hard. His fangs sliced through Malachai's leathery flesh until the barbed tip tore free with an awful ripping sound. The Beast flung the gored mass away and smashed Malachai's skull with a vicious head-butt.

The glowing eyes flickered, but the champion of the Nekropolis was not yet defeated. Malachai staggered, dazed but enraged. He reared high and strong, then surged forward, maw splayed and hungry.

The Beast braced on his good leg. He caught Malachai by the open mandibles, sliding back a few feet in the mud. The pair was matched bulk for brawn. Muscle twitched and trembled. Malachai wrenched his head, but the Beast refused to let go. Claws slashed thin air, finding nothing. The Beast dodged each swipe, keeping precarious balance by a hair's width.

A second strength surged through the Beast. Primal urge took hold, driving his instincts. In a blur, the Beast muscled an arm around Malachai's neck and clamped tighter than a rusty bear trap. He threw himself to his knees, wrestling Malachai face first to the ground. Malachai's glossy eyes widened as the air rushed free of his crushed windpipe. The Beast reached for the hinge of Malachai's wicked jaw...

A terrible ripping stilled the forest, stifling the shadow's whispering voices. The silence reigned for but a moment...

Malachai wailed and bucked. His eyes darted in all directions. Oily blood poured from the grotesque wound, cascading into a pool between his forelimbs. He collapsed with a splash into the sludge. The Beast roared his victory into the shadows, proudly displaying his bloody trophy to the Nekropolis.

He carried the detached mandible back to its former owner. An arm's length away, the Beast snapped the fang filled jawbone over his knee and flung half aside. He pointed the bony shard at Malachai and spoke words backed by the fury of thunder. "I warned you on the Road..."

Malachai gaped in horror. The bone climbed to the heavens, then flashed down. It was the final image he carried into the World After.

Chapter 33

Malachai's jaw slipped from the Beast's grasp and plopped into the mud. The rest of the monster's broken form lay in a quivering heap. The Nekropolis hovered overhead, but its domineering shadow was visibly diminished. With a final snarl, the Beast left Malachai to answer the Blight's decaying call. His body ached all over. Pain reclaimed territory annexed by the invigorating fury of battle. He wanted to drop to the ground. Just for a quick rest... Only for a moment...

His knees wobbled as he dragged himself down the path of light, his fractured leg now merely the oldest on a wizard's scroll of injuries. The Beast's chest bled into his fur, staining the gold into an iron scented mahogany. He clutched his side. Every breath tore at his insides.

The Beast willed himself on. He reached Lia and scooped her into his arms. The fountain's glorious shine called out to him, whispering encouragement. It penetrated the overpowering shadow of the black castle like a beacon in stormy seas, brightening his bleary eyes.

"Stop!" The Liche Queen boomed from her hovering palace. "The child belongs to me! She is of the Blight, it is her destiny to rule by my side."

A humming sound charged the air. The Nekropolis began to glow with a pale indigo sheen. Twisted shards of petrified wood broke free and fell. The castle fragments exploded into the earth, quickly dissolving. From steaming ash the Wakeful emerged, weapons readied.

The Beast regarded the army of obsidian steel, then his beloved daughter. A powerful, savage voice told him to put the child down and destroy each of them, one by one. He paid that voice as little mind as he had the taunting voices in the shadows. His duty was to his family. Lia shivered and shook in the Beast's arms. She needed her father. The Beast stepped over the fountain's side, climbing into liquid light of stars. He lowered the swaddled child to the fountain's cooling kiss, praying that it was not too late. *It had to work...*

The dracoliche screeched down from the Nekropolis like a diving falcon. The Beast had just enough time to drop Lia to safety on the fountain's side before being snatched by the undead dragon's deathly claws. The earth fell away while the Beast struggled to free himself, shocked the dracoliche yet lived. The splintered mast of the Reaper's Song still skewered the flying nightmare through its bony breast. The faintest hint of emerald fire flickered behind the shield of bone. The dracoliche stopped abruptly among the clouds.

And then the Beast was falling.

Wind whistled by as he plummeted towards the waiting earth. For all hi suffering, for all his sacrifice... to end like this? The Beast was filled by a melancholy calm. Maybe Polaris had been wrong and Lia wouldn't need the medallion. Maybe just being close to the fountain of starlight was enough. He opened his palms and let his arms drift from his sides.

A rippling mix of snow and mud exploded from the impact. He lay there, broken and forgotten as any abandoned marionette. With his last bit of strength he reached for the fountain's warmth. A lone claw scraped the ivory side, scratching down as strength left him.

The World After was calling.

The Beast drifted in and out of a hazy dream space, vaguely remembering the army at his back and the task at hand. He wanted only to sleep. His eye lids grew heavier and heavier. Sleep... *Peace, that was all he needed.*

A streak of indigo burst from the Nekropolis's highest tower and then cracked to the earth like forked lightning. The bolt scorched the ground, instantly vitrifying the cold mud. The Liche Queen emerged from a cloud of silver steam. "It seems to me that we too often meet this way: you, flat on your back, clinging to your wretched existence by a thread."

The Liche Queen crossed the snowy plain with a tidal wave of shadow at her back and the Nekropolis high above her shoulder. Demonic faces twisted and sneered from the dark, rolling wall. Gauntlets of dark fire consumed her hands, but could not burn away the porcelain illusion of perfection. "Beast of Briarburn, Donovan, whomever you are... you are indeed very brave. But I'm afraid being brave is not enough. The world's currency is power not courage. Look at you, lying in the mud. Bloodied.

Beaten." The Liche Queen's eyes burned with flames of the purest hatred. A wraith like hand erupted from the ground and crushed the Beast's body, squeezing free a groan.

"Powerless."

Something warm caught the Beast's flailing claw and held on tight. A smack splashed near his head: a pitter patter squishing in the mud.

Blankets fell away as Lia gathered the Breath to her. A surge of golden light quickly passed from her hand to her father's, banishing the wraith's claws back to the abyss. Lia's amber eyes blazed, as she glared at the closing wall of shadows.

The Liche Queen touched a hand to the spot on her chest were her heart should have been. "Well, well, aren't we just darling. Daughter or not, I grow weary of this game." Her shrill worlds echoed through the trees, loosing snow from branches.

"Bring me the child... And his head."

The dracoliche touched down a league away, kicking up a tempest of snow with its skeletal wings. It sounded the charge to the Wakeful ranks with a terrible wail. They closed formations and marched for the fountain. Marched for victory.

Lia raised her hand to the sky, instantly summoning a magnificent column of spiraling white light. In his haze the Beast could only vaguely recall the image of the same magic pulled Cedrik's spirit back from the World After. He remembered the toll it took on Lia's then healthy body.

He struggled to stop her.

"No starshine! Don't!" The Beast cried.

Lia kissed her father's paw. "It's my turn, *faday*. My turn to protect you." She released the claw and raised a second hand to the light, instantly doubling the intensity of the spiraling pillar.

The black army was less than a field away and closing. The dracoliche howled again and the Wakeful readied their spears. Twin tears of glittering crystal gently rolled down Lia's face, falling between the Beast's own misty eyes of amber.

"I love you, Beastly."

The Beast gasped as the tears restored his battered bones. "Lia--"

The little girl, no more than a speck on the horizon, stepped between her father and the advancing army. The light followed closely behind, like a pet obediently following a beloved master. A few steps from the fountain, Lia halted. A wall of dazzling chain erupted from the tempest behind Lia's shoulders. Interlocking links of gold shot across the field and climbed towards the clouds.

"It cannot be," the Liche Queen muttered. She raised a shielding hand, buffering her eyes from the light of Lia's barricade. "Foolish girl. The Breath's pitiful influence is nothing to the Blight." She swung her arm, unleashing a wave of concentrated Blight magic into the golden chains. The jet of souls condemned by the Blight hammered into the shield, dissipating upon impact.

Lia opened an inviting hand to the souls, offering salvation. One by one the apparitions darted into Lia's palm. The pillar in the sky pulsed as each soul took its rightful place. "No, *matar*. The Blight is beautiful, just like the Breath. They are sisters. A family. What you've done is wrong. I won't let you hurt them anymore.

The Liche Queen screeched pure fury. "Destroy them! Destroy it all!!"

The dracoliche roared at Lia's brash action and the Wakeful clapped their blades against their breast plates as they rushed for the fountain. It mattered not. The child had drawn her line. Lia channeled the pillar's lambent radiance into her hands and pulled at the sky with a single tug. The Breath fizzled from Lia's hands and she slipped away into a dream.

The Nekropolis groaned and shook, trying desperately to resist Lia's powerful magic. The groaning boomed into a deafening thunder. A mighty crack cleaved the Nekropolis down the center and the massive fortress twisted.

The Liche Queen's illusion of beauty dissolved. Her skeletal jaws widened, cracked at the hinge and dropped to the ground. The indigo fire in her eyes dilated. She reached for the symbol of her black heart like a parent reaching for a wounded child.

"No!"

Then the black castle fell. It crashed upon the stunned army and the monstrous demon at its lead. The skeletal dragon's pulsating heart was impaled on splintered bones and exploded in a wave of emerald. The

Liche Queen's mighty stronghold shattered in a gale of petrified rubble.

The Beast quickly rolled over Lia's body, pressing her into the fountain, shielding her from the wave of thorny debris. When the dust settled, he brushed away the hair from her face, hoping for the miracle of his daughter's amber eyes.

He found an angel sleeping, a curious, peaceful smile etched upon her lips.

Lia was gone.

Chapter 34

A pristine sunrise took full flight, painting the sky in wide ribbons of hazel and honey. Gentle gusts of wind swept the valley floor, kicking up loose snowflakes, scattering them about with no particular rhyme or reason. The Beast sat in silence against the fountain's smooth ivory, gently rocking Lia in his lap. Time had finally run out. All of the magic in the world could not help him now. The lump in his throat choked his breath into haggard gasps.

"Oh Lia," the Beast gulped, "I'm sorry."

The fountain babbled a condolence, pouring liquid starlight from basin to basin. He reached over the side and dipped his paw into the sparkling reservoir. Gently, he dabbed the smudges from Lia's face. He wanted to roar away the anguish, but his mouth felt full of dust. What good would it do? There was no one to hear him. He shifted his weight, settling into the soft earth.

He would be with her. It was all he could do.

The Reaper's Song materialized overhead, shedding its mysterious shroud like a reflection on sparkling water. Poogs and Polaris appeared at the rail. The pirate shouted down through funneled hands.

"Well then, is it done?"

Polaris gasped, clutching at Poogs's shoulder. "No... It cannot be." Her knees weakened. "Captain please, the ship... set it down."

The pirate landed the Reaper's Song on top of the smoking rubble once called the Nekropolis, grinding the remnants of petrified wood into dust. He cranked the starboard side winch, stepped into a loop of mooring rope and descended with Polaris clasping his neck. Polaris touched the back of her hand to Lia's forehead. She looked away from the Beast, unable to further fracture his heart. Instead, she laid her head upon Lia's chest and sobbed. Poogs fared little better. Tears freely fell from the corners of his steely eyes. He shared his hands upon the shoulders of Polaris and her grieving champion.

The Beast choked down a lump. "Is she really gone? Is there nothing I can do?" He tipped his head to the fountain, his meaning clear.

The North Star's face gravened, etching fine lines on her brow. "Do not even think it, Donovan. There are limits to *wynisahil*. Even more so if the wielder is uninitiated to the ways of its power."

The Beast's sprang to his feet, fixing a hard gaze upon his queen. "Would you have me do nothing? Would you have me sit by and lose her again? Do not ask this of me, you cannot. In all my years of service to the crown I have never asked for a single thing for myself. Can you really deny me this? Deny me my child?" The Beast's words wavered, perched on a razor's edge of pleading rage.

"I would do no such thing. If it were in my power, I would see our family restored and blissful to the end of time." Polaris took the Beast's face between her hands as she had countless times before. "The mortal soul is a tragically fragile thing. Once severed from the living realm, it travels to the World After. Interrupting that sacred voyage by wishing for its return can inspire terrible consequences, despite the truest intentions."

The Beast's ears perked up. "Wait. What was that about mortal souls?"

"Only that they are amongst the most fragile in all of Creation, like beautiful crystal strands connecting each to another. It's why you feel the death of your loved ones more vividly than we Aether do. Your precious light burns so brightly and is yet so fleeting."

The Beast abruptly threw a leg over the fountain's side. Polaris moved to stop him with an outstretched hand. "Donovan no. You must not."

Poogs was next to intervene. "Perhaps Lia was not meant for this world, my friend. Perhaps her light burned brightest for a reason."

"Of that I have no doubt," The Beast said as he waded waist deep into the pool, carrying Lia in his elbow's crook like a newborn. In his free paw, the medallion sparkled. He turned to the North Star. "You said it yourself. The mortal soul is fragile. But that is only the half that I cursed her with. The other half is of your world, of the Aether... I have to try."

Polaris smiled. "That's my Donovan. Even when the blackest night falls, ever seeing the light. Make your wish then. Save your daughter."

The Beast closed his eyes and freed his mind of emotion. He thought of Lia. Her eyes. Her courage. "I wish for my daughter to return to me."

The Beast braced for the inevitable explosion of magic, certain the liquid starlight would rise and explode to life.

Nothing...

He peeked one eye open. Then the second. Blank expressions stared back at him. "I don't understand. Why is it not working?"

The Beast looked down at Lia's pale features. Every moment passing saw Lia farther down the path to the World After. He wished again and again. He focused all his will on Lia. On the medallion.

Nothing. She had really left him behind.

The Beast sunk down, submerging Lia up to her chest in the warming starlight. He pressed his forehead to hers, whispering the words to the lullaby he first sang a life time ago. Words that no guardian, no matter how loving and kind could duplicate. Words that had been forgotten far too long for a father's heart.

In my heart, I know you're there
shining with the brightest glare.
Starlight is near
my starshine is here.
Never gone, still here in faith
in memories my thoughts shall bathe.
Darkness forces skies to dim
hopeless challenge, outlook grim.

Clouds will form and shroud the sky
always your love revives my eyes.
Glorious, with luster bright
touch the beauty of gleaming night.
Fall back home, to father's arms
free yourself of all that harms.
Starlight is near
my starshine is here...

The Beast kissed his daughter's forehead, and placed a paw on the fountain's edge. "Goodbye, starshine."

The earth suddenly shook, rippling the fountain's calm surface. A great veil of shimmering gold and silver sprang up from the starlight, blanketing its occupants in a glow that quickly spread to the fountain's crown. The Beast cradled Lia to his chest. "What's happening?"

"*Wynisahil!*" Polaris shouted back over the wail of rising wind.

The Beast stared slack jawed as Lia rose from his arms, coming to rest above the fountain's glowing precipice. A slice of twilight penetrated the morning. Millions of tiny shooting stars fell through the breach, then fused with the floating child. A minute later, Lia was cocooned in sapphire light, sparkling in a wondrous sky shared by night and day.

The dome of gold and silver dimmed. Lia's body slowly descended into the waiting arms of her *faday*. The Beast accepted *wynisahil's* gift with trembling arms, afraid to speak lest he spoil the miracle. Instead, he held the child close to his heart.

Thump, thump...

His heart beat faster.

Thump, thump... *thump, thump...*

Lia's heart echoed her father's own powerful bound.

"She's alive!" The Beast waded to the fountain's side and clambered over, pulling a wave of liquid starlight with him. The Beast motioned to Poogs for his coat, but the pirate had already dutifully pulled it free and spread it over the ground. Lia stirred. Her eyes opened a slit, then slowly widened. The Beast knelt by her side and swallowed her pink hand with the golden brown of his thumb and forefinger. "I know those eyes."

"I.. I.." Lia's lips quivered as the divine balance of Breath and Blight surged through her body.

"It's alright, starshine." The Beast's warming words soothed Lia's fear. "I am here, and I'm never leaving you again."

Lia scanned the stunned faces, finding eyes full off watery blur. "Is everyone ok?"

"We're fine, little one. Thanks to you." Poogs removed an imaginary hat and struggled with a low bow.

Lia's eyes remained fixed on the rubble. "She's gone isn't she?"

Polaris clasped a hand over her heart and then pressed it to Lia's. "Your *matar* loved you very much, but she was lost long ago. She would have been proud of the magnificent person you've grown into." She gestured to the pile of rubble smoldering beneath the healing Reaper's Song.

"The Liche Queen was a terrible perversion of your mother, my daughter's true self. An empty soul consumed by hate."

Polaris helped Lia to her feet before sweeping an arm to the twilight filled tear in the sky. "I shall tell you all about our family along the way."

The Beast's heart sank. After all that had happened, he was to lose her anyway? No. That could not be. He would not allow it. He quickly stepped in front of his daughter, shielding her with the bulk of his thigh.

"No one can take her from me. No queen, no North Star, not anybody." The Beast's chest tightened as he fought the perceived betrayal. His fists clenched and his jaws began to grind. He uttered a guttural growl...

Poogs's hand subtly reached for his flintlock. Polaris pushed the pirate's hand aside, standing firm her ground. "I warned you, my son, that *wynisahil* did not come without a price. Only the sustained magic of the Aether can fully restore her soul. If the delay is too long..."

A gentle tug on the Beast's tattered cloak ended the standoff. Lia's eyes were wide and tear filled. "I have to go, *faday*. I need to know who I am."

The Beast knew that feeling all too well. The genuine desire to fit into a world where one knew their place and purpose was the strongest, most beautiful bond connecting father and daughter. The Beast eased his stance. Lia was right. Her place was among the stars.

The Beast scooped Lia into his arms and then swung her into the sky before catching her in an embrace. Lia giggled the way only a father's princess could know, one that sang of true love and joy. One that knew for certain her *faday* would always find and protect her. If only *wynisahil* could freeze time and preserve the moment forever. But the Beast knew such a thing was not meant for eternity. Such moments were shared and remembered always in flashes of warmth and light precisely because they were so precious. Such moments spurred hope and courage, fought back shadow and would always light his way home.

The Beast placed the child gently down and took a knee. "Go little starshine, go and brighten the twilight skies." He hugged her and smiled. "For me."

Lia opened her arms wide and pressed her face into the Beast's chest. "For you, *faday*."

"It is time, Lia," Polaris said. The North Star had no desire to separate from each other those she loved most, but a fledgling Aether soul was a fragile thing that required special care. Polaris linked hands with Lia's and with a whisper the child transformed into a blazing silhouette the color of the fountain's starlight. Lia took to the air, playfully spinning as she ascended to the stars. She waved a final farewell and then vanished in a halo shaped flare.

Poogs took Polaris's hand, gently kissing it. "I suppose this is good-bye as well. It has been an honor to serve you, Lady Polaris. If you ever have need of my humble ship..."

Polaris stretched to her tip toes and kissed the roguish captain on the cheek. Sapphire star dust fell from her lips. "You know where to find me." The North Star glanced at the Beast, then pulled Poogs in close, whispering into his ear.

"Look after him for me... Lorenzo."

Poogs leaned away, face flushing over a wry smile. "How do you --?"

Polaris only winked and smiled.

"It seems so unjust, that we are parted so soon after our family has been re-united. Must you really leave?" The Beast's voice was a calm grumble.

Polaris took on a pale bluish glue and levitated to the Beast, hovering eye to eye.

"Captain Donovan," Polaris smiled, the thought of the young boy wielding a wooden sword storming the castle halls prominent in her mind. She touched the medallion at his chest, setting the firestone ablaze with radiant light. "There is a place within us all that we may always find our truest heart. Lia will never be far from yours. Someday, when she is ready, she will return and finish what she started here."

The Beast growled. "Ahriman..."

Polaris nodded grimly. "He is undoubtedly growing his power in the

Gloom, plotting his revenge. Lia will need time to prepare for his wrath."

The Beast's blood flashed to a boil, but the rage quickly faded into a knowing smile. "Then I *shall* see her again."

Polaris kissed the Beast on the forehead and phased into the shimmering silhouette of the Aether. "A little girl will always need her *faday*. And a queen shall always need her champion." The North Star sparkled as she rose to the sealing rift of twilight. "Farewell, Beast of Briarburn."

"My name is Donovan!" The Beast proudly shouted after her.

Polaris twisted in flight and smiled. "Good boy."

She disappeared with a flash and the morning sky filled itself in. A moment passed when finally Poogs spoke. "Well then."

The Beast chuckled. "Well then? Is that the best you've got?"

"It's as good a start as any! I have never heard you venture anything more profound than a grunt." The pirate clenched his jaw and did his best impression of the Beast growling. His expression softened. "Where will you go? Back to your grove? Life on the 'Road', that sort of thing?"

"Actually, I thought I may try my luck with piracy." The Beast extended a paw.

"Aye," the pirate said. He grasped the Beast's forearm, squeezing hard. "Partners it is then."

The Reaper's Song cleared the tree tops and darted into the horizon. Cloaked by Death's ancient shroud she flew for no particular heading, churning rolls of fluffy clouds into forgotten wake. The pirate's hands caressed the helm, guiding the ship along the winds. "Where to?" Poogs asked.

"First, we eat. Then we wait for nightfall. I intend to learn to sail this heap properly, under the guidance of the stars."

Poogs flashed his new first mate a knowing smile. "We will need a bearing then. Any one in particular strike your fancy?"

The Beast gazed upon the spectacular panorama the world had to offer, for once free to pursue his own destiny. The possibilities were endless and that, in itself, was frightening. But the Beast knew that the chains of the sure and certain were far worse.

He would have his freedom.

"Let's try the second star to the right..."

The End

Epilogue

Pandora's bony heels clicked through thin skin as she paced. Fiery anguish coursed through the newly formed veins crawling under her newborn flesh. Captivity offered precious little else to do.

Pace. And remember.

Pace. And plan.

Pace...

The clicks died soon after birth, forbidden to echo. She toed playfully at the cracked floor like a child, ticking years away. In the Gloom, time was as meaningless as hope.

Where a wall should have been, there was an empty stretch of sky. Dirty light poured freely through the panoramic gap, but provided no warmth. Pandora dangled her feet over the side, contemplating another plunge into the jagged mountains below.

Such was her life as prisoner in the Gloom.

Despite the dozens of deaths suffered on the rocks below, Pandora always reawakened in the cell.

She scratched at the ugly skin of her arms, hating its soft pink weakness. Being stripped of her power should have been punishment enough. But this? Restored of flesh and blood? Ahriman had gone too far.

Just outside the cell's heavy door, a pair of phantoms materialized into forms nearly human. Ahriman nodded his jeweled horn to the door, inviting his guest to view the newest addition to his gallery.

"As you can see, this one quite hates the flesh. More so than any I've ever seen."

"Indeed she does, Lord Ahriman. She seems to crave undeath. Strange for one so young." The wraith pulled back the hood of its black cloak, leaning closer to the barred portal. Shiny black hair, soft as silk, draped over its slim shoulders. A long scar of fading silver crossed its throat from ear to ear.

The wraith's hand fell to the kusarigama at her waist. The chipped blade gleamed at the thought of claiming such a prize. "Why not give her to me? She craves my touch..."

The master of the Gloom shook the prison's walls with a roar of raucous laughter. It was not often he allowed himself such a joy.

"I am afraid this one is still of use to me. And besides, you have not come all the way from the Nether Realm to parlay for a simple soul, now have you Morgren?"

Morgren's hand abandoned the eternally hungry weapon. She traced the scar at her throat with timid fingertips, memory of the dagger's kiss vivid still. The almond shape of her eyes grimly narrowed.

"No, I've come on a more personal note. Something of mine was stolen. By someone I should think you'd prefer to see punished for his role in upending your plot against the Aether"

Ahriman snorted. "Only a fool would endeavor to steal from you.

What lost trinket could inspire such wrath?"

The wraith stepped away from the door, slipping into the soothing safety of a nearby shadow.

"My ship, Lord Ahriman. I've come for the Reaper's Song."

Made in the USA
Middletown, DE
26 July 2015